When Willows Weep

When Willows Weep

Charlay Marie

www.urbanchristianonline.com

Urban Books, LLC
97 N18th Street
Wyandanch, NY 11798

When Willows Weep Copyright © 2015 Charlay Marie

ISBN 13: 978-1-62286-802-5
ISBN 10: 1-62286-802-1

First Trade Paperback Printing May 2015
Printed in the United States of America

10 9 8 7 6 5 4 3 2 1

Distributed by Kensington Publishing Corp.
Submit orders to:
Customer Service
400 Hahn Road
Westminster, MD 21157-4627
Phone: 1-800-733-3000
Fax: 1-800-659-2436

Acknowledgments

I'd like to give thanks to God for blessing me with the ability to write a second book. In no way, shape, or form am I deserving of such favor, and yet the Lord blesses me daily. That goes to show His great love and mercy for us. Even though we aren't perfect, His love is. I am ever so grateful for that love. I will always give God the glory, first and foremost.

To all my family, friends, and readers who have supported me during this journey, thank you! Your support means the world to me! I've had multiple people rave about my first book, *Under the Peach Tree,* saying they can't wait to get their hands on this book. It means so much that I can give *When Willows Weep* to all of you, as well. I hope all my readers learn something from reading this book, as it is meant to inspire, restore, and teach.

The books that I write are God's will. If they were my own, I would've written a paranormal romance series. God always has a different plan for us, a better one. Instead, He put it in my heart to please Him and to write for His glory. I like to write about the two attributes of God that are my favorite, which are His forgiveness and His mercy. He affords us forgiveness and mercy, especially when we need it most, which happens to be after some sort of life mistake we've made. He always shows us how to grow from our trials as He leads us through them. The characters in *When Willows Weep* understand these traits of God all too well, as they face their fair share of trials. Always remember that none of us are perfect, not even the highest of saints. We should always correct with love and never cast stones, as Jesus has taught us. Thank you, God, for being loving and merciful! And thank you all for reading! God bless.

Chapter One

TAMARA

"My God," I whispered to myself as I looked down at Ciara's puffy cheeks, which were stained with tears. I felt the deepest type of pain. No six-year-old child should ever have to lose his or her mother to a car accident; no child should ever have to suffer the way she was suffering. This little girl had no one. She had never known her father, and now her mother, my best friend, was gone. *Dead.*

I did everything in my power to keep the tears from clouding my vision as I drove. Lord knows, I didn't want to die the same way Ciara's mother had just died. The thought of the car accident made me want to stop my car and break down, but someone had to be strong for this little girl.

Ciara hadn't said a word to me since the funeral this morning. I figured she was mentally drained from seeing her mother in that casket. What child wouldn't be? The image of her mother lying in that casket made me weak. The sad thing was that this was only the beginning for her. Soon, children's services would be knocking on my door, trying to take her to a foster home, trying to take her away from the only thing she had left. *Me.*

I was in the delivery room the day she was born. I saw those hazel eyes stare directly at me as she smiled for the first time. I was there for every birthday, every Christmas and Thanksgiving, watching her grow and experience the joys of life. She called me Auntie Tamara. She looked to me to help her through losing her mother, and I couldn't even tell this little girl that soon she wouldn't even have me.

Children's services would take her from me. I had already asked around about the chances of me getting custody of Ciara, and none of the feedback had been positive. God knows, they wouldn't let me keep her, not with my low-paying job, and the fact that my crazy ex-boyfriend was in jail for almost killing me didn't help matters. I had also been sleeping on Candace's couch for a week, having gotten evicted from my apartment. They would deem me unfit based on those reasons and would put her in a messed-up home with a couple who probably abused children and would feed her nothing but ramen noodles and white bread. She'd get put into a school in the middle of the hood and would probably be pregnant by fifteen. Who knew what trouble lay ahead for a little girl with no mother or father? The only thing I could do was pray that the good Lord covered her and protected her, even when she got snatched out of my hands.

If only there was something I could do to make sure she didn't end up in the system. I wished there was a way I could find her father and take her to him, but I didn't even know his name. I wasn't even sure Ciara's mom, Candace, had known the man's full name. The only thing I knew was the story she had once told me about him and how they'd met.

He was a middle-aged white man, and she met him while she was at Montrose Beach, not too far from where she lived in Chicago. He showed her around, took her to dinner, and ended up in her hotel room. When Candace woke up that next morning, he was gone, but he had left behind a picture of the two of them, one they'd paid a photographer to take while they were at the beach. A few weeks later, Candace found out that she was pregnant.

I never did ask her why she never searched for him and let him know he had a baby on the way. I figured she didn't know much about him or maybe didn't care. Now I wished I had asked more questions.

"I'm sleepy," Ciara said, tossing uncomfortably in her seat. I couldn't tell if her puffy eyes were from exhaustion or crying. Maybe both. I reached over and gently rubbed her shoulder.

"We're almost home," I assured her.

"I don't have a home."

"What?" I asked in surprise, almost pushing down on the brakes, which would've caused a multiple car pileup.

"I don't have a home," Ciara said again, staring out her window. "My home is with Mama, and Mama ain't here no more."

For the hundredth time today, tears began pouring from my eyes, making it difficult to see. I quickly pulled the car over to the side of the road and turned it off. I turned as much as my seat would allow me so that I was facing Ciara, who was still looking out the window. She was such a pretty little girl, with curly hair, which her mom had always braided in two pigtails. She had big, beautiful hazel eyes that complemented her fair complexion. Her mom couldn't step outside without people coming up to her, telling her how beautiful Ciara was. She was an angel, a blessing, and I just hoped whichever family took her in saw the rarity of her beauty as well.

Ciara was a gifted little girl; she always knew when something was wrong. She could sense people's emotions without them even talking to her, and she had the wisdom of someone twice her age. I'd had to watch what I said around her ever since she was two years old, because she seemed always to understand what my words meant, especially bad words.

A word at church was spoken over Ciara about the fact that she had the gift of discernment. She would always be able to discern what was true and real and to sniff out any wolf in sheep's clothing. This minister had also said that Ciara would one day change lives, and I believed every word. She'd already changed mine.

Letting her go was something I dreaded more than her mother's death. The fact that I was powerless to help her hurt even more than having to give her over. Would Ciara blame me for not being able to keep her? The better question was, did I deserve the blame?

I took a deep breath. "Ciara, your home isn't where your mommy is, but where the memories and happy times are. Do you remember that one time we had that ice cream fight with your mommy in the kitchen and we won? Remember that?"

Ciara nodded, with a smile, but it never reached her eyes.

"How fun was that? Mommy might not be here, but that memory is. All you have to do is think about all the good times with Mommy, and you'll be okay. As long as you keep Mommy in there," I said, pointing to her heart, "then she'll always be with you, wherever your home is."

My response seemed to satisfy her briefly, but her mood changed just as quickly as a cloud passing under the sun, causing the shadows to shift. I could tell she was growing sad by the way her shoulders slumped and her head rested against the seat in defeat. When she finally turned to me with glistening eyes, I patted her knee and tried to smile reassuringly. I could only imagine how fake it seemed, but I didn't know what else to do.

"They're gonna take me away from you," she said softly. "I heard two women talking about it today. They said they felt bad because I ain't got no family, and I can't stay with you, because you ain't blood. They gonna put me in another home."

I was furious, beyond upset that some foolish women would talk about Ciara's situation without first checking to see if anyone, especially Ciara, was within earshot. Here I was, literally driving myself crazy, trying to figure out what I was going to do about her living situation and how I was going to tell her, and she already knew. Although I should've been honest with her, I couldn't. I knew Ciara would be able to tell I was lying, and yet I still couldn't look her in the eye and confirm what she had said.

"Ciara, I'm not gonna let nobody take you away from me, okay?" I knew the lie would come back and bite me, but I couldn't let this little girl worry. That was my job to do for the time being. I was going to find a way to keep her, and if I couldn't keep her with me, I'd find out who her father was and send her to be with him. She'd be better off with real family, not with people who wouldn't care about her.

And so I continued stressing over finding a way to save her.

Later that day, I tucked Ciara into bed and found myself sitting in Candace's room with a bottle of red wine. I usually didn't drink, but I found it necessary in order to deal with all my problems. I had been so concerned with trying, unsuccessfully, to find Ciara a home that I needed a form of release. I found myself sitting there for quite a while in a daze.

In a moment of inspiration, I began digging through her dresser drawers, searching through files, trying to find something that hinted at distant relatives or even Ciara's father, but I found nothing. Candace was an only child who had never known her own mother. She had grown up with her grandmother, who had passed away on her eighteenth birthday. There were no aunts and no uncles.

Just when I was about to give up, the shimmering letters on the cover of a Bible caught my eye. I slowly picked it up, feeling a sense of relief. My last resort was usually God, and He was the only one who could help me in my time of need. I held the Bible in my hand, running my fingers along the gold letters, and smiled. Yes, God was always with us.

I sat on the bed and opened the Bible, and from it, a picture fell out. I picked the picture up from the floor and examined it. My good Lord, I was staring at the images of Candace and a white man, who seemed to fit the description of Ciara's father that Candace had once given me. He was tall, with dark hair, and had a seemingly genuine smile. He seemed like the type of man one couldn't help but like. His eyes were kind.

In the picture, they stood with their backs facing a beach, his arms draped around her shoulders, her smile big and goofy. I could see why she had been with him. They looked happy, like an actual couple. Seeing her standing there, smiling brightly brought tears to my eyes. I wished I could see her smile one last time, but this picture would have to do.

I turned the picture over and saw a bit of sloppy handwriting. The message read:

> *Hopefully, we will meet again, my love,*
> *Mark Douglas*

I practically knocked over my bottle of wine as I jumped up and down with excitement. I finally had a name and a face. Candace had told me she knew only his first name, but it was as clear as day on this picture that the mystery baby daddy indeed had a last name. She must've had her reasons for never contacting him, and for a moment, I wished I could ask her what those reasons were. I pulled myself out of that sad thought and focused on the man's name. *Mark Douglas*. I was one step closer to making sure Ciara had a home. I grabbed my phone, went to Facebook, and typed his name in the search bar, hoping I'd find a match.

Chapter Two

CLAIRE

The house was spotless, my husband's favorite roast was slowly cooking in the oven, I was wearing his favorite dress—the white one with the pearls sewn into the neckline—and my shoulder-length blond hair was neatly curled, with not a strand out of place. I was the ideal housewife. I was one of those women on the TV shows with a nice house and a cool, collected demeanor. A woman who stood strongly behind her husband and took care of her family's needs. I was a woman to be valued and cherished by her husband, and yet my husband, Mark, still didn't look at me.

Most days, Mark would come home from doing whatever being a preacher and a lawyer required of him, and he'd go straight for the food, take a plate into his study, and disappear until midnight. I spent that time trying to figure out a way to make him notice me again.

I'd recently bought new lingerie to wear to bed, but he hadn't noticed. I even wore a new perfume. One time, I let the house go unclean for an entire week to see if he'd notice. Did he? Not at all. The housemaid got a free week of paid vacation for nothing.

God said a man was supposed to love his wife. One would think that my husband, being the preacher over our church, would follow this command as perfectly as he could. Looking in from the outside, people would think I got all the affection in the world. They'd think my family was happy and perfect, but then they'd all be wrong.

I did pride myself on being the preacher's wife. Every Christian woman I knew in our suburb of Highland Park in Chicago looked up to me and tried to model her own marriage on what she thought my husband and I had. It didn't help that I lied to these women. Sunday brunch was the perfect place to lie and brag about what my husband did for me. All the ladies would marvel at me like I was Martha Stewart herself . . . and I'd let them.

But they didn't know how my house was crumbling, how my daughter, Sarah, hated me and would much rather live alone with Mark, doing away with me altogether. Thank God the neighbors never saw the look she got on her face whenever I walked into a room. Sarah blamed me for everything, even when it was obvious I wasn't the cause, but they'd never know that, because Sarah knew to smile when people were watching.

Sarah and I had once been close, but that was before she hit puberty, when every other sentence she uttered was about how she loved me. I remembered how she used to run into my arms after school and spend hours telling me all about her day in a rush of excitement. The older she got, the farther the distance between us was.

I was good at hiding how my household was beginning to unravel. I was also really good at lying to myself about how willing I was to just give it all up. If I could walk away, I would; however, I was more concerned with my image and how others viewed me. I'd rather live in an unhappy marriage than leave it as long as others looked up to us as the prime example of how they wanted their marriage to be. We were Christians, after all.

The only thing that got me through my day was the false image I'd created of myself. I loved to live through other people's high opinions of me, and sometimes I almost believed them. I almost believed I had a great marriage, a wonderful home environment, and a loving daughter who adored me. I almost believed that I was happy.

Almost.

Leaving my roast slowly cooking at home, I headed to a five-star restaurant, and as I walked inside, I took in the aroma of the food, the wine, and the expensive cologne. I had a standing brunch appointment with some church members, and we met up at this restaurant every Sunday, shortly after church. We had a small church, with one service that started at eight and was done by eleven, giving us the time needed for our Sunday brunches. I took a look at myself in the long mirror just inside the restaurant doors. My knee-length white sundress looked lovely paired with the blue heels and the matching hat I wore. I'd chosen a new necklace, one that complemented my pearl neckline, and a brilliant diamond bracelet I'd purchased at Saks, knowing it would impress the ladies.

I felt confident in my outfit as I spotted my group of friends gossiping at a reserved table. They all wore white dresses but differed in their choice of hats and their finest jewelry. As I approached, trying with great effort to look as though I had no troubles, they each smiled.

"Claire, where did you get that mesmerizing bracelet?" Susan asked from across the table adorned with a white tablecloth. Her auburn hair was pinned into a fine bun, allowing her diamond earrings to stand out. On one of her fingers, she wore a ring bigger than my own wedding ring, one her fourth husband bought her a few years ago, and she would always wave her right hand when she talked so that she flaunted her ring in front of everyone. She had a pinched face and an airy disposition fit for a queen. Susan always noted what everyone else had, what jewelry they were wearing or what designer outfit they had on, and tried to outdo them.

Jen, who sat uncomfortably beside her, was the exact opposite. She didn't care about anything materialistic and spent most of her time reading romance novels because of her lacking love life. Her hair was dark brown, thin, and straight, and didn't do anything to complement her huge eyes and skinny figure. She usually wore a flowered dress, white socks, and black dress shoes, so this white dress was a definite improvement. The other girls once joked that she would make a better nun than usher of our church.

I focused my attention back on Susan as I touched the bracelet on my wrist, taking a seat at the table. "It was a gift from my husband," I lied, pleased with the looks of approval given around the table.

"What did you do to deserve this bracelet?" Susan asked, seemingly pleasant, but I could hear the sharp undertone in her voice that pointed to jealousy.

"Nothing." I smiled evenly at her. "My husband is just wonderful."

"Reminds me of my third husband," Susan began. "He'd buy me all types of jewelry for no reason. I used to think it was the sweetest thing, until I found out he was cheating and bought me jewelry only to cure his guilt."

Everyone around the table gasped, hanging on to her every word, but I understood why she'd said that. She was trying to belittle me, to insinuate that my husband was a cheating man.

"Of course, I divorced him and married Henry," Susan continued. "He doesn't buy me a thing, and I prefer it that way. I have enough money, from my divorce from number three, that I can buy whatever I want without the help of a man." She took a sip of her tea. "It's a rather beautiful bracelet, though."

"Thank you," I told her, giving her my kindest smile, although I was experiencing a sinking feeling in my stomach. I wouldn't let her know how much her words had affected me. "I'm glad that I don't have to worry about infidelity. My husband loves me and thinks I'm the greatest blessing from God."

"As it should be," agreed Carol, who was sitting next to me. Carol happened to be the most genuine and Christlike of all the women I sat with and seemed to oppose Susan as much as I did, although we had never actually stated that out loud to the others. "It says in Ephesians chapter five, verse twenty-five, that a man is supposed to love and honor his wife. It only seems fitting that a preacher would be the one who lives by this the most."

Susan turned her nose up, obviously irritated by Carol's Bible reference. "All I'm saying is that men have motives. It's never just because he wants to. He's either guilty about something or wants to butter you up to ask for a motorcycle."

"Here comes the midlife crisis story," I heard Carol say under her breath just as Susan opened her mouth to speak once again.

"My second husband used to buy me gifts just to ask for something in return. 'Oh, hey, honey. I bought you a new dress. . . . Can I get a sports car?'" Susan said, laughing to herself and not caring that no one joined her. We'd all heard this story before.

I tuned her out, focusing on my husband and infidelity. No, my husband didn't buy me gifts because he was cheating. He bought me gifts only on special occasions, meaning most of the things I had, I bought myself, using his money. But could my husband be having an affair? It would explain how distant he had been lately. Maybe that was the reason he came home every day and went straight to his study. Maybe he wasn't reading his Bible but was calling a woman or was on one of those Web sites with her.

I shook the thought out of my head. Mark might have been distant lately, but he wasn't an adulterer, and so I lifted my shoulders, sipped on my tea, and continued to pretend that everything was perfect in my life.

Chapter Three

CIARA

I peeked through the mail slot and saw a woman dressed in a black suit standing outside. She had some papers in her hands, and with her hair pulled up in a tight bun, her face was serious and almost scary. She started knocking softly, but her knocks grew louder when no one came to the door. Auntie Tamara was still upstairs, getting dressed, and probably hadn't heard anything and I wondered what I should do. Mommy had always told me not to answer the door for strangers, but Mommy was dead. I opened the door, anyways.

"Hi," the woman said with a tight smile. I could tell she wasn't comfortable being at my house. It was all in the way her shoulders tensed up. Mommy's shoulders did the same thing when she was nervous or uncomfortable. "Is there an adult here?"

"Yes," I said, looking past her at the all-black car that sat in front of the house.

"Can I speak to them?"

"She's getting dressed."

The lady nodded, and I watched her as she kneeled down so that we were face-to-face. "Are you Ciara Tucker?"

"Yes," I told her, backing away slightly. I didn't want her to take me away from Auntie Tamara.

"Don't be scared, Ciara. I'm here to help you." I would've believed her if I hadn't heard those two women talking at the funeral yesterday. I knew who she was. She was here to take me away, and so I quickly shut the front door and ran up the steps to find Auntie Tamara.

She was in my mama's room, pulling a gray sweater on over her head. She smiled when she saw me enter the room, but I could tell she had been crying. Her eyes were red. "Hey, Ciara."

"There's a woman outside, and she wants to take me away," I told Auntie Tamara. "Auntie, don't let her take me away!" I cried, running up to her and wrapping my arms around her legs.

"Calm down, girl," she said, quickly pulling on a pair of pants and then slipping her shoes on. She rushed out of the room and down the stairs just as the lady began to knock again. I watched Auntie Tamara open the door and pull it closed behind her, but she didn't shut it all the way and so I could hear what they were talking about and see them as I crept up to the door.

The woman in black began walking backward as Auntie Tamara pointed at her and yelled, telling her to get off of the property.

"I have an order to remove Ciara Tucker from this home immediately. If you refuse to cooperate, I will call the police."

"Call the police!" Auntie Tamara yelled. Whenever she was mad, she tended to get really loud and scary. "And tell them that you're wrong for being here. That girl belongs with her family."

"Records show she has no family," the lady argued but continued backing away.

"Your records aren't correct. Her daddy's name is Mark Douglas. He lives a half an hour away. I found him online. Maybe if you had done your research, you would've found him too!"

"And does he know about the little girl? Has he agreed to take her? Does the court know of this? Did he sign the birth certificate?" The lady didn't wait for a response. She just kept shooting question after question. "We need proof of this. If her father wants to claim her, he can come down to our office."

"How about this? If y'all want her, y'all can find out where he lives and come get her from her father, 'cause I refuse to hand this little girl over to you," Auntie Tamara told the woman, putting her hands on her hips the way my mama did whenever she argued with someone. "Now, you got three seconds to get your uppity self off of this property before I drag you by your hair down this lawn and put you in your car myself. Your choice."

The woman nodded and continued to back away. As she did, she pulled out her phone and called someone. Auntie Tamara barged back into the house, passed me, and headed up the stairs. I followed behind her, watching as she walked into my bedroom and began pulling my clothes from my dressers and stuffing them into my Barbie suitcase and backpack. It took her all of three minutes, and then she was shooting past me, heading into my mama's room. I followed behind her and watched as she stuffed some of mama's pictures and jewelry into my backpack. She then turned toward me and stumbled, as if she had just now noticed me watching her.

"Ciara, we need to leave," she said. "Right now."

"Are you taking me to my daddy's?" I asked her as she quickly passed by me, heading toward the stairs. She paused and stared down at me with a wrinkled forehead.

"You overheard our conversation, didn't you?" Auntie Tamara shook her head and began walking down the stairs. "If I don't, that woman will take you away."

"But I want to stay with you," I whined, following her.

"You can't stay with me," Auntie Tamara yelled, stopping halfway down the stairs. She turned toward me with so much anger on her face, I wanted to cry. She must've realized how loud she had got with me, because her face softened and she continued down the stairs. "You don't even understand half of it, Ciara. I can't keep you."

She opened the front door and guided me outside to her car. The lady in the black was now sitting in her own car. She watched us as Auntie Tamara opened the passenger door, helped me climb in, and then buckled me into my seat. "I hope she doesn't follow us," Auntie Tamara said to herself as she put my bags in the back of the car. Then she hopped in the front seat and started the car. "I'm sorry, Ciara, but this is how it's gotta be."

I watched as we backed out of my driveway, and wondered if I would ever see my old house again. Everything was changing. I had lost my mama, and now I was losing the only house I had ever lived in and Tamara. I sank into my seat and cried myself to sleep, hoping that when I woke up, Mama would be home and everything would be normal.

"Wake up." I felt someone tugging at my arm and felt a rush of cool air hit my skin. I opened my eyes and saw Auntie Tamara unbuckling my seat belt. "We're here."

I looked out at a white house that had the prettiest green grass and garden I'd ever seen. The house looked like something I had seen in the movies, all beautiful and welcoming. I bet rich people lived in a place like that. For a moment happiness spread through me as I thought about all the chocolate cake these people could afford and all the toys I might get.

"Is this were my dad lives?" I asked Auntie Tamara as she pulled me out of the car and handed me my bags. She ran her hands over my hair, pressing down the loose curls, and then looked me over with approval.

"Yes, your daddy lives here. Nice, ain't it?" she asked, turning to admire the house. "God does answer prayers. Come on."

I followed Auntie Tamara to the porch and watched as her hand went to press the doorbell button. I let go of one of my bags and quickly tugged on her jacket, momentarily distracting her before she could ring the bell. I felt scared and small, and I wasn't ready for Auntie Tamara to leave me. I wasn't ready for what lay behind that door. I wanted my mama back. I wanted to go home.

"Auntie Tamara, don't leave me." I began crying. "Don't make me stay here."

"Ciara," she sighed, lowering herself down to one knee and caressing my shoulders. "You're a big girl. You just turned six. You're so smart and strong, and you're gonna be okay."

"No, I won't," I told her.

"Do you remember *The Lion King*? Remember how Simba lost his daddy and his pack, but Timon and Pumba found him and took him in? Remember what they said to him? They told him not to worry, because everything was going to be okay. Same with you, sweetie. You're going to be okay. Remember, Mommy is watching you. She's always going to be here, and anytime you need your mommy, go into a quiet room and talk to her. She'll listen. And you can call me anytime. I'll still be in your life, I promise you."

"Can I come stay with you on the weekends?" I asked.

"How about one weekend per month, if your daddy is okay with that?" she said, picking my bag up and putting it in my hand. "But only if you promise to be a big girl. Don't give your daddy trouble, listen to what he tells you to do, and if he or anyone in that house hurts you, you call me and I'll be here. You understand?" I nodded, and she stood to her feet. "You're strong."

I didn't say anything this time as Auntie Tamara rang the doorbell. I didn't even cry. I understood that this was something I couldn't control and that I had to do what she told me to do. I had to be strong. I had to be a good girl. I had to, or else I wouldn't be able to see her. As the door to the house began to open, I prayed to God that He'd let Mama watch over me and protect me. I needed it.

Chapter Four

CLAIRE

As I stated before, I tried to dedicate my life to being the perfect mother and wife. I did additional things, made sure the house was perfect, made sure my body was fit and pleasing to my husband, made sure my daughter had all the coolest clothes, but I was never appreciated. I tried to be the best woman of God. I read my Bible daily, I prayed not only for myself but for the world, and I helped others, as God had commanded. Why, then, did I feel the Lord's absence as strong as my own family's?

Every night I found myself having a glass of wine, sometimes two and I cried. I cried because my husband didn't kiss me anymore. I cried because my daughter had no respect for me or my rules. I knew that although my friends admired me, they were all waiting to see me stumble so that they could mock me. And I was quite sure that the thin fabric enclosing all my pain was soon to rip.

After Sunday brunch, I arrived home to a burnt roast and castigated myself for staying out too long. After throwing out the roast, I cleaned the house and then found myself sitting at the kitchen table, deep in thought. Neither Sarah nor Mark was home, and neither of them had bothered to explain where they would be. I thought back to what Susan had said at brunch, about how husbands cheated and the telltale signs that accompanied this. No, Mark would never do such a thing, and yet I found myself wondering what I would do if I caught him. Prior to today's brunch, a cheating husband was not something I'd been concerned about, but now, all of a sudden, it was resting on the surface of my spirit.

Sad thing was, even if I ever did find out Mark was cheating on me, chances were I'd do nothing. I'd prefer to deal with his infidelity silently than divorce him in front of hundreds of faithful church members who admired us. We were examples, and I cared more about what other people thought of us than how I should react to him. I was completely oblivious to the fact that I should be more concerned about what God thought of my actions, versus other people.

I remembered when Mark and I used to be happy. That was when Sarah was still in middle school and she actually valued my opinions. Mark and I would go to every soccer game and cheer Sarah on as proud parents. We had a family day every Friday, where we'd play games well into the middle of the night and fall asleep on the living room floor, in front of the fireplace. I remembered how wonderful Christmases used to be back when Mark actually put thought into my gifts. He'd buy me expensive jewelry, spoil me with different perfumes from around the world, and give me nice furs. I remembered summer vacations in the islands, just the two of us, relaxing on the beach and drinking virgin margaritas. Now all he did was give me a card and flowers on my birthday. I had a garden. What did I need flowers for? And as far as vacations went, we hadn't taken one since Sarah was ten.

The changes had happened slowly, and as much as I tried to pinpoint the reason my husband had stopped looking at me, I couldn't. We had just drifted apart, as people sometimes did. I couldn't even remember the last time we'd made love. It had to have been six months ago, on my birthday. A few months after that, we had had our anniversary, which he'd forgotten about. We hadn't even made love on that day, because he'd claimed he was too tired from community work. I hadn't got upset, because I admired the fact that Mark had put himself before others, helping to build the community, which in turn, had shown our church members how good a man he was. Even church had its politics.

And here I was, turning forty in half a year, noticing the wrinkles forming under my eyes and on my forehead, seeing blemishes that hadn't been there before, and wondering if it was too late to make Mark love me again. If I were twenty, then he'd admire me. He used to love my flawless, smooth skin before the winkles came. He used to kiss every inch of me and make me feel like I was the only woman for him. If only I could go back.

But in my morning prayer, the Lord had revealed to me that we couldn't go back. We could only move forward. We had to leave the past behind and build a better tomorrow. I couldn't waste my time wishing things hadn't ended up how they had. I could only pray that things would get better from here on out.

As I sat at the kitchen table, deep in thought, I heard a knock on the front door. *Strange.* Both my husband and my daughter had house keys, and I wasn't expecting anyone to come around, since our only church service had ended at eleven and we girls had already had our brunch. Usually, our husbands went off to play golf or watch the game and left us to our gossip. Maybe one of the girls was stopping by to tell me about something that had happened after we parted ways.

I opened my front door and had to fight the urge to gasp. A black woman and a child stood at my door. That wasn't a sight I saw every day. I hoped they weren't our new neighbors. Sure, it was 2014, but our wealthy community hadn't had to deal with blacks in this neck of the woods, and I didn't want to deal with my older neighbors freaking out and calling us for a word. Some of us were still set in our ways.

I looked at the woman's dingy shirt and faded jeans, and it was apparent to me that they didn't live anywhere close by. They might live on the south side of Chicago, but not in the suburbs. I looked down at the child's worn shoes and frowned. I didn't like seeing a child who was not properly tended to. I wondered if they could sense my distaste at their appearance. I could certainly tell by the hard look on the woman's face that she didn't approve of me much, either.

The little girl stood there, holding on to her luggage and looking up at me with expectant eyes. What did she want? Food? Were they homeless? They had to be. That would explain why they had shown up in this type of neighborhood, miles away from the hood, looking for something.

"Can I help you?" I asked, forcing a smile to my face.

"Yes, you can," the woman said with a stoic expression. "I need to speak with Mark Douglas."

I laughed. "Well, you won't get anywhere by demanding things on my property, missy."

"Who are you?" the woman asked, shifting on her feet, as if getting impatient.

"Well, who are you? You're the one who showed up at my doorstep," I kindly reminded her, although I could tell by her lowered eyes that she didn't buy my politeness.

"It doesn't matter who I am. I need to speak with Mark. It's extremely urgent," she said.

"Well, I am his wife, so whatever you need to say to him, you can say to me. Mark won't be back for a few hours," I explained, deciding not to let her push my buttons. I was better than this filth.

"Okay." The woman nodded, but I could tell something was brewing underneath by how her shoulders tensed. "You're Mark's wife. . . . Well, Mark's wife, meet Mark's daughter, Ciara."

"What?" I almost laughed; I really wanted to laugh. I was sure the smile on my face looked silly. Somebody was playing a joke on me. Things like this didn't happen in real life. I looked behind the woman to see if there were any cameramen hiding in the nearby bushes. I saw nothing, which made my smile fade. The woman stared back at me with a serious expression. I looked down at the little girl with a cynical smirk. "But she's a little black girl."

"She's biracial," the woman said furiously, correcting me. I saw her fists clench and unclench at her sides.

"Still, you're mistaken. My husband and I have been married for twenty years!"

"Well, sorry to break it to you, but that doesn't stop him from messing around on you and conceiving a child out of wedlock," she explained with a nasty attitude.

If I wasn't a godly woman, I would've smacked that attitude off of her face. I thought back to what Susan had said about her third husband cheating on her. *But no. Not Mark.*

"He wouldn't cheat on me with a *black* woman!" I screamed. Before I could compose myself, the woman was in my face.

"I don't have time to deal with your prejudice hang-ups. This little girl's mother just died, and Mark is the only family she has got. If he doesn't take her, she'll end up in a foster home. I promised myself I wouldn't let that happen to this little girl. Get a DNA test and it'll prove everything. Better yet, take a look at this picture."

She shoved a picture of my husband in my hands and stepped back so that I could examine it. My husband stood next to a beautiful, young black girl, smiling brightly. I snorted. This picture could mean anything.

"So what? My husband took a random picture with a black woman. Proves nothing." I tried to hand the picture back to her, but she wouldn't take it.

"Turn the picture over," she demanded.

I sighed and did what she said. On the back of the picture was my husband's handwriting. In his note he said he hoped they'd meet again, but what hurt the most was how he called her his love. I couldn't remember the last time I had heard him call me that.

"I can't believe this," I said, trying to stay composed, but I was sure I looked as if I'd lost my composure. My husband had had an affair with a *black* woman and had had a *black* baby? *No, no, no,* I thought. *We can't take her. I can't do this. Our church. Our members. This is the biggest scandal.* "Take this back." I handed her the picture. This time she took it. "And take her back."

"I can't," the woman replied.

"Take her back!"

"I told you, I ca—"

I took a step closer to the woman, making her stop midsentence. Her look told me not to take another step forward. "What are you trying to do? Huh? Ruin my family?" I asked, ignoring the threat in her eyes.

"Your husband did that, not me," she responded evenly and then bent down to face the little girl. She rubbed her shoulders and kissed her forehead. "You're going to stay here now. I'll come back to visit you. You know my number, Ciara. If anything happens, you call me. Okay?" She then stood and began walking away.

"Hey, wait!" I shouted after her. "Come back! You can't just leave her here!" But the woman never turned around. She got into her car and drove off.

I sucked in a deep breath, fighting a round of curse words, God forbid. Looking down at the little girl with her bags, I began to get light-headed. I couldn't process what this all meant. I couldn't deal with this little girl looking up at me expectantly. I wanted to scream, cry, throw things, do anything that would make me seem ungraceful. Instead, I kneeled down to face the girl and smiled. I'd mastered putting on a fake smile years ago, yet today my skills seemed to need a little brushing up. I was sure that even this child could see how fake my smile was.

"Carmen, right?" I asked politely.

"Ciara," she answered quietly, frowning, as if she wanted to cry.

I nodded and stood up straight. "Ciara." I wanted to laugh. "Your mother couldn't think of something better than Ciara? What about good old-fashioned names like Mary or Jane?" I half expected her to answer. "Never mind. Come on inside."

I guided the little girl through the foyer and sat her down at the island in the middle of our kitchen. I watched her as she looked around my immaculate kitchen with big hazel eyes. She was a pretty little girl. Her hair was silky and was gathered in two pigtails with red barrettes on the ends. Her outfit looked worn-out, as if her mother shopped at Goodwill. I noticed her nose, which was small and pointed, much like Mark's. I found myself touching my own nose and remembering how Mark used to get picked on for having such a feminine nose, one that was rare on a man like him. And looking at this little girl and seeing that same nose made everything click into place. The part of my brain that denied any claims this little girl had against my husband was now operating at full speed.

My husband had had an affair. Susan was right. What would the church think of this monstrosity? Well, that was simple. We wouldn't tell them. But then how would I explain a little biracial girl living with us? Maybe I could say that we'd adopted her, but for how long would that falsehood hold?

I could see it now, my husband and I getting kicked out of the church, being forced to step down, being the laughingstock of the whole town. I could hear the accusations now, as most of the women would blame me for my husband's infidelity. Most of the women I knew always blamed the wife, saying how it was the wife's responsibility to make sure her husband was satisfied at home.

I couldn't worry myself with all of that, not when I hadn't even spoken with my husband. That lying, cheating son of a gun! There was nothing I wouldn't have done for my husband. I catered to him. I was the perfect wife! And the lowest thing he could ever do, he'd done. It wasn't that he had had an affair; it was who he had had an affair with. A black woman.

I was raised in a strict Christian home, and my parents had taught me to believe that dating outside of my race was low and unthinkable. If my parents saw blacks even mingling with whites, they'd go on a rampage about how the two races should remain divided. I'd never thought to question their beliefs; I had simply taken their words for truth. What would my parents think when they learned about this child? I'd surely be disowned.

I didn't realize I was holding a bottle of wine. I must've grabbed it out of the cabinet as my thoughts shifted from being disowned to getting a DNA test to make sure the child was, in fact, Mark's. For all I knew, it could be a scam to get money out of us. Even as I thought that, I knew it wasn't the case. Somehow, I knew the child was Mark's. I didn't waste time grabbing a wineglass. I had opened the bottle previously, so I pulled hard on the cork to dislodge it and then drank straight from the bottle, ignoring the glass I had sitting on the counter.

Out of the corner of my eye I saw the little girl watching me. I took another big gulp, clumsily wiped my mouth with the back of my hand, and burped. It wasn't very ladylike, but I wasn't up to being the perfect lady at the moment.

"What?" I asked Ciara, sitting the bottle down on the counter. "Never seen a white woman drink before?"

Her brows furrowed, as if she was trying to understand my question.

I shook my head. "I spent my whole life following orders. Don't drink too much wine. Wear only dresses. Posture is everything, so sit up straight. Never raise your voice, because it isn't proper. The best one I've heard, though, is, always stick by your husband, *no matter what*." I picked the bottle up and took another drink. "No matter what, they say. Even if he had an affair. Well, I'll tell you one thing, Ciara. I'm tired of following rules."

I grabbed my cell phone from the counter and dialed my husband's number. We needed to talk.

Chapter Five

MARK

"Well, boys, good game, but I have to be getting home to the wife," Daniel, my good friend, said. He gave me a roll of the eyes and laughed. "Her parents are coming into town and will be here for dinner."

"Ah." I nodded in understanding as we headed back to the golf cart. Ron and Ben, two other good friends who had joined us for an afternoon of golf, began walking in our direction. "I know all too well about visiting parents. My wife's mother is as evil as they come. Everything has to be perfect when she visits, and I count each second painfully until she leaves."

That statement earned a barking laugh from Ben as he and Ron joined us on the back of the golf cart. "Well, that beats going home to an empty house," Ben said with a grunt. He had divorced a "nagging" wife of two years against my advice. I remembered the many conversations we'd had after church in which I advised him that divorce wasn't permitted by God. I had broken down every biblical reference, offered marriage counseling, and prayed over him and his ex-wife, and still nothing had worked.

Ben once told me that he and his ex-wife had just simply grown apart. My argument was that a marriage lasted only if both parties were willing to try to make it work. Ben's response to that was that once he realized he was no longer in love with his ex-wife, it was too late. Neither he nor his ex-wife was willing to make it work.

I had a tendency to make other people's problems my own. It was a burden that came along with being a preacher. People wanted me to understand their problems and give them guidance. I had spent a lot of nights in my study doing just that.

When Ben told me how he and his wife had lost their love for each other, I spent many nights contemplating how one went about restoring what seemed to have already been lost. I came up short. Two people had to be willing to make it work in order for it to work. It took unity, commitment, prayer, and faith to make a marriage last. When one of those four components began to malfunction, it caused a ripple effect, and everything else began to crumble. That is, unless the malfunctioning component was fixed before it caused damage in the other areas. This theory of mine worked for all marriages, even my own.

But instead of thinking about my wife, my thoughts traveled back seven years ago, to one of the best days of my life. I remembered the moment I saw Candace Tucker; she was the most beautiful woman I'd ever laid eyes on. I had never been attracted to a woman of color before, but it was exactly that fact that had reeled me in. It was the way the sun glistened on her bare brown skin as she sat at the beach. I couldn't stop noticing how her teal bathing suit complemented her dark tones. And then she looked at me, directly at me, as if knowing I was watching her, and she smiled. I forgot about my wife, Claire, and our daughter, Sarah. They became distant memories as I shared a bed with Ms. Tucker that night.

That next morning, I remembered that I was a preacher with a wife and child waiting for me to return home. I made up a lie about how I had fallen asleep in my office at the church while working late. Claire seemed to buy my excuse, and so I never brought the matter up again.

The night with Candace had haunted me throughout the years, however. Never in a million years had I thought I'd have an affair.

Of course, that was the only time I'd been with Candace. When I woke up that morning, I saw her lying there peacefully, her chest rising and falling softly as she slept. But as I looked down at her, I saw my sin, and it made me sick to my stomach. I rushed to the bathroom, where I fell to my knees in prayer, asking God to forgive me my offenses, praying He'd wash them away as if they had never happened. I knew I sure would.

I then headed out of the bathroom and quickly grabbed all my things. I noticed the picture we had taken the day before on the beach, and picked it up from the table. We looked happy, and I would have believed we were a couple had my wife's face not been dancing in the back of my mind. I laid the picture down and turned to leave, but my own guilt got the best of me. I had never been the kind of man to have relations with a woman and then leave her wondering where I'd gone when she woke up. I took a pen from my briefcase and wrote something on the back of the picture. That way she would always have something to remember me by. I hoped that would be enough as I walked away from my sin.

"Are you going to start this thing or not?" Daniel joked, snapping me out of my daydream. I was once again in the golf cart with my buddies, on my way home to a wife who would never know of my infidelity.

My phone vibrated in my pocket.

"One second," I said to Daniel as I answered my cell phone after looking down at my caller ID. "Hey, honey."

"Get home. Now!" she practically screamed, making me jump and shake the golf cart. I looked over at Daniel, who whistled and shook his head, as if he'd overheard my wife's harsh commands.

"Is something wrong?" I asked, but the phone went silent. She'd hung up. I blinked a few times before putting my phone back in my pocket.

"Wife issues?" Daniel asked.

"I suppose so," I responded before starting up the golf cart. "Wife sounds upset. I probably forgot to clean my shavings out of the sink this morning."

"Want to trade wives?" Daniel joked.

I laughed. "If it were only that easy."

Chapter Six

CIARA

The white lady hung up the phone and leaned against the kitchen sink, holding on to it for support. Her arms were like Jell-O when she moved, and it almost made me laugh, but I knew I shouldn't do that. She woulda got mad.

I missed Auntie Tamara already, but even more than that, I missed my mommy. I wished I was outside, playing with my old friends. I wondered if I'd make new friends at whatever school I would go to. I wondered if this lady would be my new mommy. I didn't think I liked her much. I could tell she didn't like me, either. She had made Auntie Tamara mad, and Auntie Tamara was always nice to everyone. Auntie Tamara didn't ever do anything to hurt people. She gave to the homeless people, and she always gave her blood to people who were dying. So I knew my auntie wasn't wrong. I frowned as I stared at the lady.

"He answers the phone and says, 'Hey, honey'," the lady said to herself, storming around the kitchen. She knocked over an orange that sat in a basket on the edge of the counter, but didn't notice. I thought about telling her but didn't want her to yell at me. "He only says that when he is around his friends. Facade? I'd say so!" She suddenly stopped and turned toward me. "You," she said. I thought she had forgotten I was sitting there, watching her. She stared at me for a few seconds and then turned back around and continued blabbing. "I can't wait for him to walk through this door! I can't wait to tell him how he's ruined our lives!"

How did my daddy ruin her life? Was it because of me? I wondered. I wished Auntie Tamara would come back and get me. I just wanted to go home and lie in my bed with my dolls and pretend that everything was okay.

"Here I am, worrying about myself, and you're sitting there, looking scared," the lady said. "I'm a mess, I know. Please excuse me." She then stormed out of the kitchen, leaving me alone.

I stood there, looking around the big kitchen, noticing every detail, in awe. There was a huge black refrigerator built into the wall. It was so shiny, I could see my reflection. All the cabinets were dark brown and matched the big table in the middle of the kitchen. She even had real fruit sitting in the basket on the big table. Everything was clean and spotless, like she had a maid who cleaned for her every day.

I'd seen kitchens like this only in movies and my favorite TV shows. I bet there was food in every cabinet, just waiting to be eaten. Mama had been on food stamps and hadn't been able to buy a lot of everything. My stomach growled as I thought about eating marshmallows and mountains of ice cream.

All too soon, the lady returned, breathing evenly and seeming calm. She took a deep breath and turned to me.

"How old are you?"

"Six," I told her.

"First grade? What school do you go to? Never mind. Don't answer that. I guess it wouldn't matter now. We'd have to enroll you in a new . . ." She paused, frowning. "We, as in Mark and I. As in our marriage would survive this. Enrolling you in a new school would mean accepting you in my home. What is this world coming to?"

She didn't want me there. I felt alone and afraid. I didn't have anyone to hold me close and make me feel secure. Auntie Tamara had said everything would be all right, but then she had left me. I wanted to run away and go back home. I'd hide under my bed when Auntie Tamara was home, and I'd eat at night, while she slept. She didn't have to know I was home, as long as I was home.

I was crying, but I didn't use tears. Those were Mama's tears.

Chapter Seven

MARK

It was rare that my wife called me up, angry, and told me to come straight home, ordering me around like I was a child. In fact, I couldn't recall a time when she had actually done so. As I walked through the door, my heart gave a little shudder as I visualized my daughter sitting at our kitchen table with a police officer, waiting to tell me how he'd caught her doing drugs or something else illegal. I imagined my wife standing near the island, refusing to take a seat due to shock, blaming herself for our daughter's downfall. I quickly allowed the thought to dissipate. Sarah was an honor student with some of the highest grades in her class. She was captain of the chess team, the drama club, and the swim team, and she never missed a day of school, not even when she was sick. I couldn't have asked for God to bless me with a better daughter.

So something else was wrong.

I closed the front door behind me and could make out my wife's figure from the foyer. I could tell by the way she was acting that something was wrong. She was pacing back and forth in the kitchen, worry lines stretched across her forehead. She noticed me staring and frowned.

I tried to put on a loving smile as I walked into the kitchen, but she didn't buy it. That was when I notice a little girl sitting on one of the bar stools at the island.

Confused, I looked at my wife and then back at the little girl. The child turned her head in my direction, and her big hazel eyes began to examine me. I smiled politely at her and walked up to my wife to kiss her cheek. She pushed me away.

"Honey, what is it?" I asked, noticing the open bottle of wine on the counter. My wife stared at me, as if deciding how to approach the subject that had her in a tizzy. I could tell because she opened her mouth to speak but then quickly closed it.

"You know . . . I played this moment over and over again in my head, you know, how I'd strangle you as soon as you walked through the door, or smack you, scream at the top of my lungs, something." Claire laughed to herself, picking up the bottle of wine.

I took it from her hands before she could even take a drink. I'd bought this bottle only yesterday because she needed it for a recipe and she'd already drunk most of it. Something was definitely wrong.

"Give it back," she urged. "Better yet, keep it. You'll need the wine just as much as me."

"Is there something wrong with Sarah?" I asked, putting the bottle of wine down on the counter beside Claire.

"Is there something wrong with *our* daughter?" Claire started laughing at a joke that only she seemed to understand. "No, there isn't anything wrong with our daughter . . . but what about *your* daughter? Funny thing happened today, Mark. A woman stopped by and dropped off a little girl who, she claims, is your daughter."

Flabbergasted, I turned and looked at the little girl behind me. She was watching me with a shy and sad expression on her face. There was something about her face that was oddly familiar, but I couldn't put my finger on it. I turned back to face my wife. "I don't understand."

"Imagine how I felt when I found out my husband was a lying, cheating son of a b—" Claire raised her hand to strike me, but I quickly blocked her. "You had an affair! You had another child! A black child! Do you even know what this means? I should divorce you! I should burn your name in the church and take off with everything we own! I should—"

"Back up, Claire," I urged, not understanding what she was saying. Her words came out in a rush. "What are you saying?"

"Is my English not clear, Mark? Maybe it's my love that was never clear to you. If it had been, you wouldn't have run off with a black woman and had an affair! You wouldn't have brought hell to our home!"

Everything she had said finally clicked, and the image of Candace's face surfaced in my thoughts, as it had earlier that day. That was who the little girl sitting at our island looked like. Suddenly I was nearly seven years in the past, smiling down at Candace, who caught me staring and looked up at me with a smile.

"It's a beautiful day," Candace said, leaning back so that her elbows rested on the blanket and inclining her chin so that the sun beat down directly on her face. Her eyes were closed, and her mouth hung slightly open. I imagined kissing those lips, and I didn't even know her name.

"Can I take a seat?" I asked, and she nodded. I sat in the sand, near to where she was relaxing on her blanket. "What's your name?" I decided to ask.

"Candace. And you?" She opened her eyes and met mine with a smile.

I leaned back next to her, mimicking how she sat on her blanket. The sand bit at my elbows, but I didn't care. "Mark."

"You're getting a little red there, Mark," Candace said, looking down at my skin.

"Oh." I smiled. "I forgot sun block. Do you have any?"

She laughed to herself and inclined her chin again so that the sun beat down on her. "I don't need sun block," she said. "Black don't crack."

Claire pushed me, causing me to break away from my memory of the first words I'd ever spoken to Candace. It had been seven years since I'd seen her, and yet not a day had passed when I didn't think about her. With new eyes, I looked over at the little girl and saw both Candace and myself in her. My spirit confirmed that she was my child; it was something I just knew deep inside. I could see the fear and confusion in the little girl's eyes . . . eyes that were so much like my own. And her nose. She had my nose.

My God.

I had to look away from her. I couldn't handle it. I turned to Claire, who seemed ready to push me again.

"Where is the girl's mom?" I asked.

"Dead," Claire spat.

My heart began to sink.

"And guess who is now responsible for this little girl? You are. *We* are." Claire began to cry. "Just imagine what the church will say. Mark, you're going to have to step down. I mean, that's if we even keep the little girl. Do we have to? Can we put her up for adoption or something? Just brush this under the rug and pretend she was never here?"

"Slow down, Claire," I pleaded. My wife had just told me that my affair had resulted in a love child, and that the mother, Candace, was dead. I couldn't even begin to process everything, especially with my wife already being several steps ahead of me. She'd obviously had time to imagine what this scandal would do to our reputations;

she'd already come up with plans to have the little girl taken away. But as a man of God, would I permit it? Would I run away from my sins and brush them under the rug, or would I own up to my errors?

The most prominent emotion I felt was dread, because of the consequences of my actions. I didn't even allow myself to grieve over Candace's death or even ask how it had happened. I didn't even allow myself to pull this little girl into my arms and welcome her into my family or to see how she was holding up because she'd lost her mother. I didn't even think to reassure my wife, to apologize and let her know it was a one-time offense. No, I was selfish. I saw only my own grief.

I knew I was supposed to be a godly man, but I felt like one of the worst kinds of men there were. God had to be punishing me for what I had done all those years ago. Why else would He bring this little girl into my life if He wasn't trying to condemn me? How was I supposed to love this little girl, knowing that God was punishing me for what had happened? Shouldn't I have been happy after learning that I had another child? Why, then, did I feel the worst kind of dread? Maybe because my life was about to change for the worse, maybe because I knew I was about to lose everything I'd worked so hard for: my wife, my career as a preacher, and my way of life.

My wife was right. We couldn't keep this little girl.

Chapter Eight

TAMARA

I couldn't believe I had left Ciara with that woman. I hadn't even hugged the poor child before leaving her, and I definitely hadn't reassured her that she was with good people. As I drove home, I cried. I had to pull the car off the freeway and let it all out. I couldn't do that when Ciara was near, as someone had to be strong for her, but now that I was alone, I couldn't help but scream and punch my dashboard and blame God for Candace's death. Why did He need Candace more than her own daughter needed her?

"God, how can you do this?" I cried out to the Lord. "This little girl needs her mama, and you just take her away! It's not fair! You said you were a good God, one who was fair and just and right in everything. How can you not see that this isn't right?" I paused, as if expecting God to answer, but He didn't. I wasn't even sure if he was listening.

I remembered when Ciara was two years old. She used to call me TT because she couldn't pronounce "Auntie Tamara." Everything was "TT" to her. Every fruit, piece of clothing, and toy was "TT." Those memories were the ones I called to on rainy days. I had never really understood how those small moments would one day mean the world to me. Maybe if I had, I would have praised God more and learned never to take the small things for granted.

One thing I would never take for granted was how Candace had saved my life. I had been in an abusive relationship and would've lost my life if I had stayed with the guy. He was some wannabe thug at the time, robbing cars and breaking into people's houses. I never really knew the extent of his crimes, only that he was able to provide for me.

His name was Dominique, and we had been dating for a year before he asked me to move in with him. Dominique was a sweet boy, despite the crime. He never seemed to get angry, always showered me with love, and gave me a lot of nice gifts. Obviously, I thought he was the one for me, so when he asked me to move in with him, I obliged.

Some girls told stories about how the guy abruptly changed into a bad person, but that didn't happen with Dominique. It was a slow change. Dominique's mother passed away in the summer, and by the end of the winter, he was putting his hands on me. It was as if he wanted me to be his mother and hated every time I proved that I wasn't her. He'd lash out if I did anything slightly differently than how his mother would've done it. He started off by simply correcting me, and then the corrections turned into screaming matches, which then turned into punches.

The abuse got to the point where I wasn't even allowed to leave the house, and my every move inside the house was monitored. Dominique had become a crazy man and began spending most of his nights on the streets, getting drunk and stealing from other people. When that need was satisfied, he'd come home and start an argument with me.

One night, Dominique barged into the house after he'd probably popped some pill. I'd seen him take pills a few times before, and he'd claimed it was because of migraines. He came through the door, saying that while he was outside, he'd heard a man inside.

"Where he at?" Dominique screamed, pushing me against the wall as he walked into the bedroom.

"I don't know what you're talking about!" I cried, holding on to my arm that had made contact with the wall, as it had begun to sting.

Dominique opened the closet door and began taking out hangers full of clothes and throwing them on the floor. Once he saw that there wasn't a man hiding in the closet, he proceeded to the bathroom. I didn't follow him; I ran into the living room, intent on calling the cops. The phone was yanked out of my hand as I brought it up to my ear. Dominique then grabbed my hair and yanked me backward, and I fell to the floor.

"You callin' the cops now?" he asked and then kicked me in my stomach, causing me to scream in pain.

"Dominique, please," I begged, scooting away from him until my back hit the wall. Dominique walked toward me, his eyes low and ominous.

"You messin' with other men?"

"No," I instantly responded, looking directly up into his eyes. I wanted him to see that I was telling the truth. "I promise, I'm not, baby! It's only been you. If there was a man here, where did he disappear to? Huh? Where did he go, Dominique?"

Dominique's eyebrows furrowed, as if he was concentrating, and then he kneeled down in front of me and gently rubbed his hand against my cheek. I was so confused by his sudden show of affection and didn't know how to respond. "You right, baby," he said. "Ain't nowhere he could go."

The breeze coming from the open living room window momentarily stole Dominique's attention. He stared at the window, as if deep in thought, and then snapped his head back in my direction. "He went through the window, didn't he?"

"The window is facing the front, so you would've saw him—" Before I could even finish, Dominique grabbed my head and slammed it into the wall behind me. Everything around me went dark, but I felt every blow to my ribs as he stood and started to kick me. I hadn't believed in God back then, but I found myself praying, asking Him to allow me to make it through that beating. I promised that I'd give my life to Him and live for Him.

In mid-punch, Dominique collapsed on the floor beside me, finally crashing from whatever drug he had taken. I started crying, thanking God for allowing me to survive. Eventually, my vision cleared, and I was able to see.

Something told me to get up and leave before Dominique woke up, that now was my chance to escape. I remembered how hard it was to stand and focus, feeling seconds away from passing out myself. However, I had more than my own strength helping me get out of the house.

I walked for two miles, until I ran into a girl around my age as she was getting out of her car, which was parked in a driveway. I was going to cross to the other side of the street and keep my bruises hidden due to my embarrassment, but something told me to go to her and ask for help.

"Excuse me," I said, approaching the woman. She turned toward me and gasped. She quickly shut her car door and met me the rest of the way.

"Are you okay?" she asked.

"No," I said with a shaky voice. "I need help."

She didn't hesitate to take me into her house. She guided me to her bathroom and sat me on the toilet. She left me there, but I could hear her rummaging around for things in the other room. She returned with a basketful of bandages, ointments, cleaning pads, and different kinds of medicine. She laid the basket on the sink and began placing things on the counter.

"My name is Candace, by the way, and I'm a nurse," she said in a calm and soothing voice. "Must've been God's will that you found me, because I'm just the right person to get you patched up."

"I'm beginning to believe this," I told her. Candace turned toward me out of curiosity.

"Oh, you hadn't believed in Him before?"

"Not really," I replied. "But when you pray not to get killed and you don't, you start to wonder who answered that prayer and if He is real."

"He's very real," Candace said and poured alcohol onto a cotton ball. "Tilt your head back." I did as she commanded and prepared to feel the sting of the alcohol as she began to clean the gash in my forehead. Surprisingly, it didn't hurt as bad as I thought it would. "Who did this to you, if you don't mind me asking?"

Actually, I didn't mind her asking at all. I'd kept everything Dominique had ever done to me bottled up, and for the first time I felt I was safe enough to speak about it. I told her everything that had happened, from the very beginning.

"I'm sorry to hear this," Candace said, placing a Band-Aid on one of my many cuts. "Do you have a place to go until things blow over?"

"No. I don't have any family," I explained honestly.

"Me either," Candace said with the saddest look in her eyes. "You can stay here for a few days, or for however long you need to."

I looked into her eyes and saw the sincerity there. I couldn't believe her generosity. "Really?"

"Yeah." She nodded, smiling lightly. "I know you don't know me, and I definitely don't know you, but I believe in the goodness of God, and if He brought you to me, He'd expect me to help you the best I can."

I took Candace up on her offer, and from that moment onward, our friendship was unbreakable. A month later, when I learned that she was pregnant and single, I vowed to be whatever she needed me to be. After all, she had been there for me.

In a way, I felt like I wasn't keeping up my end of the bargain now that she was gone. Given how much Candace had done for me, I couldn't just give her daughter away to a stranger. I needed to find a way to be in Ciara's life. I owed it to both of them to try, and so I'd fight for this. It was about time I learned how to fight back.

Chapter Nine

SARAH

As I made my way home, I thought about how I couldn't stand my mother and her ideas of perfection and womanly grace. "Sarah, always sit with your legs crossed," she would say. "Always place a napkin on your lap, and tuck an edge into your shirt to avoid any accidents. Brush your hair at least fifty times a night so that it is silky and smooth. Always use your inside voice when talking to friends. It's ladylike. Never curse in front of company. It spoils a lady's image. Always curtsy when greeting guests. Never speak unless spoken to. Our guests love obedient little girls. Never wear pants. A lady always wears dresses. Sit up as straight as a board. Men don't like a woman with bad posture."

Who even curtsied anymore? *Ugh.* My mother had a rule for everything. She was too strict and solely focused on creating the perfect daughter, not realizing how she was only pushing me away.

My friends always complained about the most trivial of things. Their mothers only made them take out the trash, and that was enough to send them into a fit. Me? My mother made me take a single item of trash out to the Dumpster outside because she didn't like the idea of any trash being in the house, not even in a trash can. I wished life was as simple as throwing away unwanted things in a trash can inside my house, instead of taking the complicated route. I wished I was allowed to wear a pair of skinny jeans, like my friends were. I wished I could listen to the current pop music blasting on the radio. I wished I could go to the movies and see scary flicks with my friends. But no. Mother was too strict.

No wonder Dad ran into his study every time he came home. Who wanted to be around the Wicked Witch of the West? Sometimes Dad and I would sneak behind Mother's back and eat candy in his study, because she prohibited us from having unneeded sugar. Dad once woke me up at two in the morning to eat a whole bucket of ice cream. It was the good kind, chocolate chip cookie dough. We giggled the whole time we ate it, and I branded that moment into my memory like my childhood Christmases.

Although I couldn't stand my mother, I loved my father. Yes, at times, he could be just as strict as Mother, but he was more loving. He was always teaching me what was right and what was wrong, but he didn't go to extremes like Mother did.

Dad did have his moments, though. He was the head of our church and had to live by example. He tended to be very strict with me when we were around his church members. His expectations were high. I was his perfect daughter, the one he used as an example at church so that other parents knew how their children should behave.

Because my dad had such high expectations, I always tried to meet them. My grades were great, my friends were Father approved, and I was on the swim team because Dad loved Michael Phelps. I played chess because Dad once held the record at his old high school for the quickest win during his final game. I played the cello just because Daddy loved the sound. I admired the man my father was, and tried to please him in everything that I did.

There was one thing that I was keeping a secret, my boyfriend Ryan. He was a senior at my school, a total bad boy, and a total babe. If my father knew I was dating him, he'd just about die. Especially if my dad learned that Ryan was eighteen. And Ryan would be dead if Dad ever found out what had happened last night.

Ryan had tried to sleep with me.

No, I didn't let it happen. I mean, in many ways I wanted it to. I was a sixteen-year-old virgin, which was like a total feat in this day and age. I was a pretty girl, and I had always been told this was so. Most guys would fall at my feet to date me, but when they learned who my father was, they backed away. Ryan didn't. In fact, when he learned my father was a preacher, he tried even harder to date me. He'd leave cute little notes in my locker, telling me how much he liked me.

"You're so beautiful," Ryan had said last night, when he'd tried to seduce me. He'd been playing with the top button on my blouse as I sat next to him on his bed. I'd smiled and playfully smacked his hand away from my shirt.

"But I'm sure you already know how beautiful you are," he'd said, meeting my eyes, admiration coloring his own. "You're like . . . the first snowfall. You know how beautiful it is, that first layer of snow, before anything touches it and ruins its purity. That's you." His hands were once again trying to unbutton my blouse.

"Then we should keep it that way," I teased, knowing he was referring to my virginity. "Don't want to ruin the first snowfall."

Ryan contemplated my words. "Might as well enjoy the snow before it melts. Didn't your dad teach you that God creates things so we can enjoy them? That's why he created sunrises and sunsets, so that we can appreciate and praise Him for it."

I giggled as he successfully unbuttoned my blouse. I held it closed, not allowing him to see underneath. "For a guy who doesn't go to church, you sure know a lot about God."

He smiled almost mischievously, which caused me to squirm excitedly. I couldn't ignore the desire that arose in me in his presence. It was almost demanding. Ryan looked up at me through his thick, beautiful eyelashes, and he said, "All I'm saying is that you should let me enjoy you."

I wanted to let him enjoy me, because I would most definitely enjoy him. He was the hottest guy in our school, with dark brown, curly hair and a mischievous stare. Every girl wanted to be with him, but he wanted only me, the preacher's daughter. Although I loved my father, I often looked at his position in the church as a curse. No one wanted to hang out with the preacher's daughter. I was dull and no fun, and I definitely didn't have any edge. However, Ryan didn't see me that way. He saw my beauty as a rarity. He loved my goodness, even though there didn't seem to be much goodness inside of him.

Ryan and I had been dating for a few months, and lately he'd been getting a little touchy-feely, wanting more than I was willing to offer him. If anyone knew that I was dating him, it would get back to my father. Ryan liked the idea that we snuck around. We'd steal kisses in the boy's locker room, make out in the southern part of the library, where no one would look, and I'd occasionally go over to his house for an hour after church, which was the only free time I ever had. I'd make up some lie to my parents about how I was going to the library to study, and sometimes, like today, I just took off without telling them.

After I demanded that he stop trying to remove my shirt, I buttoned it back up and told him I needed to leave. He seemed upset at first but decided to let it go. For a bad boy, he was extremely patient.

As we walked out the front door of his house, I kept replaying Ryan's words over and over in my mind. *All I'm saying is that you should let me enjoy you.* Deep down, I really wanted him too, but I thought about my father and how good a man he was. My father would never succumb to sexual temptation, and I wouldn't allow myself to, either.

I didn't have my own car, so Ryan dropped me off at home. However, he made sure to drop me off a few houses away from mine so that my parents wouldn't see him. I watched him drive away, and then I walked to the house and headed inside. Fresh flowers engulfed the entryway. Mother had an obsession with flowers, and she had a beautiful array planted along the walkway leading up to the front door. I pulled out my keys and unlocked the door.

As I stepped inside, I heard my father shout, "Slow down, Claire!"

I could see half of my mother in the kitchen, trying to calm down by breathing deeply, but it didn't seem to be working. My father stepped into view, with his back turned to me. No one said anything for a few seconds, and then my dad decided to speak.

"How did she get here?" he asked.

"Some woman dropped her off," Mom cried.

"So some random woman shows up at our door and tells you that this little girl is mine? And you believed her?"

"Look at her, Mark. I can see the resemblance. She's yours!"

Dad turned toward the girl. "What's your mother's name?"

"Candace," she responded in a frightened voice.

"How old are you?" Dad asked.

"Six," the little girl said.

My dad sighed. "And what's your name?"

"The child's name is Ciara, Mark," Mom said, cutting into the conversation. "What do these questions prove?"

"Claire, I'm so s—"

"No!" Mom yelled, cutting him off. "Don't you dare try to apologize. There is nothing you can say or do to fix the damage already done to our marriage, our family, and our church. What about Sarah? How do you think she'll react when she comes home and finds out that she has a little *black* half sister due to your infidelity? You are a disgrace!"

My heart dropped as I began to understand the argument I had walked in on. My father had cheated and had another child. My father, who was a preacher and a husband, had had an affair. I felt stuck in one place, even though I moved toward the kitchen. My mouth seemed glued shut due to the shock of it all, but I heard the words coming out of my mouth before I realized I was talking.

"Dad? Is it true?" I realized tears were pouring from my eyes as I watched my dad tense up and turn toward me. I saw my mother cover her mouth, as if she'd gotten caught. And then I saw the little girl sitting by herself at the island. She turned to look at me, her sad eyes boring into me, as if she was silently asking me for help.

My sister?

I tore my eyes from her. I wouldn't let her make me feel compassion for her. No, this little girl was nothing to me or to my family. I couldn't believe any of it. Where was the paternity test to prove it?

Dad took a few steps toward me, but I backed away, shaking my head. I didn't want him anywhere near me.

He sighed. "Honey," he began. "You're my daughter. That's all you need to worry about. Now, go upstairs and—"

"No," I yelled, cutting him off. "Don't avoid my question. I'm sixteen. I'm not stupid!"

Dad hesitated, looking extremely troubled. "I did something unthinkable seven years ago. I had a single encounter with another woman."

"Why does it matter whether it was one time or not? It happened!" Mom screamed, but Dad ignored her, keeping his eyes on me.

"I was foolish, and I made a mistake," he said.

"She doesn't look like a mistake," I retorted, pointing a finger at the little girl.

"Well, she is," Dad retorted and then sighed, as if he had immediately regretted that he'd said that around her.

The little girl looked at our father with the saddest expression painted on her face. My heart began to break for her. I couldn't imagine my father ever disowning me as he had disowned her, and I definitely couldn't imagine the feeling it caused.

"Who are you?" I asked, looking at my father. This man standing in front of me was not my father. He wasn't the preacher I knew, with morals and values. He seemed to have aged in minutes and looked defeated. I didn't see God anywhere in him at that moment. This man, he was not my father, but a monster.

Dad sighed. "We'll talk about this later. Take the girl and go to your room."

I ignored my dad and looked at my mom, who I could tell had been drinking. The bottle of wine behind her was almost empty. "It's your fault."

"I said, 'Take the girl and go to your room!' She doesn't need to hear any more of this," Dad screamed.

"Fine." I held my hand out to the little girl. She quickly jumped up and grabbed her two bags and followed me out of the kitchen. I stopped right outside the kitchen and hid behind the wall so that I could eavesdrop on the rest of the conversation. I looked down at the little girl and raised my index finger to my mouth to signal for her to keep quiet.

My mom spoke first. "So how do we clean this mess up? Huh, Mark? How do you suppose we handle this?"

"I don't know, Claire. I'm in shock right now. How am I supposed to know what to do?"

"Well, did you pray?" Mom spat sarcastically. "Seems as though that's the first thing a *preacher* would do!"

"And it seems as though the first thing a preacher's wife should do is pray, instead of gulping down a whole bottle of wine, one you were supposed to use for a recipe," Dad shot back.

I heard Mom laugh angrily. "You did not just say that to me. How dare you turn this around on me?"

I'd had enough; I couldn't listen to my parents destroy each other with words. I also didn't want this girl to witness any more of it. How old was she? Four? Five? Surely no older than seven. She probably still played with Barbies. Had anyone stopped and thought about how she felt? Surely her world was more upside down than my own.

"Come on," I said, guiding her up the stairs and into my room. I had her take a seat on my bed as I shut my door behind me, drowning out my parents' screams. I joined her on my bed, noticing her interest in all my things.

My room wasn't up to my taste, since Mom wouldn't allow me to hang up pictures of my favorite boy band. Instead, I had one poster of Jesus on the cross. The little girl was staring at my stuffed animals that were sitting on a big shelf that protruded from my wall. I stood, walked over to the shelf, and grabbed a cute brown teddy bear. I handed it to her as I sat back on my bed.

"This is Teddy Eddy," I told her. "My first teddy bear. I got him when I was two and never let him out of my sight. You can play with it."

She smiled and hugged the teddy bear close but said nothing. I tried to think of something to say, something to distract both of us from the drama below.

"What's your name?" I asked.

"Ciara," she muttered barely above a whisper.

"That's a pretty name." I smiled. "Ciara, where is your mommy?"

"With Jesus."

"Oh," I said with a nod. "No wonder you're here."

The little girl finally met my eyes and asked, "Are you my sister?"

I tried to blink away my tears, but a few escaped, and I was forced to wipe them away. I started crying, because I wanted so badly to say, "No, I am not your sister," but I couldn't. No one really knew for sure. Even if she turned out to really be my sister, I would never be able to say that we were blood. It just didn't feel right. My world was changing, and there was nothing I could do to stop it. I thought about God and how He saw all of us as brothers and sisters. He wouldn't approve of my thoughts, so I sucked it up and smiled at Ciara.

"I don't know."

"What is your name?" she asked me, seeming to accept my answer.

"I'm Sarah."

"That's a pretty name, too," Ciara said, finally beginning to play with the teddy bear. I could see her already opening up to me, but did I want her to? Did I want to bond with her? "I'm hungry." I heard her stomach begin to grumble.

"One sec," I said, reaching under my bed and pulling out a wooden box that I used to hide things in. I sat it on the bed and pulled out a bag of chips, then handed it to Ciara. "Don't tell anyone I gave these to you. If my mom finds out, she'll go crazy. She is against snacks."

Ciara frowned. "I don't like your mom."

I sighed. "I don't like her much, either."

"But your mommy likes you. She doesn't like me," Ciara said, leaving me shocked. "My daddy doesn't like me, either." She lowered her head. "Nobody loves me here."

That did it. My tears started pouring from my eyes in waves. I tried to compose myself, but I couldn't. I had been right. No one in this house would ever feel the pain that this girl was going through. Knowing my mother and her prejudices, she wouldn't get past Ciara's skin color, and knowing my father, he wouldn't move past his own shock and his mistake to actually see his daughter. And me? I saw everything just as it was. I saw a little girl being destroyed by a family who would never love her the way she needed to be loved.

I didn't know if it was God or me, but in that moment I promised myself that even if no one else loved her, I would. The color of her skin or how she was conceived didn't matter. I decided that she was my sister, and that I would love her, just as God loved me.

Chapter Ten

MARK

My back was aching from sleeping on the sofa last night—the result of the wife kicking me out of our bedroom. I didn't blame her. In fact, I had seen it coming. I replayed in my mind the details of last night's argument as I stared at myself in the bathroom mirror. I looked like a wreck, and quite frankly, I felt like one. I had had everything together. I had had God, the church, the car, the house, the wife, the all-star daughter. Everything had been right in my life, and somehow I had allowed my own desires and stupidity to ruin it all. I wanted to break the glass mirror, destroy my own image worse than I'd already done, but instead, I directed my anger at God.

"You knew," I said, my voice menacing as I raised a single fist in the air toward God. "You knew I had a daughter. Why didn't you keep her away? Why did you have to take the girl's mom? See, everything could've worked out perfectly fine, had you covered me! Isn't that what you promised? That your grace would always cover us? Well, where is your grace now, God? Huh? Where is it?

"The only thing I see is condemnation. But, God, you knew I regretted what I did. I repented! I begged for forgiveness! I thought you forgave me, but clearly, you haven't. What am I supposed to do now? I'm the man who people come to for answers, and I can't even solve my own problems."

I continued to stare at myself in the mirror and noticed all the worry lines that had formed due to the stress. I was staring at a stranger, a man who was laughing back at me, pleased to see failure written across my face. I turned the knob on the faucet and cupped my hands underneath as the water began to pour out, and then I splashed my face, washing away my sins. I looked back up into the mirror and the same stranger was staring back at me. Who was I? Surely not a man of God.

I heard a knock.

"Dad." Sarah's voice came through the door. "I'm going to be late for school."

I could tell by her monotone voice that she hadn't forgotten last night's events. I had spent most of my night contemplating how to explain everything to her. Sarah had looked up to me and she had seen someone who was true to himself and to God. But now? Now I wasn't really sure what she saw.

I opened the bathroom door and found her standing right outside it, Ciara holding on to her hand. Sarah stared down at her phone and didn't even bother looking at me. However, Ciara's eyes were glued to mine. I had forgotten about Ciara last night. I had been so caught up in my own pain; I hadn't thought to check on her after I told Sarah to take her upstairs.

"Where's your mom?" I asked Sarah.

She shrugged, still seemingly preoccupied with her phone, although when I looked down at the screen, it was apparent she hadn't been browsing at all. The screen was black. "How am I supposed to know?"

I frowned, not used to Sarah speaking to me with sarcasm, but I deserved it. "Well, what am I supposed to do about her?"

"You're the parent. Figure it out," Sarah said and then sighed. "Dad, she's six. She needs to be enrolled in a school. Take her down to the elementary school. I looked through her bags. Whoever packed them left her Social Security card, her birth certificate, and her mother's obituary in there. Go through whatever legal stuff you have to do to verify that she's really yours, Dad. You are a lawyer." Sarah sighed. "This is such a weird conversation to have with my dad. This really sucks, you know that?"

Ignoring her last statement, I thought about how most of the staff at the school attended my church and how questions would arise if I tried to enroll Ciara in school as her parent. No, I couldn't do that. I still hadn't figured out whether or not I was going to keep the girl if she was mine. My wife and I still had a lot of discussing to do. But first, I needed a DNA test. Until I got the results, I'd treat Ciara as if she was my daughter. I wasn't going to add salt to that child's wounds.

"Can you stay home from school today and keep an eye on her?"

"What?" Sarah looked bewildered. "I have a huge math test today. I can't miss it. Why won't you take her to a school?"

"Because," I began, but then I stopped. How could I explain to my sixteen-year-old daughter that I was embarrassed to flaunt my mistakes around town? She wouldn't understand. "Look, no one can know about this situation right now, okay? Not your friends, not other relatives, no one. Understand? I can't take her to school just yet."

Sarah finally met my eyes. "Well, I need to go to school, so it looks like you're the one who's going to be playing hooky." Sarah looked down at the little girl and sighed. "Dad, she needs you, not me. You are her dad, and as hard as it is to accept that, I'm doing way better at it than you are. No one even came upstairs last night to check on her. I gave her a bath and let her sleep with me. All she had for dinner was a bag of chips. This morning I got her dressed. She has only three pairs of clothes, Dad. And I made her cereal, because no one else thought to make her something to eat. Why is it that Mom made me pancakes before she left, but didn't think about Ciara?"

Sarah shook her head. "So now it's your turn, Dad. How about you take her shopping for clothes, get her situated in the guest room, take her to the park, bond with her, and be her *father*. Now, can you take me to school?" Sarah didn't wait for my response. She stormed off, leaving Ciara standing there, waiting for me to do something.

The car was silent as I drove Sarah to school. She pretended to be extremely occupied with her phone again, and she leaned against the passenger door to keep her distance. She hated me, and the one thing I wished was that there was something I could do to win her love back.

"Sarah," I began.

"Busy."

"On your phone?"

"Yes," she said exasperatingly, as if I was disturbing her. Sarah had never been this short with me. "Studying."

"How can you study on your—"

"New technology, Dad. I can download the study guide onto my phone. Gosh."

I decided to leave her alone, but my silence didn't last more than two minutes. "Sarah, I know you're angry with me."

"Angry? That's an understatement." Sarah smirked.

"What can I do to fix this?" I asked, pulling up to her school and slowing to a stop behind a school bus.

Sarah finally turned toward me, momentarily forgetting her phone. I could see the desperation in her eyes as she searched my own. "I spent a lot of my life picking you over Mom, siding with you in every argument. I looked up to you, sometimes even more than I did to God. I walked in your footsteps because you were my role model. But now I don't even know who you are anymore. Do you even know who you are?" She laughed spitefully. "You want to know how to fix this? Give me a reason to believe in you again."

Sarah got out of the car and slammed the door shut. I sat back in my seat and watched her disappear into a crowd of kids.

Chapter Eleven

SARAH

I was standing by my locker, frustrated because I couldn't get it to open. I kept messing up the combination because my hands were shaking from all the pent-up anger I wanted to unleash on my father. The only thing that had kept me sane during the drive to school was knowing that Ciara was in the backseat, watching us. She was a very observant girl, and somehow she understood every single thing that was going on. I tried to not revisit the conversation we'd had last night, but pieces of it kept popping into my head as I opened my locker and got my books.

"If I leave, your mommy and daddy won't be angry anymore."

"Ciara, they aren't mad because you are here. And he is your daddy, too."

"My mommy said I don't have a daddy."

"Hey, beautiful," a familiar voice said from behind me, causing me to jump as I shut my locker door. Firm hands settled around my waist, relaxing me. "It's just me. Chill."

I could hear the laughter in Ryan's voice. I turned toward him and gave him a hug, fully aware that we had an audience. I didn't know one girl who didn't want my boyfriend, and they all kept a close watch on us. I was sure new rumors would spread just because of our little embrace.

Ryan lowered his eyes as he studied me. "Something's wrong. Where is your smile?"

I sighed, not wanting to get into the drama, knowing that if I told him, it would get out and back to my father. Even though my father didn't deserve my loyalty, I'd keep Ciara a secret. "Nothing. My dad just irritated me, that's all."

"Maybe a kiss will make you feel better." Ryan grabbed my hips and pulled me close, causing me to spin away from him quickly.

"Not in front of everyone," I said and began walking down the hall with my books in hand. I didn't have to look back to know that Ryan was following behind me.

"Who cares what these people think?"

"I do," I told him, rounding a corner while managing to keep from running into other kids. "My dad knows half of these kids' parents."

I heard Ryan sigh behind me, and then he wrapped his hands around my waist, bringing me to a halt. He stepped in front of me, oblivious to the fact that he was blocking traffic in the hallway. I looked around at the kids passing by us and wanted to apologize.

"When are you going to stop living by your dad's rules and start living by your own?" Ryan asked, and I was sure he didn't even understand the significance of his question.

He was right. My whole life had been run by my father and the church. I'd always had to keep up an image, as if I were royalty, but if my father could break his own rule of being the best person he could be, why should I observe it? A big part of me wanted to rebel. I wanted to let my hair down and be a teenager for once, to allow myself to make mistakes, just like Dad had. I wanted to go to parties, drink, do more than make out with my boyfriend, and stay out half the night without my parents knowing. If Dad could mess up, why couldn't I?

"You're right," I told him, smiling for the first time. "What are you doing tonight?"

Ryan's eyes lit up. "Nothing. Why?"

"Can I come over?"

"Don't you have a swim meet tonight?"

"I'll miss it," I told him.

"Sarah? Skipping a swim meet? That's, like, your favorite extracurricular activity at the moment. Something has come over you, princess."

"No. You're totally right. I'm done living by my parents' rules, especially if they can't follow them."

Ryan kissed me before I could protest, not that I would've at that point.

"See you tonight," he said before walking off.

I headed to my classroom, ignoring the hushed conversations about Little Miss Perfect kissing a boy in the middle of the hallway. As I entered my classroom, I immediately spotted my best friend, Alex. He was actually the only boy my father approved of me hanging out with. Alex was an aspiring preacher who ushered at the church and helped my dad out with his sermons and other work after service. I was not really sure what else it was they did to bond, but I knew my father loved him.

Alex and I were strictly friends, though. Sure, he was cute in a boy-next-door kind of way and had plenty of girls who would've dated him had he been interested in them. But I'd known him since I was a toddler, and there was no attraction there. Sure he had electric blue eyes, unruly, dirty blond hair, and the body of an athlete, but we are just friends. No doubt about that.

"Hey," he said as I took a seat next to him. He was already prepared to take notes; his pen and pad were sitting neatly on his desk. The teacher was writing something on the chalkboard and wasn't paying attention to the conversations of her students.

"Hey." I smiled, trying to hold everything together before he noticed that something was off. If Ryan could tell, surely Alex would.

If Alex noticed, he said nothing. "Ready for the math test?"

"Crap!" I'd forgotten about the test that fast. "I almost forgot about it."

"That's unusual." Alex laughed.

I could feel his eyes on me as I dug through my book bag for a pen. I must've forgotten my supplies in my locker.

"Here." Alex leaned over and offered me a pen. I took it without meeting his eyes. "Sarah, is there something—"

"All right, class," Mrs. Tomkins began, cutting Alex off.

From the corner of my eye, I saw him straighten and face forward. I let out a small sigh of relief and paid attention to the teacher.

"Everyone knows what today is right? Big test! The one that will determine half of your overall grade . . ."

Somewhere between Mrs. Tomkins's speech and ringing of the bell, I zoned out. I looked down at my test, at the answers I barely remembered writing, and sighed. I had spent the whole hour thinking about my dysfunctional family. I wasn't even sure if my answers were correct. Worse than that, I wasn't even sure if I cared anymore.

I walked up to the teacher's desk, handed her my test, and left the classroom. I was quickly joined by Alex in the hallway.

"How do you think you did?" he asked, and I shrugged.

"I don't know. Good, I guess." I sighed. "Actually, I'm not sure. I don't even remember taking the test."

"How is that possible?"

"I zoned out," I admitted, and everything my father had told me not to say was on the tip of my tongue. Alex was the one person I couldn't keep anything from. I grabbed his arm and pulled him into a quiet hallway where there were no kids.

"What is this about?" he asked in confusion, and everything I had tried to keep from Ryan surfaced. My tears began with a shudder that rolled through my whole body. "Hey, don't cry." Alex pulled me into his arms.

"My life is ruined," I told him, not caring that my slobber was getting all over his jean jacket. "My dad had an affair on my mom."

"No way."

"Yes way!" I screamed. I pulled away from Alex, wiping my tears, but it made no difference, because they just kept falling down my face. "He has another daughter, and she's now living with us. But do you want to know the crazy part? It's a little mixed girl. Her mom is black. And I'm not saying that because I'm racist. I'm saying it because my mom is. She's been freaking out since yesterday, and it's not fair to the little girl.

"She's so cute and sweet. She doesn't deserve to go through this. The girl told me last night that her mom just died, and now she's staying with us. And everyone is being too selfish to even notice her needs. And my parents just want to hide her, because they are afraid that she'll change our lives. They're afraid of what everyone is going to think. I heard them say it last night! I heard everything! My dad could lose his job. If that happens, we'll lose our house, I'll have to go to another school, and—"

"Slow down, Sarah. You don't know that," Alex assured me.

"Everything is changing. Even I am," I told him. I had plans to go over to Ryan's house and do things my father wouldn't be proud of. Yes, even I was changing. "But you can't tell a soul, Alex. If anyone else finds out, our lives are ruined. Can you keep this between us?"

"Yes, I will," Alex promised, and I believed him. "You said that you were changing. What does that mean?"

What did that mean? It meant I was about to grow up, and fast.

"I just mean I'm not Daddy's little girl anymore," I said, choosing my words carefully.

Ciara is.

Chapter Twelve

TAMARA

A knock on Candace's door caused me to jump out of my sleep and land on the floor beside the couch. I grabbed my phone, which had landed next to me, and looked at the clock. It read 8:34 a.m. I sighed and stood up, wondering who would be knocking on Candace's door this early. I was hoping it wasn't the lady from the day before, trying to get Ciara again. Or maybe it was the cops, with an order to hand her over to children services. Good thing I no longer had her, which made me feel a sense of relief. I knew that leaving her with strangers wasn't much better than letting children's services take her, but at least they were her family. She needed family. I was family to Ciara, but I wasn't blood.

I stood, fixed the scarf wrapped around my head, and then headed to the door. Before I opened it, I looked through the peephole and saw half of the face of a white man. Most likely a cop sent by that woman. I open the door reluctantly.

"Look, I ain't got time to be dealing with the police. . . ." My words trailed off as I stared up at the man, who watched me curiously. I knew him instantly from the picture. He still had the same dark hair. However, it had begun to gray around his temples. His nose was the big giveaway: it was just like Ciara's.

"Hi, Auntie Tamara," Ciara said, standing beside him with her hand wrapped in his. I hadn't even noticed her standing there, and I was so happy to see her big hazel eyes, I almost started to cry. But I quickly came to my senses, understanding what a visit from both Ciara and her father meant. He was returning her, and even though I wanted to take her back, I couldn't let it happen. I simply couldn't provide for her.

"Are you Tamara?" he asked politely.

"You can't bring her back," I said, ignoring his question. "It doesn't work that way! How did you even know how to get here?"

"Ciara gave me the address, plus it was on the birth certificate. Just listen to me," he said, trying to reassure me, but I was already losing the will to keep myself composed. I was ready to break down, and I'd do it in front of Ciara if he didn't back away. "I just need to understand."

"You want to abandon her!" I cried. "She ain't got nobody!"

"Listen—"

"Her mama died, and now you trying to bring her back! How much more can she deal with?"

"Listen!" Mark screamed, surprising both himself and me. I could tell by the way he paused and cleared his throat. He then lowered his voice, but the urgency in it remained. "Everyone is suffering here! And the only way to figure out how to best handle this is if we both work together. I just want to talk," he said, holding his hands up in a sign of peace. "That's all. Just talk."

I studied him for a second, making sure he wasn't going to turn and run away, leaving Ciara standing there. I blinked away a few loose tears and nodded. "Come on inside."

I left Mark sitting in the living room and took Ciara up to her room to play. I shut the door behind me and then returned to Mark, who was standing near the fireplace, staring at the family portraits. Even though his back was turned to me, I could tell he was having a moment. It was in the way his shoulders tensed . . . the way he barely moved an inch as he stared at the picture of Ciara and Candace at the park, one of them at the beach, and another of Ciara on her first birthday, with a cake-covered face.

I remembered that day like it was yesterday. Candace had cut out a big chunk of cake and had let Ciara have her way with it. After about ten minutes with the chunk, she was covered from head to toe in icing. Candace had taken the picture, laughing harder than I'd ever seen her laugh. Sometimes I wished I could hear a picture; sometimes it wasn't enough to just see someone's happiness. I'd do anything to hear Candace laugh again.

"How did she die?" Mark asked, somehow sensing my presence. I walked into the room and took a seat on the couch. Mark joined me with the picture of her and Ciara at the park in his hand.

"Car accident," I said softly, understanding this wasn't the time for an attitude. He deserved to mourn the way I had been. "She died instantly."

He lowered his head to his hand, allowing the picture to hang loosely in the other. "I didn't know," he said.

"It happened just a few days ago."

"No," he said, snapping his head in my direction. "I didn't know about Ciara. If I'd known, I would've . . . I might've . . ."

"You might've what? Accepted her then? Would it have been any different if it was Candace showing up at your doorstep six years ago versus me showing up now? I think we'd still be in the same predicament, because from what I gather, you're married. You have a family and this beautiful life, and I'm sure there is no place for

Ciara there, even though you have, like, eight bedrooms probably. So please don't tell me what you would've done back then."

"I might've left my wife," he said.

"Oh, really?" I laughed. "You would've left your wife for your one-time black lover and child? Please."

"You don't know."

"No, I do know," I spat. "If you had cared about Candace at all, you would've visited or found a way. If you cared for Ciara, you wouldn't be here right now. You'd be enrolling her in school and fixing things."

"I'm here because I want to fix things!"

"Oh yeah? And what is your definition of 'fixing things,' Preacher?" I asked, tasting the bitterness in my own words. "You thought you could come here, give me some sad story, and bribe me to keep her?"

"No. I . . ." Mark sighed. "Okay, yes. Maybe that was in the back of my head, but I'm also a man of dignity."

"And what does that mean?"

"I went to the drugstore this morning and got a DNA kit. I tested Ciara. She's mine. What I'm trying to say is, I will not back down from my responsibilities, but I am also admitting that I need your help." Mark sighed again, and worry lines creased his forehead. He seemed to have aged in minutes. "Let's think about Ciara here. Her mother passed away, and now she's with a new family in a new home. That's got to be hard on her, right? She needs familiarity. She needs you."

"I told you, I can't keep her! Candace left me her house in the will, and I'm barely keeping up with it without any help! I can't afford a child as well."

"What if she came over a few nights during the week or on the weekend? I could drop her off and pick her up, pay for her expenses. I'll pay you too."

"I don't want your money, Mr.—"

"But she needs you just as much as she needs her blood family. Can we arrange this?" Mark waited for my answer and then continued when I didn't speak. "Just until she is comfortable enough to stay with my family full-time?"

I thought about his proposal, and it did make sense. Ciara would still have me, and she'd have her father. But what about that crazy wife of his? Would she be okay with this arrangement? Was Mark even thinking this through clearly? There was still a possibility that one day, Mark would drop Ciara off and never return. Ciara didn't need another parent leaving her behind.

I also had to ask myself what my own reasons were if I decided to reject his offer. Honestly, I had none. I'd love to be able to spend every day with Ciara if I could. I knew she wanted me more than anyone else at the moment. Mark had stated that he would pay for her expenses and take care of the transportation, and all I had to do was keep her a few days out of the week. It almost seemed as if a big weight had been lifted off my shoulders. Maybe this arrangement could work.

"How is she gonna get back and forth to school?" I worked early mornings and couldn't be responsible for getting Ciara back and forth to school. Hiring a child-care provider was out of the question, unless I could find somebody to do it for free.

"I'll have my driver come get her," he said.

"You have a driver? Are you rich?"

"I'm well off, but we have a driving service at our church for elders and children needing transportation to school. You wouldn't have to worry about her and school."

"And you said you'd pay me? That's my biggest concern. I can barely rub two pennies together."

"Yes," Mark said, nodding quickly. I could tell he was positive that I'd succumbed to his offer. "All her expenses . . . and some."

I sighed, feeling guilty for allowing a man to bribe me into caring for my goddaughter, when I should've taken her back the moment she showed up on my doorstep. I prayed for Candace to forgive me, but I needed the money. I had had no idea what I'd do about Candace's bills, especially since I planned on staying in the house. Mark's money would be enough to give Ciara a decent home again, even if it was just for three days a week. At least she got to enjoy some normalcy.

"Okay, I'll keep her three days out of the week," I told Mark. "You have a deal, but only because I care about Ciara's best interests, and I hope that's your real reason as well."

"It is," Mark said. "I'm looking out for Ciara. Last night wasn't the best situation for her to witness between my wife and me. I'd prefer if she stayed away for a few days, just long enough for me to settle things with my wife and daughter."

"And you need me to keep her," I said. It was more of a statement than a question.

"For a few days. Here." Mark stood and pulled his wallet out of his back pocket. From that wallet he pulled out a wad of cash and counted out two hundred dollars. "This is to show my appreciation. Take it."

I wanted to argue with him, but what reason did I have this time? I swallowed hard and took the money out of his hand. "Three days."

Chapter Thirteen

SARAH

I sat on Ryan's bed, with a heart that wanted to escape from my chest because it was beating so hard. Ryan was emancipated, and so there were no adults to walk in on us or catch us doing things we weren't supposed to be doing. To Ryan, having his own place was a plus, but I was scared out of my mind. Ryan had gone into the kitchen to grab us some drinks, and as a distraction from what I knew was going to happen, I busied myself with studying his room.

He had a few posters of swimsuit models on his walls. One was particularly graphic, and I looked away, blushing. I focused my attention instead on his nightstand. There was nothing on it but a simple black alarm clock and a white lamp. I scooted closer to the nightstand and opened the drawer out of curiosity. Inside it laid a black notepad with the word *Conquests* written on the top page. As I moved to grab the notepad, I heard Ryan's footsteps echo in the hallway. I didn't want to be caught snooping, so I quickly shut his drawer and took a seat on his bed just as he entered the room with two cups in his hands.

"Hello, beautiful," he said with the biggest smile. He kissed my forehead and took a seat next to me. "Miss me?"

"Of course, even though you were gone only for a few minutes." I smiled shyly, brushing an unruly piece of hair behind my ear. Alex had once told me that I did that whenever I was nervous, and now I understood why he'd said that.

Ryan smiled and handed me my cup. "Here."

I took the cup with shaking hands, only now realizing how parched I was. I lifted the cup to my mouth and took a big gulp. My throat instantly started to burn, and I began coughing. "Oh, my God! What in the world did you give me?"

Ryan chuckled, placing his hand on my back and rubbing it softly. "I spiked it with a little bit of alcohol."

"You drink liquor?"

"No, but I figured this would be the right occasion. I have a friend who was able to get me some."

"Well, I don't drink, Ryan," I said, fuming. "And you know that!"

"It'll calm your nerves, Sarah. I was just trying to help. Look, I'm sorry if you're upset." Ryan scooted closer, and I noticed how his voice dropped an octave as he spoke in an almost seductive manner. "Let me make it up to you."

If I thought my heart was pounding its hardest before, I was wrong. I was sure Ryan could feel its vibrations as he pushed me down on the bed. He slowly moved on top of me, and I tensed up. My arms instantly shot out, pressing against his chest to hold him at bay.

He chuckled. "Relax," he said, pushing his weight against my hands, which collapsed under his chest. He was fully on top of me now, and he lowered his lips down to my neck. I gasped as he started to trail kisses down to my collarbone, and even though I was afraid, I started to feel pleased. A soft moan escaped my mouth, which caused his kisses to intensify, as if he was getting more excited.

He rose up slightly to look down at me. "I've always wanted you." He lowered himself to kiss me again, but I stopped him.

"But do you love me?" I asked.

"So much," he said and then stole a soft kiss.

"What if I told you I didn't want to?"

"How could you not?" he asked, placing a hand under my shirt. "We were meant for each other." He looked down at me with a serious expression. "You love me, don't you?"

"Yes," I told him, truly meaning it.

"Well, then, show me how much you love me."

I stared at Ryan, wanting to cause more distraction, but then an image of my father flashed across my mind. This image of his kind and caring face should've been enough for me to stop what I was doing with Ryan, but it wasn't. Instead, it fueled my anger, which triggered vengeance. Having sex with Ryan was my way of getting back at my father for his affair. It was my way of lashing out.

I brought a hand up to Ryan's neck and pulled him down, fully welcoming him. He moaned in surprise and then kissed me deeply. I knew it was going to happen. Ryan was going to take my virginity.

Just then my phone went off in my purse, which was lying on the floor beside his bed. I was once again tense, wondering if it was my mother wondering where I was, or if it was my father wanting to apologize again. I tried to ignore the buzzing, but my instincts told me to answer. I managed to get Ryan off of me with much protest and rolled over to the edge of the bed clumsily. Digging in my purse for my phone, I pulled it out and stared at the screen. I was confused to see Alex's name pop up. He couldn't have picked a worse time.

"What do you want?" I asked with a hushed voice.

"Well, hello to you too," Alex said, and I could tell by his tone that he was smirking. "Why do you sound weird?"

"I'm busy," I told him.

"With what?"

"With stuff, Alex!" I almost screamed it.

"Wait, you're talking to Alex?" Ryan asked behind me.

"Is that Ryan in the background?" Alex asked.

I didn't know how to answer either of their questions, so I said nothing.

Alex was the first to speak. "Where are you? Your parents would never let Ryan near you, and if you were on schedule, you'd be at practice. Where are you?"

"None of your business, Alex!" I said, pulling away from Ryan as he tried to pull me closer.

"It is my business when my friend is doing something out of character." Alex paused. "Is this because of your dad?"

"I have to go," I said, not in the mood to discuss my feelings, especially when he was right.

"Sarah, don't do anything you'll regret," Alex warned. "I'm coming to get you."

"You don't know where I am."

"Not hard to find someone in a small suburb where everyone knows each other. My best guess is Ryan's house, and if that's the case, I'm only five minutes away from there," Alex reminded me. I heard a door slam on his end of the line. "And, Sarah, I would've expected better from you." He hung up.

I quickly sat up, adjusted my clothes, and brushed my tangled hair down with my hands. I heard Ryan moan in frustration, but I had a bigger problem on my hands. Alex.

"I have to go," I said, moving toward the door, but Ryan quickly stood, pulling me back to the bed.

"What did Alex say? And why the sudden change?"

I could tell Ryan was extremely irritated, but not as much as I was. I pushed him away and rushed to his bedroom door before he could stop me. I quickly opened his door and ran down the stairs, trying to make it out of the house before Alex started pounding on the door, causing a scene. I heard Ryan shout for me to come back, but I closed his front door behind me, drowning out his pleas.

Alex had just pulled up to the curb and wasted no time getting out of the car. As he approached the porch, I was able to make out his face. He looked impassive. That usually meant he was storming inside. I quickly walked down the steps to meet him, but he walked right past me and was up on the porch in one step. He banged loudly on the door.

Within seconds, Ryan opened the door, wearing nothing but his pants and a cocky grin. "I knew you'd come back, babe. . . ." His words trailed off when he saw Alex standing in front of him.

"You have five seconds to explain why she was in your house. You have two seconds to explain why your shirt is off, and one second to explain why her hair looks tousled."

"What?" Confusion marked Ryan's face.

"One . . ."

"Alex!" I shouted, running up the porch steps and latching on to his arm in hopes of pulling him away, but his stance was firm and intimidating. I'd never seen him so angry. I wanted to tell him to calm down and ask himself what Jesus would do, but I was in no position to act righteous.

"Did you touch her?" Alex took a step closer to Ryan, who smirked.

"Maybe."

Alex fumed at Ryan's response and slammed him against the door frame.

"Nothing happened, Alex," I said, hoping by God that he'd back off. "Just take me home already."

It seemed like an eternity passed before Alex backed off. He spat on the porch, turned, and began walking away. He didn't have to look back to see if I was following him. He probably heard my exasperated breaths as I walked behind him, completely overwhelmed. I didn't even bother to turn around and mouth a good-bye to Ryan. For all I knew, that relationship was over.

Chapter Fourteen

CIARA

When I grew up, I wanted to be an angel. That way I could help all the boys and girls with no mommies and daddies. I'd give all of them parents who would love them unconditionally. I once saw a movie called *Annie,* about an orphan girl who went to live with a rich man, and at first, he didn't like her, but then he started to love her. I could only wish my daddy started to love me.

I was happy to be back in my room, playing with my toys. When I was in my room, I felt like my mom was right beside me, smiling as she watched me play. I pretended Mommy was there, sitting beside me, holding up two dolls as she made them talk. Mom had always made her dolls say the funniest things. I started to imagine what she'd say if she was with me.

"You stole my Pizza Bites," Mom made the blond-haired Barbie say to the redheaded one.

"No, I didn't!" the redheaded Barbie said.

"I ate the Pizza Bites!" I said, holding my look-alike Barbie in the air.

Mom gasped. "Oh, no, you didn't! I declare war!"

"We are good Barbies, Mom! We don't start wars," I told her.

"Well, then, I declare a Pizza Bite–eating contest!"

"You ate all the Pizza Bites! We can't have a contest!" I laughed.

"Well, then . . ." Mom paused to think. *"Let's have an ice cream–eating contest!"*

"But we don't have any ice cream!"

"Well, if we don't have any Pizza Bites or ice cream, and we are peaceful Barbies and can't have a real war, then I declare a thumb war!"

I giggled. "Barbies can't have thumb wars!"

"Well, my Barbie is special," Mom told me. *"But do you want to know what's even more special?"*

"What?"

"You." Mom smiled, laying her Barbie doll down. *"Come here."* She held out her arms for me, and I crawled into her lap. *"I love you. You know that, right?"* I started to feel sad, knowing what she was going to say next. *"You have to be a big girl for Mommy, okay? Be strong for Auntie Tamara and your daddy. He loves you too."*

"He doesn't act like it," I told Mommy.

"Well, he'll come around soon. He loves you."

I nodded, but I couldn't stop thinking about how she was going to leave me. "Don't go."

"I'm right here," she said, rubbing my back. *"How about I tell you a story?"*

I nodded, relaxing against her chest and readying myself for her story.

"Once upon a time, there was a young girl who lived in the trees."

"Why did she live in the trees?" I asked.

"Because she loved the trees. They were always kind to her."

"How were they kind to her?" I asked.

"Because the trees' leaves gave her shelter from the rain. The water would bounce right off of the large leaves and splatter on the soil. One tree also gave her food."

"How?"

"It was a fruit tree. It produced any kind of fruit you could ever ask for. It had strawberries, blueberries, cherries, apples, bananas, and oranges. It even had tomatoes!"

"Ew!"

"But she loved tomatoes. So, one day, a man and a woman found the girl in the tree, eating, and took pity on her. They told her that they didn't have any children and that she could live with them and be their child, but the little girl said no."

"But didn't she want a mommy and a daddy?"

"She already had everything she needed in the tree. She didn't need the man and the woman. Instead, she told them that they could come live with her and eat from her tree. And guess what?"

"What?"

"The man and the woman thought the tree was so beautiful that they decided to live there too. Days later, an entire family saw the girl, the man, and the woman living in the tree, and they asked why they were there. The little girl told them that they lived in the fruit tree because it gave them everything they needed. The family asked if they could live there as well."

"That's a lot of people in one tree," I told my mommy.

"It's a tree so big that it can feed every single person in the world."

"Is there really a tree like that, Mommy?"

"No," she said, gently kissing my forehead. "But there is a God who is like that. His name is Jesus. You know Jesus, Ciara. Anytime you are feeling lonely and afraid, you can call on Jesus, and He'll give you everything you need."

I looked up at Mommy. "You promise?"

She smiled down at me. "He promises." Mommy kissed me again and removed me from her lap.

"No." I buried my face in her chest, fighting against her. *"You're gonna leave me."*

"But I'll always be with you."

And then she was gone.

I was alone in my room with my dolls. I knew Mommy ain't really come and see me, but I loved to pretend like she did. I knew that if she could, she'd really say those things. I had seen it in a movie once, where a boy lost his brother and would imagine they would go and play baseball together like they did when he was alive. I liked to think of Mommy that way.

Whenever I got sad, I liked to pray to God. When Mommy had prayed, she'd got down on her knees and bowed down. I did the same now and closed my eyes.

"God, I miss my mom. Can you tell her that I love her and miss her? And tell her I'm being a big girl. Amen."

I sat up, feeling better. Mom wasn't with me, but she was with God, and she had always said that He was with me. I knew God would tell my mommy those things for me. The Bible said we could ask for anything. I couldn't wait for Him to tell her.

Chapter Fifteen

SARAH

Alex climbed into the driver's seat and put his key in the ignition. I expected him to speed off, but he just sat there, breathing heavily. Eventually, he started the car and began driving. I wanted to punch him in the arm for what he'd just done. How dare he invade my privacy and force me to go home. If Ryan dumped me, I was going to seriously hurt Alex.

"I hate you," I told him with folded arms. I kept my face pointed toward the passenger-side window, glancing at the dark and distant trees as we drove through the night.

"You'll thank me later," he said. "And what were you thinking? Are you stupid? Ryan?"

"No, I'm not stupid!"

"That guy is known for deflowering virgins."

"Well, good thing we aren't in the seventeenth century, then, huh?" I replied.

"You know what I mean, Sarah. You're smarter than that! You should know that talking to Ryan is like playing with fire! You're a good girl, but more than that, you know the Lord."

I groaned and covered my face. "Please don't bring God into this."

"He's been here this whole time! I'm sure God is the one who put the thought in my head to call you, because if I hadn't . . . ." His words trailed off.

"Why is it so important to you, huh?" I finally turned toward him, wanting to see his face as he answered my question.

He remained stoic as he said, "Because your father asked me to watch you."

"My father?" I wanted to laugh. "My father is a hypocrite! He's the one who needs to be watched! I don't even know who he is anymore. And after everything I told you, you still have the nerve to take his side? What kind of a friend are you? I expected you to say something different, but to say it's because of my father?"

His expression softened as he stole a glance in my direction. "You're father isn't the only reason I'm here, and you know it. I also came because I care about what happens to you. I know you're going through a hard time, and I want to make sure you get through this without a scratch on you. What you did back there was just plain stupid."

"Don't judge me."

"There is a big difference between judging and stating the obvious, Sarah," he said. "Stop trying to play the victim, like I was so wrong for saving your butt back there! You were wrong, not me. You were."

"Like father like daughter, huh?" I laughed sarcastically. "Go figure."

We rode the rest of the way in silence, and when Alex parked, I quickly jumped out of the car, hoping he didn't follow behind me. I heard his car door shut behind me, and I knew I was in for it. He was going to tell on me. I would hate him if he did. I spun around to face him, causing him to almost bump into me.

"Are you going to tell my father?" I felt betrayed, regardless of how wrong I was. If he was my friend, he wouldn't put himself between my father and me. But who would go directly against their preacher's request?

Before he had the chance to answer, my front door opened and my father stepped onto the porch, with a welcoming smile.

"I was starting to worry, Sarah, but I see you are in good hands." My dad nodded at Alex.

"Good evening, sir," Alex said, his tone reminiscent of an army private's, which made me roll my eyes and cross my arms over my chest. "Yes, your daughter is in good hands now."

"Now?" my father asked curiously. "Was there a problem before?"

I turned to Alex, knowing what was going to happen next. I wanted to hurt him, but there was nothing I could do.

"Yes, there was a problem, Preacher. I found your daughter alone with a guy from our school, and they were on the verge of—"

"Studying," I lied, cutting him off. I surprised myself, having lied only a few times in my life, and it was never to my own father. "All we were doing was studying. Big science test tomorrow. Alex thought something else was going on, but I told him he didn't have to worry. I'm fine."

"You were alone with a boy?" my dad asked, placing his hands on his hips as he contemplated the scenario.

"It's not what you think," I said.

"Yes, it is, sir," Alex told him. "The guy was shirtless, and her hair was messy. I'm not stupid. She even told me what she was going to do."

"You're lying!" I pushed Alex away from me in anger. He was shocked by my sudden outburst and looked at me like he no longer knew who I was. "I hate you, Alex. Don't you ever talk to me again."

I turned around and began walking up the porch steps, ignoring him when he called my name. I purposely bumped into my father as I passed him. Something was coming over me, a change was happening inside me, and it was all my father's fault. I hated him more than Alex.

I entered the house, and when I was halfway up the stairs, I heard the front door close, and my dad called out my name. I sighed, turned around to face him and then headed back down the stairs.

"Can we talk about this?" he asked, looking up at me with a solemn expression. I could only imagine what he was thinking, and I would do whatever I could to avoid hearing him say it.

"There is nothing to talk about," I spat.

"You lied to me. You said you were stud—"

"You lied to me! You have another daughter!" I retorted. "Where is she, by the way? Huh? Worry about her. I don't need you."

"I'm your father!" he shouted, and I could hear the hurt in his voice, but it could never match the pain I was in. He'd never understand what he had done to me. "Sarah, please, let's talk about this."

"No. How about I talk for once?" I told him. "Alex said you had him watching me. Why? You don't think I'm trustworthy? Maybe Mom should've had Alex watching you. Maybe then we would've known you had another child! Maybe we would've figured out a long time ago that you are a fake and a fraud! And now you're mad because I did something that normal teenagers do? They kiss, they flirt, and they hang out with their boyfriends.

"Every day I come home, and I make sure I'm perfect for you. I study for two hours a day, I take my piano lessons, I do my chores, and I even hated Mom for you! Everything I did was for you!" I started crying, not even caring how stupid or vulnerable I looked. "I don't get to do things that normal teenagers do, and for once I let my hair down, and I'm wrong? Who are you to call anyone wrong? Who are you to be in the position to play father when you're more like a stranger?"

I turned around and stormed up the steps. My father, he didn't even call after me. He probably just stood there in shame, the way he should've been.

Once I was in my room, I flopped down on the bed and cried into my pillow. I tried to muffle my noises for fear that my father would return to antagonize me. The last thing I needed was him. I felt like everything was caving in on me, and the only thing I could do was just sit there and allow those walls to flatten me.

My father had taught me that when I had problems, I must turn to God. I didn't feel like listening to anything my father had taught me at that moment. Mother had taught me that when things got rough, you should drink a whole bottle of wine and then pretend with your hypocritical church friends in the morning that nothing happened. I guessed we all had our secrets.

I remembered the half-empty bottle of wine downstairs. It seemed more appetizing than ever. Maybe today would be the day when I took my mother's advice instead of my father's.

I stayed up and listened for my mother's return home. I heard them argue briefly before her footsteps sounded on the stairs. She slammed her bedroom door, and then the house grew quiet. I waited another hour or so, until I was sure everyone was asleep, and made my way downstairs. Dad was passed out on the couch, with a thin white blanket covering him, and even though he slept, his worry lines stayed planted on his forehead. It was as if he dreamed about his life crashing down on him.

I made my way into the kitchen and kneeled before one of the cabinets. I reached into the far recesses of the cabinet, a place where my father would never think to look, and pulled out a half-drunken bottle of wine. I was surprised and happy to find that my mother hadn't finished it yet. She was most likely still keeping company with the bottle my dad had bought.

A thought did occur to me. What if I drank the wine and my mother found the empty wine bottle or no bottle at all? Well, hopefully, she'd think either my father found the wine and got rid of it or that she'd drank it all and didn't remember doing so. It was still possible that she could blame me. Either way, she wouldn't mention anything to my father for fear that he'd find out she had a secret hiding place.

I tucked the bottle under my arm and made my way safely back upstairs, reassuring myself that I wouldn't get caught like I had with Ryan today. I had to learn how to be more discreet if I ever wanted to be a normal teenager. Once in my room, I locked my door, sat on my bed, and started to gulp down the tangy, pungent liquid, which seemed to mirror how I felt inside.

Chapter Sixteen

TAMARA

That night I watched Ciara as she played with her doll babies on the floor in her room. If she could have it her way, her whole room would be filled to the ceiling with dolls and accessories. It was hard on most days to get her away from her toys, and I was so thankful to see her playing with them. At least something still remained the same.

Ciara finally looked up and noticed me staring down at her from her bed. She smiled, and I smiled back, feeling a ping of hope in seeing her smile. It had been days since she'd lifted those cheeks into a smile. It had been days since she'd actually played. Maybe in a sense, things were returning to normal, or at least as normal as they could be.

"Auntie Tamara, am I living with you again?" Ciara asked.

"Sometimes you will stay with me, and sometimes you'll stay with your daddy, Ciara."

I watched her pout as she said, "But I don't want to live there."

"Why not, Ciara?" I asked, scooting down to the floor so that I was eye level with her. I wanted her to be comfortable enough to open up to me about how things had gone at Mark's house. If I found out they had hurt her in any way, I was going to flip.

"My daddy's wife doesn't like me. My daddy doesn't like me, either," she said as a matter of fact, but I could hear the pain in her little voice. My heart tightened from sadness.

"Did they hurt you?"

"No."

"Are they mean to you?"

"No, but the lady doesn't like me," Ciara told me.

"I know she doesn't, baby, but she'll come around. They are going through a hard time. See, your daddy is supposed to have babies only with her, but he had a baby with your mommy, and so the lady is mad. Do you understand?"

"Yeah," Ciara said.

I hated having to tell her the truth, but I figured she'd already guessed it by now. And if she hadn't, it was still better to tell her than to let her guess or feel bad about herself. In that moment, I hated Candace for dying on us.

She had left me with her child, another human being with feelings and needs that I had no control over! She had left me alone to take on this world without her. There wouldn't be any more girl talks, any more late-night confessions, any more sisterly arguments and making up. She couldn't get on my everlasting nerves again. Now her memory would always make me cry.

Sometimes I asked myself if there was something I had done to deserve this. If I had somehow sinned and invited God's wrath. I thought back and tried to come up with things I could've done, but I could think of nothing. I was a good woman to God and to His people. I minded my business and worked for everything I had. I followed His commandments, repented daily, and had fellowship with God. I knew it was just the devil trying to put negative thoughts in my head.

One thing I had learned was that I had to fight the devil off at all times. He was constantly waiting for an opportunity to latch on to our thoughts and tell us things, things we might have secretly felt. He was the ultimate deceiver, as he was so skilled at making us believe his stabs at us were our own thoughts. Well, the devil was a liar!

There wasn't anything I had done to bring about Candace's death. I'd find a way to make Ciara's life as comfortable and trauma free as possible, and I'd continue being a strong, independent woman of God. I had to. The Lord had put it in my heart that the only direction was forward, and I knew there was nothing left but to keep pushing toward the cross.

Chapter Seventeen

CLAIRE

The next day, I took off to Saks. A lot of times, shopping was the only therapeutic thing that happened in my day, well, aside from a glass of wine, which I usually snuck when no one was watching. There was something about buying something new that excited me, whether I was buying just a pack of gum or a pair of new shoes for Mark. New things were a distraction, and for the time being, they made me forget I had problems. The only thing that really gave me a sense of relief about my mess of a home was buying something shiny and expensive.

I was standing at the jewelry counter, glancing at gold and diamonds, all wonderful gifts indeed, but then my breath caught when I looked down at a brilliant pearl pendant with the word *mom* encrusted on it. This pendant shimmered, begging me to buy it, to wear it proudly as if the title "mom" was my best asset. My daughter would beg to differ. Her Mother's Day gifts were merely thoughtless items that neither held true meaning nor came from the heart. If she only knew what it took to be a mother, maybe she'd appreciate me more. Well, in the face of my daughter's lack of support, I'd support and encourage myself.

I asked the saleslady to remove the pendant from the display, and I tried it on to see how it fit me. I made sure to put the word *mom* directly above my heart, and then

I stood in front of the little mirror mounted on the glass counter. It was a beautiful pendant, one that should've made me melt, but I knew I wore a lie above my heart, and I couldn't stand to look at it another second. I almost snatch it off before hurriedly handing it back to the woman behind the counter. She seemed a bit surprised by my sudden outburst but said nothing as I walked away.

Maybe clothes were a better option. Buying a piece of fabric was hardly enough to bring up memories of how I had failed as both a mother and a wife. As I began walking toward the women's section of the store, my attention was diverted to an African American couple with a little girl around the same age as Ciara. She was a cute little girl, without sadness outlining her eyes, the way it did Ciara's. This little girl was completely oblivious to what loss was, having both parents near her side. Ciara was a sad, quiet little girl, and although I hadn't spent much time with her, I could tell she was mature beyond her years.

Ciara deserved a family like this, one with two parents who were happy and in love. She needed two black parents, ones just like her, not a white father and a dead mother. America didn't work like that. America had its order. Blacks stayed with blacks, and whites stayed with whites. It'd always worked that way. Once that order was disrupted, children were hurt and everyone became confused. Ciara belonged with a black family, not ours.

One would think that over the course of two days, I'd grow accustomed to the thought of this child being a part of my life, and yet I was only growing more and more repelled by this very notion. I refused to continue on in my marriage with a black love child. I would be forced to give Mark an ultimatum. Me or Ciara. Me or his sin. I had grounds to leave my marriage, namely, adultery, and the Lord had commanded it to be so. I was not the type of woman to force my husband to pick between me and his child. But the truth was that he'd already made that choice a long time ago, when he'd decided to have an affair. I was only finalizing a decision he had already made.

I noticed a cute white couple as they passed by, holding hands and sharing a joke. They didn't notice me watching as they passed me, seemingly completely oblivious to anything going on around them. Theirs was young love, the kind where nothing else mattered but the two of you. The world could be burning down, but as long as those two hearts had each other, nothing seemed wrong. It was the kind of pure, untarnished love that could withstand such a test as infidelity.

Were Mark and I ever that in love? Had I once been that happy and naive, ready to dive headfirst into what would become my worst heartbreak? Had I known then what I knew now, would I have given Mark all these years?

It was a question I couldn't answer, not with a clouded mind.

"Claire?" Someone nearby called my name.

When I turned, I was greeted by Elizabeth Moore, a member of our church and one of the biggest gossipers in town. She was also a substitute teacher at the high school my daughter attended, so she knew everything about everyone's children. I could taste sourness in my mouth as I greeted her, but I kept a pleasant, kind smile on my face.

"Elizabeth," I greeted. "How are you?"

"I have a day off from work. Just shopping for a wedding outfit. My daughter is getting married in two months," she bragged. "And you?"

"Shopping for nothing in particular," I said, hoping my short answer would cause her to lose interest in our conversation. I knew these thoughts weren't very Christian-like, but I wasn't in a mental state where I could easily pretend to be light and happy. I was going through a crisis.

"Nice," she said. "Well, soon you'll be the one shopping for a wedding dress. That daughter of yours is one striking young lady. Men will be lined up to take her hand in marriage."

"Well, we are hoping for med school, so boyfriends and marriage are out of the question for the time being," I joked lightly.

"Speaking of your daughter . . ." Elizabeth said with a mysterious tone, which concerned me. Whenever she began to gossip, her voice would take on that tone. "I've noticed a change in her attitude lately. She was once so precise and cautious with everything, and it seemed like yesterday she was reckless and uncaring. There's been talk of a new boyfriend, one I'm sure you would not approve of. I've noticed in my years of teaching that when a child begins to lash out at school, it's because something is happening at home. Claire, is everything all right at home?"

I gave her my best smile. "You are talking to the first wife, a woman very much in control of her home's environment. A woman whose home is blessed by God. I assure you, there are no problems at home. I do appreciate your concern, and I will talk to her about this sudden change in her character. Thank you."

I tried to walk away, but Elizabeth stopped me by gently grabbing my arm. When my eyes met her face, I saw concern and alarm there. "Sarah isn't the only one acting strange. I hear your husband has been a bit out of it as well. Last Sunday's sermon seemed a bit forced, don't you think?"

"Elizabeth, why are you so concerned about my household?" I asked, not hiding one ounce of my irritation. My husband's sermon last week was actually great. Elizabeth just wanted to make something out of nothing.

"Well, as Christians, God instructs us to help each other through our infirmities."

"That hardly means prying into someone's personal business and imagining things that aren't there," I said with firmness and authority. "I appreciate your concern, but my family is well."

I began walking away, completely bothered by her ability to perceive things that were supposed to be hidden. It seemed as though I was the only one trying to keep things a secret. I thought that maybe I should give up, tell the whole world that I was not perfect, that my marriage was struggling in the worst way. Maybe I should've admitted that I'd failed as a wife and a mother.

I was already losing my mind from worrying about keeping the church and the scandal in my marriage, about how everyone would blame me. I needed to let my feelings out, or I was going to explode. I turned around to face Elizabeth, feeling myself on the verge of breaking down.

"Actually, there is something," I said, watching Elizabeth's greedy eyes light up.

Chapter Eighteen

SARAH

"Just talk to me!" Alex said, following closely behind me in the hallway at school the next day, not caring about the stares that we were getting.

"Stay away, Alex," I warned, trying my best to make my way down the hallway, filled with students, to get away from him, but he was determined. I broke free from a cluster of students and turned down a fairly empty hall. I started to run, but Alex reached out and clasped my arm, bringing me to a stop.

"Jeez, Sarah," he sighed, exasperated, and ran a hand through his dirty blond hair. "Just listen. I did what I thought was best. Guys like Ryan are bad news. One day you'll thank me."

"Why does everyone feel the need to think for me, as if my own brain isn't capable of doing the job?" I asked with a raised voice. "I'm sixteen, and perfectly capable of handling myself. I don't need you or my father trying to keep me locked in a cage."

"Is that what you think? I want to keep you trapped?" Alex sighed again. "You know me better than that. Sarah, look at yourself. You've changed, and you're going crazy. You need a friend."

"Friends don't snitch, Alex. Friends worry, but they don't run and tell parents things. If you were my friend, you would've tried to talk to me first."

"I did! I am! How many times do I have to tell you? Ryan is bad for you."

"Well, lately, everyone has been bad for me, even my own father," I argued. "If you want to help me, then leave me alone!"

I snatched my arm from his grip and continued walking down the hall, intent on getting out of the building. I had a few more classes before my school day was over, but I couldn't handle the thought of another one. I needed air.

I burst through the side doors and took a seat on the steps facing the student parking lot. I then buried my head in my hands, ready to cry. I wondered where God had been the past two days, when I'd needed Him most. I lifted my head, ready to pray, but loud music from the parking lot broke my train of thought. I saw Ryan sitting in his black truck, bopping his head as he smoked a cigarette. I was instantly relieved and started making my way over to his car. We still hadn't talked about how Alex had ruined our night, but I was perfectly content to forget it if he didn't bring it up.

"Hey, gorgeous," Ryan said as he exhaled in my direction as I slid into his passenger seat. I caught a whiff of smoke and made a face.

"What is that?" I asked, eyeing the rolled-up cigarette in his hand.

"Pot," he said, taking another hit and then holding the joint out to me. He exhaled as he said, "Here."

I hesitated, thinking about how, moments before, I was completely content when I was about to pray to God. And here I was, now, sitting in my boyfriend's car, watching him get high. I had never thought I'd stoop so low.

"No thanks," I said.

"Come on. It'll take away all the stress, and, babe, you look stressed." He held the joint out for me again. "Try it. Won't hurt anything. At least that way you'll know whether or not you like it."

He had a point. If I didn't like it, I wouldn't have to try it again. Also, I needed a stress reliever, and I started to doubt that my prayers would help much. It was nothing but the devil toying with me, but I pushed the idea of turning to drugs instead of God to the back of my head, and I took the joint from Ryan's hand. He eyed me curiously, seeming almost proud, as I raised the joint to my mouth. There was no going back at this point.

An hour later, Ryan and I stumbled into a tattoo parlor, holding half-eaten cheeseburgers, which we'd grabbed from the nearest fast-food restaurant. I'd never been so hungry in my life, and every bite of the burger was like heaven in my mouth. When we left the burger joint, I had noticed the tattoo parlor and had had the craziest urge to get a tattoo. Thankfully, Ryan knew the tattoo artist and could get me a tattoo with no parental permission needed.

I watched as he chatted with the tattoo artist, who had tattoos on every inch of his body. If my mom saw him, she would instantly begin judging him, calling him sadistic and the devil, not realizing her own judgment of him could condemn her. We all had a way of pointing out others' flaws while hiding our own, but this tattoo artist wore his flaws on his skin. His tattoos must've represented former pain, love, betrayal, and sin. To me, he was more honest than my mother. She had those same markings, but she just wore them on the inside.

I flipped through a book of different tattoos, trying to figure out what I wanted, but nothing seemed appealing. Nothing seemed to match what I felt inside. Maybe I should get a tattoo on my forehead that read "I hate my life." That would've been accurate.

"Find anything?" Ryan came up behind me and kissed my neck.

"Can't figure it out," I told him.

"Well, whenever I don't know what I want, I just have him do whatever. I tell him how I'm feeling, and he goes off that. You should try it," Ryan suggested.

"Come on, toots. I ain't got all day," the tattoo artist said, and I nodded, making my way over to his seat. He probably sensed the nervousness I possessed, because his expression softened up a bit. "First tattoo?"

"Yeah," I whispered, feeling my nerves get the best of me.

"Do your parents know?" tattoo man asked.

"Screw them," I said, tasting bitterness in my mouth, and it was enough to give me enough strength to go through with my stupid idea.

"Well, what tattoo do you want?"

"I—I don't know," I admitted. "Can we wing it?"

"Sure thing, princess."

"Don't call me princess," I said. "My dad calls me that, and I hate it."

"Ah." Tattoo man chuckled. "You're a rebel, I see."

"Rebel." I smiled and look up at Ryan, who watched me with a lustful look on his face. "I like the sound of that. Give me a tattoo that says, 'Rebel,' right here." I pointed to where my shirt met the top of my pants, right where my bikini line began. "Put it right there."

Chapter Nineteen

CIARA

I was hiding under Mommy's bed and could hear Auntie Tamara's footsteps as she tried to find me. She started downstairs, and then she looked for me in my bedroom. I could hear the panic in her voice as she called my name, but I didn't move or make a sound. I knew she was gonna make me go back to my daddy's house after I'd stayed with her for three days, but I wanted to stay forever. I didn't want to go back to my daddy's house ever again. Auntie Tamara was good to me; she fed me, played with me, and was nice to me. My daddy barely looked at me. I didn't like him much.

"Ciara, where are you?" she called. "This ain't funny!"

I could see her feet from under the bed as she had stopped just inside the room.

"Are you hiding from me?" She walked over to the closet and opened it. "You ain't in there. Hmm . . . where else could you be?" Auntie Tamara lowered herself onto her knees and looked under the bed and found me. "What are you doing under here?"

"Hiding," I admitted, scooting even farther under the bed.

"From what? The monsters are usually *under* the bed."

"Not the real-life monsters," I told her. "The real monsters don't even look like monsters. They just act like us."

"Tell me more about these real monsters," Auntie Tamara said.

At first I was afraid to speak, but her warm smiles gave me strength. "Some real-life monsters don't even know they are monsters, but you can tell by how they act. My daddy's wife is a monster. My daddy is turning into a monster too, but he doesn't know it."

"How does one turn into a monster?"

"Bad things happen to them."

"Why is your daddy's wife a monster?" Auntie Tamara asked.

"My teacher said that anyone who hates another race is a monster," I told Auntie, and she seemed okay with my answer.

"Well, how about you come out from under the bed so we can talk more?"

"No," I told my auntie.

"Ciara," she sighed. "Your daddy is on his way to come get you."

"I don't wanna go."

"Ciara," Auntie began, but the doorbell rang, distracting her. "Ciara, that's probably your daddy."

"He's not my daddy."

"Yes he is, and you're going to go stay with him for a few days. Now, get out from under that bed."

The doorbell rang again.

"No."

"Ciara!"

"No!" I screamed, closing my eyes tightly and wishing Auntie would go away. I heard her stand and leave the room, and I was thankful. Just when I began to believe that Auntie was giving up, she returned with my daddy. I watched his feet stop at the edge of the bed. I heard his grunt as he lowered himself onto his hands and knees.

"Hey there, kiddo. What are you doing under there?" he asked, but I didn't answer. I just scooted even farther under the bed. "Are you ever going to come out?"

"No. I'll stay here forever."

"Well, now, how will you eat? What happens if you have to go to the bathroom?" my daddy asked. "Or when your favorite cartoon comes on?" I didn't answer. "Well, if you stay under there, who will I take to the zoo today? Maybe I can find another little girl who wants to see the lions and tigers and bears, oh my."

I looked at my daddy, who was smiling at me, holding a hand out. I'd never seen him smile at me before. And he wanted to take me to the zoo. "Is there cotton candy at the zoo?"

"You bet," he said with an even wider smile. I looked over at Auntie Tamara, who was kneeling beside him, with the same smile, one that looked hopeful.

"Doesn't that sound like fun?" Auntie asked me, and I nodded. "Come on then!"

Chapter Twenty

TAMARA

"Thanks for the invite," I said to Mark as we sat on a bench, watching Ciara feed the geese at the pond in the zoo. She seemed almost happy, like how she'd been before her mother died. It was nice seeing her so free from worry and sadness, seeing her just play like a child. "I'm impressed. You're showing effort, trying to be active in her life. I was afraid."

"That I'd bail?" Mark asked me. "To tell you the truth, I sure did think about bailing. But God didn't raise me up to be the type of man who ran from his problems. I laid in that bed, and I'll make it."

"What changed?"

"Well, I spent the past three days watching both my wife and my daughter pull away from me. I still haven't told them about the paternity test. I messed everything up. Here I was, trying to fix it, trying to get my wife to look at me, to get my daughter to talk to me, but it was out of my control. I then decided to focus on the things I could control."

"And those are?" I asked him.

"Bonding with Ciara. Showing her who I am, opening my heart to her. At the end of the day, I have a daughter who will go away to college in a few years and a wife who could leave me for good reasons, and the only thing I'll have is a daughter who doesn't know me." He paused, looking up at the sky. "I made my mistakes, but does that make me less of a Christian?"

"No. We all have our faults."

"Well, I won't let my mistakes keep me from being a great Christian man now," he told me. "I was concerned . . . afraid of what the church would say and think about my situation. Surely, I'd have to step down as preacher. Surely, I'd lose the respect of family and friends around me. I was willing to hide Ciara, keep her as a skeleton in my closet, but what kind of a Christian man would that make me? What kind of example would I be to my oldest child and my wife?

"I mean, eventually, the truth would come out. Eventually, everyone would know me as the adulterer. Why not embrace it now? I mean, what am I really losing? God showed me that it's all about perspective. I'd be losing my wife, my church, possibly my home, but I'd still have God, and I'm gaining a child, another piece of me. That life, that little girl over there, is worth my love."

I smiled, feeling a weight lifted off my shoulders. Ciara's father was finally accepting her. It was a great move in a positive direction.

"She's a good kid," I told him, trying to hide my tears of joy as I watched her be young and free. "She's so smart, sometimes too smart for her own good. She's really hurting, though, and I hate it. I wish I could take her pain away, but I can't."

I paused and looked at Mark, who was watching Ciara with a fascinated expression on his face. "You can, though. She needs you. She needs you to fill her mother's shoes. To pick up where she left off. There is nothing more powerful than a parent's love. Promise me that no matter how cracked your family foundation gets, no matter how damaged, that you'll always do right by Ciara. Promise me that you won't neglect her or hate her or blame her for your own actions, and that you won't let your wife hurt her out of spite or to treat her like she's less. Ciara deserves to feel equal. She—"

"Tamara, yes, I understand," Mark said, cutting me off, but I was too far into my emotions to stop.

"I don't think you understand the challenges you are going to face when you walk out in public with a biracial daughter and the whole world is staring. You might be able to handle it, but what about Ciara? How will she feel when the kids at school start to pick on her? When she notices all the curious and hateful stares and overhears the whispers? She'll be affected by it the most. And you have to be willing to understand her, help her, even when you need help yourself. You'll always have to put her first. Can you really do that?"

Mark looked me directly in the eye without wavering and said, "Yes."

And I believed him. He had a look of determination in his eyes, like that of a father dedicated to his child. I nodded and turned back to stare at Ciara. We were quiet for a few minutes before Mark spoke again.

"Let's take her to see the lions."

Later that day, I came home and curled up on the couch. I was at peace with a few things and thought I'd be able to nap. As soon as my eyes began to close, the doorbell rang. I sighed and wiped my sleepy eyes, then clumsily made my way to the door. I opened it, ready to yell at whoever had disturbed my sleep. My heart sank when I saw who was standing before me.

Dominique Coals, my abusive ex-boyfriend. The very reason I originally moved in with Candace all those years ago, after she patched me up. I'd stayed with Candace a total of three months before I was able to get on my feet and get my own apartment. My life without him had been great. The last I'd heard, he was in jail. Seeing him standing before me, with that same lazy, knowing smile, made all my anxieties resurface.

"I thought you'd be happy to see me," Dominique joked. He looked behind me, observing the house. I noticed a new scar under his eye, as if he'd been cut open, and wondered how he'd gotten it. "Are you going to invite me inside?"

"No." I tried to say it as firmly as possible, but I was cowering under his constant gaze. My mind kept reverting to images of him lashing out at me, striking me across the cheek, choking me. I remembered the feeling of losing the air in my lungs, the desperation, not knowing if I'd live or die, and being completely helpless under his hands.

"Why not?" he asked, challenging me, his eyes low and calculating.

"You know why. How did you find me?"

Dominique chuckled. "I followed you from the zoo. I saw you with your husband and child. A white man? I thought you could do better than that, Tamara."

I thought about telling him that I was single, but that wouldn't help my case. Instead, I kept my mouth shut.

"What surprised me was seeing the two of them head to a different car than yours," he added.

"My husband, he . . . he took our daughter somewhere else. I . . . I met up with them briefly, but we had our own daily agendas. Why is it your business?"

"So you *are* married," Dominique smirked. "Where is the ring?"

"At the jewelers," I lied, growing impatient. I was ready to shut the door in his face. "My husband is having more diamonds added."

"Hmmm . . ." Dominique pondered what I'd said as he leaned against the door frame. "Well, can I come inside and catch up? See how life has been treating you?"

I didn't trust him. There was something off about how he stared at me, how he smirked. I was afraid for my life all over again. I had spent years trying to erase the damage he had caused in my life, and with one visit, he had brought it all back.

"My husband wouldn't like that idea," I warned him. "You need to leave now."

"Ouch," he said, taking a step back and holding his heart, as if I'd punctured it. "This is how you treat an old friend?"

"You ain't nobody's old friend. You know what you did to me. If my husband ever found out that you dared to step on this porch, he'd have you killed," I told him. "My husband is a cop, Dominique. If you ever step foot on this property again, you're dead."

The corners of Dominique's mouth turned up into a menacing sneer. He started to back away slowly, but his eyes never left mine. "If you think a cop could stop me from getting back what belongs to me, even after seven years in jail, then you're still that same stupid, clueless girl I knew. I'll be seeing you, and your husband, around."

And with that, he left.

Chapter Twenty-one

SARAH

My tattoo burned below my stomach, and I was thankful for the bandage that kept it from rubbing against my jeans. I felt powerful with my new tattoo. Powerful and alive. I'd spent so much of my life staring at the world from behind my Bible and my father's protection. Now? Now I was experiencing things the way normal teenagers did. I was distancing myself from my father's image of me and forming my own image of myself. This tattoo was more than just a tattoo; it was a stepping stone.

When I came home, I entered the kitchen and almost didn't notice my mother sitting there, watching me with curiosity. I hadn't really spoken to her in days, not since we'd learned of my father's infidelity. Even before that, we had barely talked, and I preferred it that way. Even more so now. I hated that woman.

"Well, hello there, daughter," Mom slurred, and I instantly knew she'd been drinking again. So unchristian, but who was I to judge, with the new tattoo burning my skin? I almost wanted to laugh at how backward we were. How could God still love us?

"Mother," I responded in a monotone voice, leaning against the counter with folded arms. All our conversations ended in an argument, so I was preparing myself for the inevitable. "Drinking again, I see."

"Wouldn't you?" she asked, taking a drink out of the wineglass, which hadn't been there before. She must've hidden it under the table when she heard me come through the door. She had probably thought I was my father, which meant he wasn't home yet.

"I wouldn't mind a glass," I said honestly, expecting her to lash out, but instead, she shoved her wineglass in my direction. I hesitated, not understanding her intentions.

"Drink," she said.

I slowly walked toward her, then took a seat at the island. I grabbed her wineglass, aware that she was watching me like a hawk, and I gulped down the rest of her wine in seconds. I wiped my mouth and looked back at her. She leaned over and picked up a bottle of wine from the floor, hidden under the table, and poured me some more. I drank it the same way, in a hurry, as if I'd never drink another thing again. Once I was done, my mom just stared.

"How do you feel?" she finally asked.

I took a moment to evaluate myself. I did notice a warm feeling coming over me. I also felt myself begin to relax. "I think I'll need another glass," I joked, but Mother didn't even crack a smile.

Seconds later, a harsh laugh escaped her mouth, followed by a burp. We stared at each other, and then we both burst into laughter. Mom stood, grabbed another wineglass, and poured us each a glass. We'd spent so much time arguing with each other, and I'd spent a lot of time watching her try to be the perfect Christian and hating her for trying to make me the same as her, but now we sat there, finally bonding in the most unconventional way. We had to be losing our minds.

When the laughter died down and the wine dried up, we almost had a breakthrough.

"I'm sorry," Mother began. "For how I raised you. For the amount of pressure I put on you to be the perfect child. You know what my mother taught me? How to be a perfect lady. She taught me all my mannerisms and class and raised me to go through the motions of being a Christian woman, but never to be truly on fire for God." Mom stopped and thought to herself, and I wished I could read her mind. She noticed me staring and started to speak again. "If she wasn't correcting me, she barely glanced in my direction. I never truly felt loved by her, especially after Father passed. Everyone used to say how much we looked like him. . . . Maybe she couldn't stand to be reminded of the love she'd lost.

"I told myself when I was around your age that I'd never be like my mother. I told myself I'd be active in my child's life and make them the best person they could be. That's what I tried to do with you, but in the end, I was still my mother. Yes, I have looked at you, stared at you the way she never stared at me, but have I really seen you? I figured if I had seen you, we'd have a better relationship. You're probably wondering why I allowed you to drink. Well, I thought maybe you'd understand why I drank if you had some yourself. I like the way it makes me feel . . . free and without a care. Free and open to see things how they really are. I can see you. I can also see how bad I messed up. Sarah, would you let me fix it?"

I thought about her question, which somehow angered me. This family was in no shape to be fixed. We were beyond reconstruction. If we tried to fix it, we'd still be standing in the middle of a building that was seconds from collapsing on all of us. The damage was done; there was no going back.

"It's not your job to fix everything," I told her, instead of saying what I was thinking.

"I can try."

"You should've tried!" I yelled, feeling my anger rise to new levels. "Maybe then, Dad wouldn't have had an affair. If you had been trying, none of this would've happened!"

"That's not fair, Sarah!" Mom cried. "How can you put all of this on me, as if it was my fault? I didn't tell your father to sleep with another woman! And I did try with him. I gave him a beautiful, smart daughter! I gave him a clean home and a cooked meal every night! I gave him the affection a wife is supposed to give her husband, and he still rejected it! When are you going to learn that it's your father's fault? Stop blaming me for everything!"

"You pushed Dad away, Mom," I told her. "I watched it all happen. In your head you were the perfect wife, but you weren't." I stood up, and as I took my glass to the sink, I stumbled. I grabbed the counter for support, surprised the wine had affected me so quickly. I didn't realize my shirt had lifted, revealing my bandage, until my mom stood and walked over to where I stood putting my glass in the sink. She lifted my shirt and touched the bandage. I jerked away.

"What is that?" she asked.

"Nothing," I said all too quickly. "Just a . . . bruise. That's all."

"Let me see it," she said with concern, and I pulled away more.

"No, I'm fine," I retorted. "Just leave me alone."

But Mother was too quick. She pulled on the bandage, revealing the tattoo on my side. I heard her gasp, and I immediately became defensive.

"Wow, Mom. You act like you've never seen a tattoo!" I quickly hid the tattoo behind the bandage.

"Not on my sixteen-year-old daughter!" She looked mortified.

"You just let me drink wine with you, and now you're complaining about a tattoo?" I laughed. "You're unbelievable."

"Wine is nowhere near as bad as a tattoo!"

"So now you're God?" I asked. "You have the power to say which sin is greater? It's because of you and Dad that I got this tattoo, so blame yourself, not me!"

"So we made you a rebel?" Mother looked stricken.

"Yes," I said confidently, not affected by her pain.

"No!" Mother yelled. "I made you into a kind young lady, not one who goes and gets tattoos out of spite!"

"Well, Mother, it's already here. Yelling about it won't change my tattoo. It's here for life! Nothing you or Dad can do about it." I sighed as I walked away from the kitchen sink, my back turned to my mother.

"I don't even know who you are anymore," Mother said, in tears.

"In fact, you never did." And with that, I left the kitchen.

I went to my room and lay in bed for a few hours. I heard Dad when he came home, accompanied by a child. My guess was that Ciara was back. *Good.* Finally, someone else was around to take the attention off of me.

Chapter Twenty-two

MARK

When I returned home, I took Ciara upstairs and tucked her into bed in the guest room. She lay there, looking up at me so peacefully, and I could tell she was beginning to trust me, although we had got off on the wrong foot. Eventually, her eyelids began to droop as she tried to fight sleep. I walked over to her window and drew the blinds. When I was a child, the moonlight had kept bad dreams at bay, and I was hoping it would do the same for Ciara. The moonlight cast the perfect light over the tree outside the window, making it look glorious and stand out in the night.

"Daddy," she said, calling me that for the first time. I felt my heart soften even more as I smiled down at her. I thought she had drifted off to sleep.

"Yes, sweetie?"

"That tree outside the window, why does it hang so low?"

I took a seat on the edge of the bed and rested my hand on her leg. "Because it's a weeping willow tree."

"I know, but why does it weep? Does it miss its mommy like me?"

Her words broke my heart, and I did everything to keep my next words even. "Weeping willows don't have mommies. I like to think that when willows weep, it's God crying over the sins of the world, especially our family's sins."

"So the tree is crying because Jesus is crying?" she asked me.

I looked out at the tree, whose branches were hanging lower and lower with age, and I asked myself if I truly believed the explanation I had given my daughter. Maybe that tree represented all of us, every soul in this house, and the pain that we all shared, a pain that was rooted deep beneath the foundation of this house, just like the roots of that tree. We were all crying and hurting, but I believed it was Jesus who wept the most. After all, He was the one who had to die for our sins.

"Yes," I told her. "It is God mourning over our home, and may He save us all."

Once Ciara was asleep, I made my way down to the kitchen, which was where my wife had been spending most of her time as of late. And there she sat, slumped on the island, with an empty bottle of wine. That was becoming her regular routine. I watched as she slept lightly with her forehead pressed against the back of her hand, a light snore escaping her mouth. I headed over to the sink to pour myself a glass of water. Claire lifted her head and stared at me.

I felt terrible that my actions were causing my family to break up with such a force, and there was nothing I could do to stop it. All I could do was watch from a front-row seat. I sighed and took a seat next to my wife. I had yet to tell her about the paternity test.

"Ciara's mine, you know. I took a paternity test from the drugstore. Can you believe you can just buy those things there?" I looked over at her. She was still slumped against the island. She had heard what I said but was probably too intoxicated to respond, I guessed. "Look at us," I said, shaking my head. "Look at what we've become. We've allowed the devil to come right in and party in our home."

"You've allowed it," she slurred. "It's because of you that the devil has entered our home. That paternity test obviously proves that to be true, although it was already obvious." Claire paused and began fluttering her eyes, as if trying to hold back tears. "Sarah got a tattoo today. Right above her hip bone. And you know what it says? Rebel. Our baby is rebelling because of you. And you want to know what sucks about it all? She blames me for the affair, not you. She says I led you to cheat. Everything is my fault in her eyes."

"She hates me too, Claire. And it's not your fault," I assured her.

"No, it's not. I mean, I tried to get your attention, to get you to look at me like you used to. I'd dye my hair, hoping you'd notice, and you never did. I'd buy new clothes, cook new recipes, everything. I tried everything, and you had to go cheat." She laughed through her tears, but I knew it was not because she found the matter funny. It was an angry laugh. "But what hurts my ego more than anything is the fact that she was black. Don't judge me for being raised to believe that blacks are inferior to us! But that's how I feel, and to see my husband choose a black woman over me? I feel less than the blacks. I feel like the dirt you walk on."

"That's a low way to think, Claire. God has taught us that we are all equal," I told her.

"And God has also taught us not to commit adultery. Does it mean we always listen? No! I'm flawed too. And, Mark, I don't think I can bring myself to love this little girl. I will always be reminded of the dirt that I am."

"But—"

"And the looks we'll get from everyone when they see a white couple with a mixed child. They'll say, 'What a beautiful child. Did you adopt?' And I'll have to say, 'No.

My husband had an affair with a black woman.' Shame!" she screamed. "I can't live like this. I won't."

"What are you saying, Claire?" I asked, but I already knew. The way she looked at me said it all. She was going to leave me.

"I'm asking you to choose. You're daughter or our family."

I hesitated, wondering if I had heard her correctly, but I knew I had.

She slapped her hand down on the table with an impatient grunt. "Choose . . . now!"

"It's not that simple."

"It's very simple!" she insisted. "At Saks I almost told one of our church members about your scandal. She asked me what was wrong, and I almost told her everything, but I told myself to hold off, to wait one more night. Wait to see whose side my husband is on before I expose him. If you choose us, the little girl goes, and we can work on fixing our marriage. If she stays, I go."

"Then you'd be alone."

"I've been alone in this marriage for far too long. I think I would survive," she told me. And I stared back at my wife, at the distaste etched across her face. She hated me. Even if I chose her, she'd hate me.

Even if she didn't hate me, I couldn't choose her. Sure, she was my wife, but I had a child with no one to depend on. If I put my own child out, what kind of a man would that make me? Jesus didn't abandon me. Why would I abandon my own child?

Even though I was a sinner, one who deserved no mercy from the Lord, I was still a Christian, and I still needed to live my life for the Lord. I was done with allowing the devil to distract me. I had the power to choose whether Ciara would be my biggest curse or my best blessing. I'd choose her as my blessing.

I looked over at my wife with confidence, but at the same time I felt remorse for having to choose.

"I choose Ciara."

Claire laughed in disbelief. "What?"

"I said, I choose my daughter."

Claire watched me with a stoic expression, and then she jumped to her feet and walked slowly toward me the way a lion stalked its prey moments before attacking.

"I've given you twenty years of faithfulness and dedication, and this is how you repay me?" Claire asked, bewildered, her emotions now painting a vivid picture on her face.

"You're pushing me into this decision."

"I didn't push you to cheat! You did that! Everything that comes after that one important fact would be due to your infidelity! Do you think I want to make you choose?"

"Then don't," I told her. "We can work through this, Claire."

"And how do you suppose we do that?"

"We try. We can go to prayer, allow God to heal our family. Claire, nothing is too great for God to fix!" I tried to reason with her. "We could try to find a way to explain it to the church, a way that they'd understand. If I lose my job, so be it, as long as I still have my family and God."

Claire listened, and I could tell by the look on her face that she was actually considering the possibility of us working it out. In that moment I said a silent prayer, asking God to guide this moment and to allow His great will to happen.

Tears poured from Claire's eyes, and she fiddled with her fingers. "I can accept what you did, but I can't accept your daughter."

"Why can't you? Because she'll remind you of what I did?"

"Because she's *black!*" Claire shouted, and I could tell by her contorted expression that she hated what she'd admitted to me, that my daughter's color was the sole reason. I'd heard Claire's comments about other races every blue moon, but I hadn't guessed that her hatred toward colored people was that extreme.

"What kind of Christians are we, Claire?"

"Obviously, the kind who hides behind lies, shame, and guilt until it all boils over and reveals that we are just as messed up as the rest of the world," she explained. "I can't love your child. I cannot love her, because of her skin. I cannot love her, because she is not my child! I cannot love her, because she is the bad omen of our marriage. She is the result of your sin, and to love her would be to accept your sin against me. I cannot."

"Then what do we do now, Claire?" I asked, feeling just as exasperated as she looked, standing there with her shoulders slumped.

"Just imagine the people who will stare!" she continued, as if I hadn't asked her a question. "They'll say, 'Look at that couple with the black child!'"

"Then let them talk," I told her.

"They'll wonder if she's adopted or the result of an affair," Claire explained. "They will all wonder."

"You stated that already. Then let them talk! Claire, you should be more concerned about what God thinks. Galatians one, ten, clearly states—"

"For do I now persuade men, or God? or do I seek to please men? for if I yet pleased men, I should not be the servant of Christ," Claire interrupted in a rush. "I know what the Bible says, Mark. I've been a first lady for fifteen years! I know the Bible inside and out!"

"Then live by it," I told her.

She laughed. "How dare you tell me to live by the Word when you've been living by a lie the past seven years? You are in no position to correct me!"

"Claire, we just keep going in circles," I sighed, completely exhausted. "Maybe you need to go away for a few days, clear your head, seek the Lord."

"Yeah, maybe I should," she said, sounding a bit defeated, judging by how low her voice got, but at least her fight had died down. "I'll . . . go get a hotel room or something." She started to walk away with her head lowered, but I caught ahold of her arm and brought her closer. I was surprised that she didn't try to break away from my grasp. I cupped her cheeks in my hands, staring at her intently, so that she'd understand the truth in my words.

"Claire, I love you," I told her. "I truly do. I wish I could change the past, but I can't. We are here now, and right now, no matter what happens, I love you. We can get through this together."

She stared up at me, and I could see the conflict she felt as she processed what I'd said. She blinked a few times, quivered her lips, and sighed. Eventually, she backed away with a slight nod.

"I just need to get away and think, Mark," she said as she began walking out of the kitchen. "I just . . . I need time."

I heard the front door close as she left, and I prayed to God she'd soon return.

Chapter Twenty-three

TAMARA

That night, after Dominique left, I slept with every house light on and with a few knives under my pillow. If I told anyone I knew about how I'd slept, they'd laugh, but they had no idea what he had done to me. The countless scars, the emotional damage, and the fact that I had no children were all because I couldn't trust men after what he'd done to me. On my drive to my job at a local clothing store, I couldn't help but to replay in my mind everything he'd done.

I started with the very first time he put his hands on me. We were standing in my kitchen, and I was making his favorite dish, macaroni and cheese. It was his mother's famous recipe, and after she passed away, he had no one to make it for him. I took him asking me to cook it as a test to see if I could re-create his mother's specialty. If I succeeded, maybe then he'd consider me wifey material.

Dominique was a good boy at heart, but he prided himself on being a hood boy who earned his street credits by selling dope and intimidating all the other competition. He wanted his name to be known and feared. I'd heard about his last relationship and how it had ended with the girl going to the hospital after a fight. But being young and stupid, I blamed her and didn't question him. If I had, I might've saved myself a year of torture.

I was making the macaroni and cheese just the way his mama did, and he was standing over me, watching. I'd seasoned it just right, added the right amount of cheese, everything, but I hadn't put the glass dish on the first rack of the oven. Instead, I'd put it on the second. I learned of my error as soon as my head slammed into the oven. I saw blood dripping into the macaroni and cheese from my head. I unwisely placed a hand on the rack to balance myself and I burned my hand. I hadn't realized how hot the oven was.

Before I could react further, Dominique pulled me backward, tossing me to the floor. I held my bleeding head with one hand and sat my burnt hand on my lap. I looked down at the smoldering blisters and the red, damaged skin.

"Is you stupid?" he asked in a rage, pacing back and forth in front of the oven. "Mama would never put it on the first rack. It cooks the top too quick. You just about dumb!"

"I can't believe you hit me," I said, still in shock, still watching him pace, still very afraid of him.

"Ain't gonna be the last time if you keep acting stupid!"

Funny thing was, I tried so hard not to do anything stupid after that point. Everything was done with precision, and yet he still found a way to hurt me for not being his mother. Once, he whipped me with a belt because I didn't wash his dishes for him. Another time he choked me to the point where I passed out, because I had complained about him leaving the toilet seat up.

It was sad that a woman would start to blame herself; she'd trick herself into believing the beatings were her fault. She'd start to hide the truth from others, make excuses for his actions, and defend him, as if she deserved it all.

I spent a year defending him to Tara, an old Latina woman I once worked with. Tara had seen bruises appear on my arms repeatedly. At first, I was able to brush the bruises off as accidents, but eventually, she started questioning things. It took Tara sitting me down and delivering her own testimony for me to want to change. I remembered the day like it was yesterday.

Tara took me to a quiet bench, away from all the employees, who were enjoying their smoking break, and we sat there, quiet at first, just enjoying the scenery, the view of downtown skyscrapers from the nice hill. Then Tara pulled up the sleeve of her shirt and showed me a bruise the size of a nickel, round and ragged from healing over.

"That's a cigar burn," she told me. "My ex used to love his cigars. He got them illegally imported from Cuba. He had a huge display of cigars he'd never smoke, just to impress his friends." She paused, looking up at the sky with a bright smile. "I just love it when God uses me. It's a beautiful thing."

"What do you mean?" I asked, confused. Tara turned to me with a smile.

"I was abused by my boyfriend too. This mark on my arm, he put it there. He took one of those cigars from the case, lit it, and put it to my skin. He was so angry, he didn't even care about his precious collection. That was the first time he ever put his hands on me, and funny thing is, I can't even remember why he did it. But I'll never forget that he did it. I have other bruises from other fights, ten in total, and I wear them as a reminder of what God brought me through.

"I was seriously contemplating suicide from the pain I had to go through with my ex. One day, I woke up, tired and ready to give in, and the Lord spoke to me. He told me to get up, get out, and live for Him. I got out of that

bed, and I walked across the street to the church, and I gave my life to the Lord. After that, He made it so that I was able to get all my things out of that house and start a new life. Two years I spent with that man, and all it took was a few words from God to change it all. Whatever you are going through with that man, God says, 'It's over. It's time for you to get up and go.'"

I felt a sense of relief, a sense of knowing it was finally over. I felt God near, a presence I hadn't contemplated much, but in that moment, I could feel Him. I turned to Tara, whom I could barely make out due to the tears clouding my eyes.

"Thanks for the advice," I told her, truly appreciating her words.

It was crazy how the past could come back to haunt you, how you could have the same nightmare for the second time. I found myself in the middle of Candace's room, crying and praying, asking God not to allow this bad omen back into my life. But I also knew that God was a being. If Dominique was meant to come back into my life to give me another lesson, I prayed God would make me strong enough to handle it.

Chapter Twenty-four

SARAH

School sucked. The whole learning ordeal was a bunch of crap. I sat in science class and didn't even bother trying to learn. It was something I'd never use in life, anyway, especially if I was going to be a stupid stay-at-home mom like my mother. Ugh, I wanted to be nothing like her. I'd prefer to work than to be anything like her. Maybe I did need science.

By the time I decided to pay attention, the bell was ringing, dismissing the class. I rose from my chair and followed the crowd out into the hallway.

"Sarah." I turned around at the sound of the teacher calling my name. He sat at his desk, pushing his glasses up on his nose. "May I have a word with you?"

I sighed and began heading over to his desk. "Yes, sir?"

Mr. Calmaster held a piece of paper in his hand and briefly read over it. "I have a compilation of your test scores from your different classes over the course of this week. On each test you've scored under an eighty percent, which is unusual for you." Mr. Calmaster removed his glasses and sat them down on the piece of paper. "I'm afraid that you are no longer number one in your class, and if you keep this level of performance up, you won't be your class's valedictorian in two years. I am deeply saddened by this, Sarah. You barely paid attention in class, and your name is being tossed around the school.

I've heard rumors about you dating a particular student, and I am extremely displeased."

"Mr. Calmaster, everything is okay," I lied. "I have got my period this week and have been a bit off. That's all."

Mr. Calmaster coughed once and nodded, seemingly uncomfortable about my revelation. "Very well, then. I expect to see an improvement. You're a bright young lady, Ms. Douglas. I'd hate to see you go down the wrong path."

"I won't. You have my word," I said through gritted teeth. I then practically ran out of his classroom, only to bump into a strong body in the hallway.

"Whoa there." Ryan chuckled and pushed me against a locker. I didn't care who was staring at us, as we were now being completely open about our relationship. I was happy. "Why the rush?"

"My teacher just pounded me about my tests lately," I admitted, watching people in the crowd as they watched us. Ryan tilted my head toward him, so I had no choice but to look him in the eye.

"Who needs school, anyway?" he asked. "Wanna skip?"

The old me would have said no. The old me would have first thought about God and then about my father. I would have said no to his suggestion in two seconds. But I was no longer that stupid, innocent, naive girl. I was becoming my own woman. I remembered the tattoo that I had gotten yesterday, and thought about how cool I was now. *Forget school,* I thought. I was totally a rebel.

I smiled up at my boyfriend and locked my hand in his. "Sure. Let's skip."

Ryan smiled down at me and then led me down a hallway that ended with a set of doors that opened out onto the side of the building. I felt my nerves kick in, and my heart pounded as adrenaline began pumping through my blood. We reached the doors, and Ryan opened them, stepping aside so that I could exit first.

"Rebels first," he said and smiled, looking charming and mysterious, looking like a total bad boy.

I giggled and walked outside. Ryan quickly joined me, wrapping his arm around my waist as we began to walk.

"Have I ever told you how much I love your brown hair? Your mom is a total blond babe, but you are beyond her beauty. Brown suits you. Don't ever dye it," Ryan told me, which happened to be the sweetest thing he'd ever said. No one knew how much I wanted blond hair, but my mother would never let me dye it, so to hear Ryan compliment me on what I thought was a flaw made me like him even more. I knew he was the guy I wanted to give my virginity to.

"Sarah!" I heard my name being called as I crossed the lawn to the student parking lot. I spun around and saw Alex standing on the steps by the side doors we'd just walked out of. I cursed silently.

Alex started jogging in my direction and caught up to us before I could warn Ryan, who only watched with mild interest.

"What do you want, Alex?" I asked as he stopped before us. He kneeled down, slightly out of breath.

"I . . . I came to stop you from doing whatever you are about to do," Alex answered, finally straightening. He looked behind me at Ryan and gave him a menacing stare. I heard Ryan chuckle behind me.

"What I do is none of your business," I retorted.

"She's right, man. Back off," Ryan chimed in, taking a few challenging steps toward Alex. Alex showed no sign of fear as he stood his ground.

"This time, when I take her away from you, I won't be so nice about it," Alex threatened, which made Ryan laugh.

"I know what this is. You can't stand seeing her with someone other than yourself. Do you like my girlfriend,

Alex?" Ryan took another step forward, barely leaving any space for Alex to breathe. They were literally chest to chest. I needed to de-escalate the situation before it got out of hand.

"Alex, just leave us alone," I shouted as I tried to pull Ryan away, but he was firmly planted to the ground. His eyes never left Alex.

"So what if I do or don't like her? Right is right, and wrong is wrong. She can't skip. I won't let her," Alex answered. He finally turned to me. "Sarah, look who he is making you turn into. You'd never skip."

"If you think he is the reason, you're wrong," I told Alex. "This was my decision, so back off. I told you I never want to talk to you again!"

Alex's face fell, as if my words had hurt him. "You think that'll stop me from protecting you?"

"I don't need your protection, Alex! I don't need anything from you!"

"You heard the girl," Ryan chimed in. "So back off."

Alex turned his menacing stare on Ryan. "No."

"No?" Ryan laughed, but it was far from an amused sound. He was angry. Ryan pushed Alex back, making him stumble. "I was trying to be nice in front of my girl, but you're pushing my buttons. Back off."

"No," Alex said, standing his ground once again. Before I could say anything, Ryan punched Alex in the face, causing him to fall to the ground. I let out a scream and automatically ran to Alex, kneeling down before him. He was holding his nose as blood seeped through his fingers. I heard Ryan laugh behind me, and my blood boiled.

"You didn't have to hit him, Ryan!" I yelled, keeping my eyes trained on Alex. I gently moved his hand away from his nose and saw the fracture. I was disgusted. "Are you okay, Alex?"

"Oh, what? Now *I'm* the bad guy?" Ryan asked incredulously. "Now you're on his side? This is unbelievable."

"Just go, Ryan," I told him, still keeping my eyes on Alex's nose. I didn't even want to look at Ryan. I heard him breathe heavily as he began to walk away. I met Alex's eyes. "You're either stupidly brave or bravely stupid, Alex. Either way, you're so stupid."

"It worked." He smiled, and I helped him stand to his feet. "So does that mean you're coming back inside?"

I smiled, feeling my anger toward him dissipate. "Who else is going to take you to the nurse?"

Later that day, I was sitting on my bed, surfing the Internet for something to cure my boredom, since homework was the last thing I wanted to do. When I found nothing, I closed my laptop and pulled out my phone. I had a text message from Mom, telling me that she'd be gone for a few days to clear her head. *Figures.* I also had six missed calls from Ryan and three voice mails. I hadn't realized my phone had been silenced. I sighed and decided to listen to his messages.

"Sarah, I'm sorry. I spazzed out. That dude has been testing me. I did what I thought was best." Silence. "I know you're probably thinking that violence isn't the answer. You're right, so I'm apologizing. I was wrong." Silence. "Please call me back."

The message ended, and so I skipped to the next one. "Sarah, baby, are you still mad at me? Please don't be. I'll make it up to you. Just answer your phone!" The message ended. I went to the next one.

"Dang it, Sarah. You're being unreasonable. I'm coming over. I'm on my way. I need to see you."

Crap, I thought. I checked the time the message had been sent. Twenty minutes ago. That meant he was very close to my house. I picked up my phone and called him. He answered on the first ring.

"I knew that last message would get you to call me," Ryan said as soon as he picked up.

"Ryan, don't you dare come over here!"

"I'm not." He laughed. "I just knew saying that would make you call me."

"Well, you were right!" I said, feeling my anger rise. "You're a trickster."

"Only for you," he said. "Sarah, I punched him for you, too. Okay, so I don't make the best choices, but that's why I have you. You're my better half, Sarah. You make me want to be better and do better. I could've had any other girl, but I wanted you."

"Gee, thanks," I said sarcastically. I wanted to laugh at how cocky he was being. He could have any girl? *The jerk.*

"You don't get it. Yes, I could've had any girl, but they aren't as good as you. You are pure and angelic, you are my opposite, and together we balance each other out. You get it now?"

"Yes, I do," I told him, feeling a bit elated.

"Do you forgive me?"

I sighed and nodded, even though he couldn't see me. "Yes, I forgive you."

"If you tell me that we can have makeup sex, then I'll really be on my way," he joked, and I found myself laughing.

"You're not as bad as Alex makes you out to be, Ryan."

"I bet he gave you an earful about me." Ryan laughed.

"He did, actually. The entire walk to the nurse's office, he complained about how you were a bad boy who didn't really care about me. He told me not to believe anything that comes out of your mouth."

"And what do *you* think?" Ryan asked me.

I took the time to think about his question before I answered. Yes, Ryan had his flaws, but at this point, I didn't think there was anyone worse than my dad. Ryan was rough around the edges and had his fair share of girls, but I truly believed he had a genuine interest in me, regardless of what Alex had said. Speaking of Alex, why did he care so much? I began to wonder if maybe Alex was just jealous because he was in love with me. Maybe his excuse was that he wanted to protect me because of my father, but what if he was protecting me only because he was in love with me? He had always been overly protective of me when it came to boys, he had never seemed interested in having female friends besides me, and he seemed to be jealous of Ryan. Suddenly, I couldn't think straight anymore. I needed to talk to Alex. I needed some answers.

"Ryan, I have to call you back." I didn't wait on his response. I just hung up.

I was going to call Alex, but how would I broach the subject of his interest in me? Was I supposed to just flat out ask him? What would he say? Knowing him, he wouldn't admit to it. And what if he didn't like me? Better yet, if he did like me, what was I going to do about it? I'd never thought about Alex in a romantic way. I didn't even know if I could. And it wasn't like I was willing to break up with Ryan to date my best friend. *Too weird.*

Nonetheless, I found myself dialing Alex's number. Just then I heard talking coming from another room. It sounded like Ciara's voice. Out of curiosity, I found myself walking toward the guest bedroom, sitting the phone to the side.

Chapter Twenty-five

CIARA

Daddy took me to a new school today. We got to walk around and look at everything, just to make sure I liked it. The school had a big playground with lots of things to play with. My old school had only monkey bars and a swing set with only one working swing.

The lady at the front desk looked at me weirdly when I walked in with my daddy, though. She smiled at me and asked my name, but I could tell she didn't like me much. She had the same look on her face that Daddy's wife had when she first saw me. I knew it was because I looked different than Daddy.

She even asked Daddy if I was adopted, and I looked up at him to see what he'd say. Daddy put his arms on my shoulders and told the nosy lady that I was his biological daughter. I didn't know what that meant, but Daddy said I was his. It made me feel happy.

After school, Daddy called Auntie Tamara and got the location of my mommy's grave. Daddy said that he wanted to take me to go see her and wanted to say his own good-byes. I thought it was a great idea. I wanted to talk to my mommy more than he did, and I couldn't wait.

When we got there, Daddy led me past different headstones, and some looked so creepy, I wanted to cling to Daddy for comfort. There was one headstone that looked like it had been struck by lightning. I was really scared, but then Daddy stopped in front of a grave and laid the flowers that he had been carrying on the ground by the headstone. I forgot all about the other scary headstones as I stood next to Daddy and read my mommy's name on the gray stone. I knew her name as it was one of the first things I'd learned to write after I'd learned to write my own name.

"I'm so sorry," I heard Daddy whisper as he stared down at the grave with watery eyes. I wondered if he had meant for me to hear him, and even more, I wondered why he was saying sorry to my mommy. Daddy cleared his throat and looked down at me with a smile that looked sadder than anything. "Anything you want to say to your mother?"

I looked down at the headstone and thought. What did I want to say to my mommy? There was so much I wanted to say that I couldn't think of one thing that inspired me most. I kept wondering why my daddy was sorry.

"Why did you say you were sorry?" I asked, looking up at him. I watched his lips shake as he opened his mouth to speak. He quickly turned to me and kneeled so that he could look me in my eyes.

"I said that I was sorry to your mother because I wasn't able to be a father to you. I'm sorry that she had to raise you by herself," Daddy told me. I didn't know what to say, and I guessed he didn't expect me to. "I'm here now, right?" Daddy let his eyes drift to the headstone. "I came to tell your mother that she doesn't need to worry about you, Ciara. I wasn't there before, but I'm here now."

Daddy turned to look at me again, and this time he smiled at me. I smiled back, believing in what he had said. My daddy was starting to love me, and I was starting to love him too. Afterward, Daddy let me stand alone, and I told Mommy not to worry about me, either, and that she was right about what she had said to me in the bedroom. My daddy was finally starting to come around.

After we left the graveyard, Daddy took me shopping and bought me all new clothes. He even took me to get toys and things for my new room. I decided that another reason I was beginning to like my daddy was that he had a lot of money. He even told me that there was a pool in the backyard and that he would get it cleaned out just for me to swim. He said Sarah liked only to tan herself, and so there was no need to clean the pool if it wasn't going to be used. I told my daddy that I couldn't swim, and he said he would get me swimming lessons with a mermaid. I knew he was just being silly about the mermaid part.

On the way home, Daddy asked me all about Mommy. He wanted to know where she had worked, what her favorite things were, what she'd done for fun, and he especially wanted to know how good of a mommy she'd been.

"She is the best mommy ever," I told him with excitement, but then I got really sad. I shouldn't have said, "She is the best mommy ever." She *was* the best mommy ever. Daddy must've seen how sad I was getting, because he patted my leg.

"Hey," he began with a soft voice. "Mommy loves you, and she's listening to you in heaven right now, telling me how she *is* the best mommy."

His words started to make me feel better, but not all the way.

We finally went home, and I watched Daddy make me pancakes for dinner. He said that pancakes were the only thing he could make and that his wife would be gone for a while, so the only thing I could eat was pancakes. I was happy. I loved pancakes.

After I ate, Daddy took me to my room and helped me put all my new clothes into my dressers. He then helped me put my new pink sheets on my bed and tucked me in. The new teddy bear he had bought lay next to me, and he scooted it closer with a smile. He then walked over to the window and opened the blinds.

"What are you going to name your new teddy bear?" he asked me, walking back to the bed. I looked down at my new teddy and smiled.

"I'll name her after Mommy. That way she'll always be with me."

Daddy smiled at me and kissed me on the forehead. "I'll always be here too. Ciara, I know I haven't been the best dad to you, but I promise I'll make it up." Daddy smiled again and then left the room. Not being in my life must've really bothered him. He kept apologizing for it.

I lay in my bed, looking out the window at the willow tree. At night, it seemed even sadder. I didn't want the tree to be sad too. Trees weren't supposed to be sad. I got out of my bed and went to my window, then opened it so that I could see the tree better. If I reached far enough, I could touch its leaves and talk to it. Maybe then it wouldn't be sad.

I hung over the windowsill, stretching my arm out to the tree. All I needed to do was scoot just a little bit closer. "It's okay, tree. Don't cry anymore. You have a nice home and a family and me. I'll be your friend." I could almost touch the tree. All I needed to do was scoot just a little bit closer.

"What are you doing?" a voice shouted behind me, and I quickly got off the windowsill. Sarah stood by the door, watching me. She looked very angry. "You don't hang out of windows! You could've killed yourself! Where is the window screen? Out of all the rooms in the house, this is the only one missing a screen. Somebody should've made sure this window had a screen. Even I have one!"

"I just wanted to tell the tree something," I told her, holding back my tears. I had never seen her so angry, and the fact that she was mad at me didn't help matters much.

Sarah sighed and moved over to the window and closed it. She then grabbed my hand and led me to the bed, tucking me in again. She sat down next to me and looked away, as if deep in thought.

"Ciara, if I didn't come into your room, you would've fallen out the window, and you know what would've happened if you'd fallen out the window?" I shook my head. "You probably would have died."

"But then I'd be in heaven with my mommy," I told her, and I could tell that my words made her sad by the way she sighed. I didn't want to make her sad after I'd just made her angry at me.

"This is where you belong now," my sister told me. "With us. Tell me, how is Daddy treating you?"

"He took me to a new school and we went shopping and he made me pancakes for dinner!" I said in a rush of excitement, almost forgetting that I was in trouble.

Sarah giggled, as if she had forgotten too. "Daddy used to make me pancakes too whenever my mom couldn't cook. Best pancakes ever!" Sarah paused, and I could tell she was thinking about something by the way her eyes wandered around the room. "This used to be my room when I was your age."

"Really?"

"Yeah, but I got older and wanted the bigger room," she said. "Under all that wallpaper lies a magical land of princesses and evil witches." Sarah stood up and walked over to the wall, trailing a line with her finger. "Right here is where the castle is. It's a big gray castle with a princess trapped in the tower, and below, the prince awaits on his horse, ready to rescue her. But above the tower is an evil witch on a fire-breathing dragon, and she knows the prince is there. She is furious!"

"I wanna see the wall!" I begged. "Please!"

Sarah's eyes became unfocused as she thought for a second and then nodded her head. "I'll be right back," she said and then left the room.

Moments later, she returned with a pair of scissors. She went over to the wall, near the spot she'd previously been standing by, and sliced the wallpaper, which was really a nice contact paper, down the middle with the scissors. I could faintly see the paintings beneath the wallpaper and got excited.

Sarah turned to me with a smile. "All you have to do is pull the wallpaper away and reveal the magic. Help me!"

I got up and rushed over to where she stood. I looked up at her, a little unsure of myself, wondering if I should really do what she had said to do. Sarah nodded encouragingly, and without another moment of hesitation, I started pulling the wallpaper away. It felt like I was unwrapping a really big present, and so I did it as fast as I could, wanting to get to the gift underneath. It was like finding buried treasure deep in a mountain by the sea. It took several minutes for me and Sarah to remove all the wallpaper, and then we sat on my bed, looking around at the walls.

It was even more special that I had imagined. Each wall told a different fairy tale; each wall had a princess with her own story. I looked up at Sarah and could tell that she wanted to cry by the way her eyes were watering. I scooted closer, wanting to make her feel better.

"Don't cry," I told her, laying my head down on her shoulder.

"It's just . . . I almost forgot about these walls," she told me. "I almost forgot how innocent I once was, before boys and cheating fathers and puberty. I wish I could go back. I remember how close to God I used to be. We were best friends, and now . . . I barely pray. I think in a way, I'm mad at Him. He's just letting me slip out of His hands, and He's not doing anything to stop it. He's just, like, 'Go ahead and be stupid. You'll learn.' But I'm, like, 'No! Keep me! Hide me until it's all over.' But He won't."

"Sometimes we gotta go through things," I told her, knowing it was something Mommy would've said to me, even though I didn't really understand it. Sarah looked down at me like I was an alien, and I wished I hadn't even spoken.

"You're too wise for your age," she told me. "I know that in the end, God will have His way. I know He's up there somewhere, watching and guiding me, but it still sucks, you know?" Sarah sniffed. "It sucks so badly. But it's time for you to go to bed. Okay, kiddo?"

I nodded my head, crawled under my covers, and watched Sarah leave. She turned around and smiled at me before completely closing my door. I got out of bed and got on my knees, and I prayed the way Mommy used to pray, asking God to never let Sarah go. Mommy used to say that everyone needed someone to pray for them. I didn't know if anyone was praying for Sarah or not, but I told myself I'd start adding her in to each prayer at night. She was my sister, after all.

Chapter Twenty-six

CLAIRE

I spent my first day away from home at a luxurious five-star hotel, relaxing in a Jacuzzi and drinking enough wine for both my husband and me. Then I spent a few hours being pampered at the spa. I ended my evening with a nice dinner by the fireplace in my suite. I then lay in bed and ordered a movie, which I watched until I fell asleep. The entire time, I barely thought about my husband.

I wondered if this was what heaven was like: relaxation, free from worry or stress, no outside troubles threatening to shatter my world, bliss. Ah, if only heaven was a spa.

The next morning, I woke up and took an early morning swim while the majority of the guests still slept. I floated on my back and stared up at the rising sun and watched God's glory. I hoped today would be better than a lot of the days leading up to it. I had an appointment to meet with my lawyer about the divorce, and then I had a date planned with the girls, during which I planned to tell them everything. I was grateful that the girls had agreed to switch the dates for our brunch. I didn't know if I had until Sunday to inform them of Mark's infidelity. Who knew if Mark would even stand up and preach without feeling compelled to confess his sins in front of all his members or if someone else would blatantly point out what he had done?

I had already received a phone call from one of the elementary school teachers. She told me that my husband had enrolled a little black girl, who, he claimed, was his daughter. As fast as news traveled in a small town, I wouldn't be shocked if all the other wives already knew about this. Well, if they didn't, I was sure going to give them a story.

Indeed, staying in a nice hotel did wonders for the mind, and I was starting not to care about what people thought of this situation. I wasn't going to let myself look bad. No, I'd make sure my husband's name got dragged through the dirt, if it was the last thing I could do. Although I was starting not to care about what people thought, I still felt my need for vengeance grow at a rapid rate. I was ready to tarnish Mark's name.

Later that day I walked into my attorney's office with purpose and took a seat, ready to handle business. Mr. Carter, my lawyer, was a younger man with an airy disposition, which most likely helped him win cases. Dressed in a tailored black suit, he definitely looked the part of a man who divorced the wealthy. He also looked like the type of man who could win me every penny my husband had. "Mr. Carter," I said, resting my purse on the chair next to me. I met his eyes with a firm gaze. "I'm hoping you have some great news."

"Well . . ." Mr. Carter began, pulling a file from his desk drawer. He sat it on the table and opened it. "I have the divorce papers right here. As far as your concerns, you are entitled to the house, the car, and a lot of his assets. As far as how much of his assets you will receive, I don't know how—"

"He had an affair. That should entitle me to everything," I said out of anger, cutting him off.

Mr. Carter nodded in agreement, causing his dark curls to bounce on his head. "However, if Mark hires a good lawyer, that lawyer will negotiate heavily. They could dig up things on you that would make you want to settle for a lot less."

"Like what?" I asked. "They can't pull a thing on me! I've done nothing wrong."

Mr. Carter glanced at me and shook his head, as if I was foolish. "Do you know how many women have said that?"

I sat up in my chair, giving Mr. Carter the firmest look I could manage. "I hired you to make my husband regret that affair, and I'm telling you to make sure he does."

Mr. Carter sat up in his seat as well, as if to show me that he wasn't intimidated. "I want you to ask yourself one question. Are you divorcing your husband for revenge or because you truly want a divorce? Sounds to me as if you are doing this out of spite." Mr. Carter handed me the divorce papers, as if he was done with the conversation already. "Really think about what you are doing. If you act out of anger now, you could regret it."

"I'll keep that in mind," I said, standing up. I felt offended that he had blown me off so easily, but then again, I didn't want to discuss my deepest emotions or accept that what I was doing could be a mistake. In a way, I was happy to leave. "Have a good day."

Truth was, I wanted to make Mark suffer, and that desire won me over. After I left Mr. Carter's office, I went to his receptionist and asked for a pen. Without a moment's hesitation, I signed the divorce papers. I couldn't wait to see the look on Mark's face when I sat those papers in front of him.

I was the first to show up at lunch, due to the fact that my meeting with my lawyer had been cut short. I sat at the head of the table, picking the seat that would allow me to face all the girls directly. I wanted to see their reactions once I told them about the affair. I had my sob story memorized, every detail implanted in my mind. I was going to make sure that everyone felt pity for me, as they should. Maybe then I could escape this scandal with dignity and a reputation still intact.

Carol was the second one to enter, and she wore a beautiful off-white maxi dress with brilliant pearl earrings. She greeted me with a kiss on both cheeks and took a seat across from me.

"How are things?" she asked genuinely, and I could tell she didn't know a thing about the affair, which meant that word hadn't traveled as fast as I had expected it to.

"Things are going," I answered as I caught a glimpse of Susan entering the restaurant. She was tall and stunning for a middle-aged woman, with a presence that always demanded attention, and red hair so vibrant, it caught everyone's eye. She walked with her chin up and her shoulders back, enlarging her chest area. She was wearing a formfitting, knee-length tan dress with a matching clutch. She paused for a moment, glancing around, before finally spotting Carol and me. She gave us a small wave and made her way over. I stood, greeting her kindly.

"Well, aren't you lovely?" Susan said, assessing me almost earnestly." Your skin is glowing. A new baby?"

If I was suspicious, I would've thought she was truly referring to the new child in my life, but instead I smiled and said, "I went to the spa. They have this amazing pineapple and coconut facial that is to die for."

"Oh, really?" Susan asked while taking a seat. "Sounds amazing. I haven't been to the spa in ages . . . and by ages, I mean days."

"You were always the one who loved to get pampered," I said.

"And yet I had a few husbands who barely lifted a finger to spoil me," Susan retorted. "Thank God for my access to their accounts, or I'd be a poor rich wife." Susan turned to Carol. "How's life, darling?"

"Life is the same. Nothing new for me. You?" Carol asked.

"I found a new love interest. This one is seventy-three." Susan glanced at me. "He's almost as old as his money."

"That's not how a Christian woman should think," Jen said, taking a seat next to Susan. I hadn't noticed her enter the restaurant, but she was one of those women who tried not to draw much attention to herself, and so I wasn't surprised. "You worry too much about money. You idolize it."

"We all have our flaws, Jen," Susan retorted with a sour expression. "Mine just happened to make me rich."

Jen rolled her eyes and focused her attention on me. I could tell by her sullen and grim expression that she knew something. Suddenly, I didn't feel so confident sitting before these three ladies, but I had promised myself I'd make Mark take the fall while I played the victim. After all, I was the victim.

"Claire," Jen began, saying my name slowly while placing a white cloth napkin on her lap. "There is a small rumor going around about how Mark enrolled a little black girl in school. Have you adopted?"

Susan gasped while taking a sip of her water. "Adoption? A black child?"

"Claire, that's so wonderful," Carol said, chiming in. "What a great way to set an example for all mothers, although I'm shocked you hadn't mentioned this sooner."

"I hardly adopted a child, Carol," I said, taking a confident sip of water. I kept my chin raised as I glanced at each one of them.

"Well, the rumor is that it's really Mark's child," Jen practically whispered, gaining Susan's full attention. She practically whipped her head around in Jen's direction.

Every sad and desperate feeling I'd tried to stomach over the past three relaxing days hit me with full force. My confident facade quickly faltered as I started to sink in my chair. Any other time, I would've tried to hold back my tears, but I needed as much sympathy as possible if I wanted everyone to be on my side. The first teardrop made Carol gasp.

"It's true. It is his child," I told them. "He had an affair almost seven years ago. A love child was the result. She showed up on our doorstep about a week ago. She . . ." I couldn't hold my deep sobs in, and this gained me curious stares from the guests at other tables. "She has his eyes and his nose."

"The preacher had an affair," Jen said, more to herself than to the others. "We're all damned."

"My *marriage* is damned," I said, correcting her. "Everything we've worked so hard for is ruined. The church, our daughter's education, our reputation as a strong Christian family . . . It's all shattered. Just imagine what people will think of me! They will blame me!"

"No," Carol said, caressing my shoulder. "It's not your fault."

"I feel like it is. I could've tried harder, done better," I explained.

"It's just amazing to me. The perfect couple has now revealed just how imperfect they truly are. I can see it in the papers," Susan said, amused.

"You find this funny, Susan?" Carol asked with a bewildered look in her eyes. "This woman's life is ruined, and you're worried about what the newspapers will say? Do you realize what this means?"

"Enlighten me, Carol," Susan said, clearly irritated, judging by the way she slammed her hands down on the table. Carol turned toward Susan, accepting the challenge.

"They could divorce, Mark will lose his job as a preacher, and their family name will be dragged through the dirt. What about their daughter, Sarah? She'll be forced to choose sides while dealing with the emotional damage. Not to mention the little girl they now have. This is big, Susan, so stop being a ditz."

"A ditz?" Susan laughed.

"Yes, a ditz," Carol confirmed.

"Ladies," I sighed, irritated by Susan's indifference to my crisis, though I had suspected as much. I continued on with my sob story, although it wasn't faked. I truly felt every emotion being displayed. "I didn't mention all this for you to fight about. I need support. It's true what Carol said. I'm going to lose everything. My daughter now hates me. She blames me for the affair. My husband is choosing his new fatherly responsibilities over his old ones. I don't know what to do. I mean, I do know what to do, and it's the only thing I can think of." I paused and took in a deep breath. "I saw a divorce attorney today. I got the divorce papers."

"You can't be serious," Susan mused. "A divorce?"

"You can't divorce him, Claire," Jen added, placing a warm hand over my own shaking one. "What will that say to the church? To give up on a marriage when things get bad? No, Claire, you must stick beside him, no matter how much it hurts. You have to be the example for wives whose husbands have cheated. God can still get the glory!"

"That's easier said than done, Jen," I explained. "But the Bible does give permission to divorce on these grounds."

"Moses gave his people permission to divorce simply if the man had not found favor in his wife. That doesn't make it right! Jesus came back to say we should divorce only for certain reasons as well, but it doesn't mean you should!" Jen argued. "Stick with your husband. If he's done with the affair, move on."

"And what's the deal with the woman he had an affair with? Why did she wait until now to show up?" Susan asked. "Did she just pop up and say, 'Hey, you da baby daddy'?"

"She's dead," I told them. "The child had nowhere else to go. It was the child's aunt who dropped her off."

"That's truly sad, Claire." Carol shook her head and made a sound in her throat. "I assure you, no one is going to blame you. Whether you decide to divorce him or not, I am here for you, supporting you. We all are. And don't forget, God is here too."

"I appreciate it," I said, wiping my tears away with the white cloth napkin I had laid across my lap. I suspected these three women would soon tell the whole town the news, and at least they'd be on my side, which meant the rest of the town would be on my side as well. Mission accomplished. Mark had it coming to him.

Chapter Twenty-seven

MARK

Church was in service. The choir had already sung, and the praise was great among the congregation. That was the Lord's doing. I said a silent prayer before taking the podium, asking God to work through me, the way I always did. I saw Sarah sitting separate from her mother toward the back of the church, with Ciara planted by her side. I noticed a few curious glances in their direction, but nothing too much out of the ordinary.

Claire sat in the first row, the same place she'd always sat, which gave me a sense of comfort, even though I knew how upset she was with me. I could only hope we'd make it through this with minimal damage done.

I stood in front of the crowd, assessing everyone. I noticed a few women whispering to each other and pointing at me. To my right, I saw a few men begin to talk and shake their heads while watching me. My heart started to race, and I hoped it was all just my imagination.

"It is a blessed Sunday," I began. "The good Lord has brought us all together in thanksgiving as we offer ourselves to Him in—"

"Adulterer!" someone shouted from the crowd, cutting me off. I tried to find the person who had done this, but all I saw was a crowd of people watching me expectantly.

"God has brought us together in His n—"

"Cheater!" another person shouted. I explored the crowd, looking for the individual who had shouted, but at this point, everyone began whispering to one another. An uproar started in the congregation. I looked at my wife, who stared at me with a conniving smile, as if she was the one behind the chatter. They knew. Everyone knew what I'd done.

An older woman stood up and shouted, "You don't deserve to stand before God! You are not a godly man!"

Everyone started talking at once, shouting and pointing at me. I didn't notice Alex as he came to my side.

"Come on, sir," he said, pulling me away, but I wouldn't move. I had known this would happen eventually, but I hadn't envisioned that it would be like this. What kind of a man would I be if I ran from my problems? I needed to face them. I owed it to my congregation.

"Everyone, please, calm down," I instructed, but they continued to fuss. "I am an adulterer, as some people in the congregation apparently already know. I'm also a liar. As we all are. I am not the saint you think I am, but merely a sinner redeemed. As a preacher, I am expected to live a sin-free life. However, I stand before you today to explain that even I sin. I've sinned not only against God, my wife, and my child, but also against all of you. I am not fit to stand before you and preach the Word of God. I do not ask for your mercy, as true mercy comes from God, but I ask that you please listen." I looked around the crowd, watching the congregants begin to settle down and take an interest in what I had to say. I thanked God for that.

"I had a one-time affair, a moment of poor judgment, and due to that one mistake, a child was born. Due to that one mistake, my family has been shattered, along with my image. I wish I could go back and change it, but then I never would've met the most amazing young girl. My daughter Ciara." I took a moment to rest my eyes on my youngest daughter, who was staring up at me, her facial expression indicating that she was slightly confused and yet seemingly comprehending. She knew what was happening in her own way, and her little face gave me the strength to continue. At first, I had rejected her, but I had found myself starting to love her. She was my child, after all.

"King David was an adulterer, which is a prime example that even God's chosen make mistakes. It is not an excuse to sin, but a beautiful reminder that God forgives. The Lord has forgiven me of my trespasses and is teaching me how to accept my current fate. I only ask that all of you show the same mercy, as none of us can cast stones. But if you can't, I understand. If I must step down, I will. I want to say that I am sorry to all of you, especially to my wife and my oldest daughter, who are hurting the most. Thank you."

The church crowd was silent as I walked out of the pulpit. I was hoping my truthful words had spoken to them. That was all I could hope for. I'd know by the next day if I'd be disowned by my congregation, and I was going to pray the whole time before then.

Chapter Twenty-eight

SARAH

I knew that after church service, I'd have to take the walk of shame down the school hallways Monday morning. I knew I'd hear people talk. I knew they'd whisper, find some way to shun me or pity me. *Ugh*. I couldn't handle it. I wanted to distance myself, hide in a dark corner and never come out.

On Monday I stood at my locker, looking around at the sea of students. Some were gossiping, others were engaged in horseplay, and one couple in particular was having a make-out session in front of the biology classroom. I grabbed my books from my locker and prepared to take my walk of shame to physics.

"Want some company?"

I stopped and turned to find Alex standing next to me, watching me curiously.

"You look like you could use the distraction." He knew how I was feeling somehow. Maybe it was due to the fact that we had grown up together or were good friends, but the main thing was that he knew. It reminded me of what I'd meant to ask him the other day: if he liked me or not. That question would have to wait, though.

"Yes, I *need* a distraction," I answered. He nodded in understanding, and we began walking.

"My dad knows the dean at Harvard, and he pretty much said I'll get in after I apply next year," he told me, but he wasn't beaming with excitement. Instead, his lips were pressed together in a firm line, which gave his irritation away. I wanted to jump out of my skin with excitement for him, and I didn't understand his sudden mood change.

"Oh, my gosh, Alex! That's awesome!" I said, trying to cheer him up, but then I paused, finally understanding why he didn't seem happy. "But I thought you wanted to be a preacher?"

He nodded, and I could see the unease etched across his face. "I want to, but my dad has other plans for me. He's . . ." He paused, as if trying to find the words.

Before Alex could continue, Ryan threw his arm around me, pulling me away from Alex. "I can take it from here," Ryan said through gritted teeth.

Before I could react, Ryan pushed me against the lockers and kissed me deeply. "Did you miss me?" Ryan smelled of fresh laundry and cologne, a wonderful combination, and I almost forgot Alex existed. Almost.

"Hey, man," Alex said, pulling Ryan away from me. "You make her look trashy when you throw her up against the lockers like that, dude. Lay off."

Ryan faced Alex, breathing quickly, and I could tell by his reddening face that he was angry. I didn't want a repeat of last week, when Ryan almost punched Alex's face off.

"I didn't know you were a hall monitor, loser," Ryan retorted. "She's my girl, I do what I want."

"She won't be your girl for long," Alex threatened, but I could hear the fear in his voice. It took a lot for him to stand up to someone like Ryan. "Her father—"

"Has enough on his plate at the moment, from what I hear," Ryan said, wrapping an arm possessively around my waist and pulling me close. "Now back off."

At this point, the entire student body seemed to be watching. The last thing I wanted was to see Alex get knocked out in front of everyone. I needed to find a less humiliating way to make him leave.

"Alex, it's okay. Just go," I said reassuringly.

Alex looked at me as if I'd hurt him. "Yeah, you really have changed, Sarah. I thought there was still hope."

"I'm a rebel now," I said, pulling the side of my shirt up to reveal my new tattoo. I heard a few gasps from the people watching, but it was Alex's shocked expression that won my guilt. However, I preferred this method of making him leave versus Ryan punching him. Alex looked at Ryan once more and stormed off into the crowd. Ryan pulled me in for a hug.

"Good job, pumpkin," he said. "Let's get you to class." I followed Ryan through the crowd of students with my head hung low. I didn't like who I was becoming, and yet I wasn't willing to go back to the old me.

By lunchtime, I couldn't handle the stares and whispers. Every conversation was about me. Every head turned in my direction, just to see what I'd do next. I couldn't escape hearing the words *cheater, another child, tattoo,* or *bad girl.* I needed to escape before I passed out from the stress.

Mr. Calmaster was writing part of the periodic table on the chalkboard, and I was vaguely paying attention to this. I was more interested in watching the clock like a hawk. We'd been sitting in his class for only twenty minutes, but it felt like three hours. I could hear the clock slowly ticking away, taunting me. I was chewing impatiently on my bottom lip because I couldn't take it. I stood up, grabbed all my things, and walked out of the classroom before Mr. Calmaster could register what had happened. The farther I got down the hallway, the more certain I was that he hadn't seen me leave his classroom, or he would've stepped into the hallway and shouted for me to return to class.

I didn't know where I'd go or what I'd do. I just knew I couldn't stay at school. I decided to put my books in my locker, because I just didn't feel like carrying them around. I shut my locker door and began walking down the hallway again. As I walked, I saw a door open, and a teacher stepped out of the classroom. It was too late for me to hide.

Mr. Brown, a pouty-faced English teacher, frowned when he saw me. "Shouldn't you be in class?"

"Cramps," I lied, grabbing my stomach for effect. "I'm going to the nurse's office."

"Where is your hall pass?" Mr. Brown asked, looking down at my empty hands.

I froze, racking my brain for an excuse. "I'm in so much pain, my teacher said to just go," I said, then pressed my hand to my stomach and moaned. "I need to go."

I walked right past Mr. Brown, thinking he might stop me, but he let me go. I sighed in relief as I rounded the corner. I quickly ran to the girls' bathroom and hid in a stall. I felt a strange thrill from getting away with a lie. I had rarely told lies before, and now I was a master at them. Alex was right. I was changing.

I walked out of the bathroom stall and stood in front of the mirror, looking at myself. Somehow I seemed older. My round, fat cheeks seemed to sink in a bit, or maybe it was my imagination. My bottom lip was slightly bruised from me biting down on it in class. I also had darkness around my eyes from a lack of sleep. I reached into my purse and pulled out my compact and put foundation on my face to liven it up. It barely helped.

"Slap your cheeks," a girl said, walking out of one of the stalls. "It'll bring color back to your face. That's what I do whenever I vomit."

"Vomit?"

"I have an eating disorder," she told me, walking up to the mirror next to me and fluffing her hair.

She was a pretty blonde, but the skin on her face sank in, exposing her cheekbones. Her eyes also appeared lifeless and pale in the low light, making her look a little scary. I could only imagine how pretty she must've been before her disorder. I didn't understand why such a pretty girl felt the need to get sick, but I didn't judge. We all had our problems.

"My doctor said I need to talk about it more, in case you're wondering why I just blurted that out," she added.

"You're beautiful. You don't need to do that," I told her, slightly jealous of her looks, even in her current state.

"It pays to look like this," she said sarcastically. She then reached into her purse, pulled out a cigarette, and lit it up in the bathroom. I was shocked. She noticed and chuckled. "Want a square?"

"I don't smoke."

"Oh, yeah, that's right. You're the preacher's daughter," she said, blowing smoke in my direction. I fought the urge to cough. "Little Miss Perfect, almost didn't recognize you. So is it true? Did your father really cheat on your mom?"

"I don't want to talk about it," I told her, feeling my emotions rise again. "I just wish people would stop talking about it already."

"Hey, I know how you feel," she told me. "Last year, my eating disorder got really bad. I weighed, like, eighty pounds. The whole school talked about me. I had to go to rehab for a while, and when I got back, people were still talking." She laughed to herself. "I started not eating again, because of the constant stares and judgment. Smoking helps. When I get the urge to vomit, I just light up a cigarette. Sometimes you have to fight fire with fire."

She reached into her purse and pulled out a cigarette and extended it to me. She waited patiently before I took it out of her hand. "My name's Ranya, by the way."

"Sarah," I responded.

"I know," she said and then lit my cigarette by holding it up to her own. "It's gonna be harsh at first, but it will calm your nerves. You'll thank me later."

I nodded, taking a puff of the cigarette. My eyes began to water as the smoke burned my throat. Ranya watched me, amused and pleased with herself, I was guessing.

"You're not the preacher's perfect angel anymore, I see." Ranya turned toward the mirror and began fluffing her hair again. I turned toward the mirror as well, watching myself as I took another puff of the cigarette. "Welcome to the real world."

Chapter Twenty-nine

TAMARA

It almost seemed like another storm had come in just as the previous storm had passed. I'd finally found peace in knowing Ciara would be taken care of. I had thought I had nothing left to worry about, well, besides Candace's bills and dealing with her death as best as I could. Then Dominique showed up, and everything I had tried so hard to heal from smacked me in the face. There was no way I would let him back in my life. I was hoping that the story of my husband would suffice to keep him away, but I wasn't so sure with him.

I was thankful the day was almost over as I walked up the porch steps. I said a silent prayer as I pulled my keys out to unlock the door. I was so thankful to make it through another workday. I put my key to the keyhole and then paused when I noticed the door was open a crack. *Strange.* Did I forget to close the door this morning? Ciara had a habit of never closing doors, and so doors would stay open a crack until someone caught it. It was very possible I'd done the same. I shook my head, criticizing myself for my goof up, and walked inside the house.

I laid my keys down on the stand by the door, removed my jacket, and hung it up in the closet. I took my shoes off, slid my house shoes on, and proceeded to walk up the stairs to take a nice shower. Halfway up the stairs, I paused, having seen from the corner of my eye somebody sitting on the living room couch. My heart sped up as I slowly turned toward the person.

Dominique sat on my couch, with his intense eyes planted on me. He'd probably been watching me from the moment I walked in my house. Every inch of my body told me to run, to lock myself in one of my rooms, but an image of him breaking down the bathroom door many years ago kept me frozen in place. Dominique slowly stood and made his way over to the staircase.

"Happy to see me?" he asked with a cocky smirk. "I took the liberty of showing myself around your house, and the funny thing is, I found no traces of a man living here. I thought you were married, Tamara."

"I am," I said, continuing my lie. I was too afraid to do anything but lie. If he knew the truth, he'd beat me blind. "My husband and I have been separated for a few days."

Dominique nodded once and took a single step up onto the first stair. Instinct told me to do the same, but I couldn't move.

"That's not what you said originally. I also noticed all the pictures hanging on the walls. Nice family pictures, by the way, but there was something real suspect." Dominique took another step up. "They were pictures of your daughter with another woman. Matter of fact, I saw only two pictures of you."

"It . . ." I paused, trying to think of a reasonable lie. I realized I had a death hold on the railing and loosened my grip. "It's my sister and my daughter. She passed away, so I recently removed the old pictures and put the ones of her and my daughter up. I couldn't stand looking at my husband's pictures with him gone."

Dominique nodded and took another step up. There were now six steps separating us. All he had to do was reach out, and he'd have me. I wanted so desperately to move, but I knew that at this point, it wouldn't make a difference. He had me right where he wanted me. The only thing I could do was pray.

Jesus, don't let him kill me. Lord, please don't let him kill me.

"Where is your daughter now?" he asked, taking another step.

"With her father," I said, thankful that it wasn't a lie. If she were here with me, if she witnessed his craziness, I wouldn't be able to live with myself. "What are you doing in my house?"

"I wanted to see you." He smiled.

"You saw me. Now leave."

"Naw, baby girl," he said, taking another step. "I wanna see all of you."

I knew what he meant in that moment. He wanted to have his way with me, the way he used to so many years ago. He wanted back in my life. He wanted control again. What scared me the most was that Dominique always got his way.

He took another step, and I could almost feel his body heat radiating off of him. The look in his eyes was one of pure desire, and something darker, much darker. There was a warning in his eyes, one that said, "Danger. Stay away," and yet once he had his grip on someone, getting away seemed impossible.

I needed to be smarter this time. Stronger. I couldn't keep running and hiding from him, and if jail didn't stop him from getting to me, a restraining order sure wouldn't. I had to trick him. Make him think I wanted him, buy enough time until I could figure something out.

I stretched out my hand to cup his face, and I smiled. "You can see all of me." And then I led him to my bedroom with another silent prayer.

***

When I woke up the next morning, Dominique was no longer in my bed. I didn't even try to think about what had happened the night before, wishing I could forget, trying to trick myself into believing that I hadn't let him seduce me. I felt depressed, hopeless.

First, I lost my best friend, then I had to deal with having to give Ciara away, and now my worst nightmare was coming true. Dominique was slowly making his way back into my life.

I got out of bed hesitantly, thinking it was possible that he was still in my house. I quietly walked toward the bathroom door and peeked inside the bathroom. The toilet seat had been left up, my shower curtain was drawn back, and wet footprints marked the tile floor. Judging by the wetness of those footprints, I guessed he was still here. I then heard a noise coming from downstairs.

I pulled a long T-shirt over my body and made my way slowly down the stairs. I headed to the kitchen, having smelled bacon and eggs. As I approached the doorway to the kitchen, I heard rap music playing. Dominique stood in front of the stove, flipping pancakes and nodding his head to the music. He quickly turned toward me, probably having sensed my presence, and smiled.

"I hope you're hungry after last night," he joked lightly, seeming to be in a good mood.

"Starving," I managed to say, taking a seat at the kitchen table. I watched Dominique freely, as his back was turned to me, and noted that he wore only his boxers, which was a sign that he was making himself right at home. I couldn't have that with Ciara around, and I needed to think up a plan to make him leave.

Dominique interrupted my thoughts by walking a plate over to me and sitting it in front of me. I was shocked by his kind gesture, and it made me wonder if he was only trying to butter up to me. It was hilarious, considering he had broken into my house. No amount of breakfast could make me forget the beast he truly was.

Dominique returned to the stove, turned it off, and then walked back to the table with his plate. We sat for a while, barely speaking, he gulping his food down while I picked at mine. When I caught him watching me, I made sure to take large bites, as if I was enjoying his meal. He seemed content with that.

"I was thinking," he said while chewing a piece of bacon. "We should start a family."

He was delusional. "I have a family." I watched the veins in his neck bulge, which was a sign his anger was beginning to flare. I needed to watch what I said at this point, which meant that I needed to agree with everything he said. I hated being this weak. I hated the person he always made me be. "But a family sounds good," I said hurriedly.

"Did you miss me?" he asked, dropping his fork and leaning over.

"Sure," I said. "Yeah, I did. I'm . . . glad you're here."

He smiled, taking a bite of his eggs. "I was in the joint for some years."

That didn't surprise me. "Oh, really?"

"Yeah, I did six years. Got out early. I got charged for murder." Dominique lifted his eyes from his plate to meet mine. "I ain't kill nobody, though." I had a hard time believing that. "As soon as I got out, I started looking for you. I spent a lot of time in that cell, regretting the things I did to you. A real man don't beat his woman. He loves her, cooks for her. It took for me to get locked up to realize that. I want you to know that I've changed."

For a while, I sat there, not able to say anything due to shock. Was he telling the truth? Had he really changed? One thing was obvious: he still had some bad habits. For one, he had broken into my house; for two, he had invited himself back into my life. Based on those two things alone, I'd say he hadn't changed. Even if he had changed, I couldn't let him back in. I couldn't just trust this man's word, not after what he'd put me through, but I put on my best smile, lying to him the way I knew he was lying to me.

"I believe you."

Chapter Thirty

CLAIRE

I waited patiently for my husband to walk through the double doors of our home. I was sitting on our lush off-white couch, the one he'd gotten accustomed to sleeping on last week. I bet he'd enjoyed the bed while I was gone. I hadn't been gone the full three days, because I couldn't wait any longer to serve the divorce papers.

I had to admit, something had taken over me. The woman I was becoming was strong and fierce and definitely past negotiating. When I looked in the mirror, I also saw a woman who was beginning to distance herself from her God. A lot of my actions definitely did not scream, "Saint." However, I could only handle my situation the best I could. Once emotions got in the way, it was hard to act the way Jesus would have. I wished I could, but I was too lost.

As a woman, my self-worth had diminished, disappeared like the sun behind raging storm clouds. Some would think I was being irrational, serving my divorce papers with spite. Others would say they'd do a lot more to hurt their husband for his infidelity. I'd watched movies where raging wives threw their husband's clothes from buildings or set their things on fire. I'd seen women lose it. At least I still had some dignity.

As I waited, I imagined how he'd react once I served him the papers. In one scenario, he took the news with a silent nod, accepting what he knew was inevitable without a fight. In another scenario, he upturned the love seat in a fit, ending with a plea that I stay with him as he wept at my feet. Both scenarios were pleasing to me, because in both scenarios, he was the wounded one, and I was the exalted one.

I then moved on to the thought of being a single woman. I had a feeling that Sarah would stay with her father, even though she hated him for causing the family such pain and humiliation. I saw it in her eyes at church. That meant I'd be alone, which I didn't mind, so long as I didn't have to stay in this house with my soon to be ex-husband and his black child.

Maybe I'd find a new husband, one who was attracted only to successful Caucasian women. One who would notice me, give me compliments on my newly dyed hair or new dress. One who would take the time to hear what was on my mind and learn all my ways, as if it was his passion. Mark, he was once that way, long ago. *Funny how life changes. Actually, I take that back. It's not funny at all.*

I heard the latch on the door turn, and in walked both my husband and his child. He was a handsome man, always had been. His graying hair was always groomed: it looked as if it had been washed by Jesus's hands. His clothes were pressed and proper, and he looked as if he was on the cover of a golf magazine. He had always carried himself like a man with authority. When I first saw him, I knew he was a strong man of God, but as I looked at him now, I noticed only his clothes. It was almost as if God had left him.

The first thing Mark noticed as he walked through the door was me sitting on the couch. He leaned down and whispered to his daughter. I watched her in disgust, almost hating myself for hating an innocent child, and yet I wanted to blame her for everything.

The child looked up at me and then nodded at Mark and headed up the stairs. Mark's chest rose as if he was sighing, although I couldn't hear it, and then he made his way into the living room. He took a seat on the love seat, the same one I'd envisioned him tossing around once he learned of the divorce. I almost wanted to smile.

"I wasn't expecting you to be here," he said, looking at anything but me, I noticed.

"I live here," I reminded him. "I can come and go as I please."

"I know," he began. "I just—"

"It doesn't matter, Mark. I'm here for a reason." I studied his expression, but I wasn't able to read it.

"I figured you'd want to talk soon. I was waiting." He paused, clearing his throat. "*Hoping* you'd want to talk."

"Ah." I nodded. "Well, I'm sure this isn't the conversation you were hoping for."

"What do you mean?" Confusion marked his face as he sat up, resting both elbows on his knees. I was surprised he hadn't noticed the stack of papers at my side. I grabbed them, handing them over. It took Mark almost a minute to take the papers from my hands.

"Read through that and sign on the line, please," I said with nonchalance. Mark flipped through the papers, face scrunched up in confusion, eyes beginning to water. I had to look away. I had imagined this moment to feel good, and yet I felt torn inside.

"A divorce," Mark stated blandly.

"Yes." It took me a moment to answer. Why did I hesitate?

Mark instantly sank from the love seat and dropped down on his knees, allowing the papers to fall out of his hands. His body shook as he let out his first heart-shattering cry. I couldn't take it.

"No, no, no," he cried, and then he lifted his head up to the ceiling. "Jesus, please fix it! No!"

"Don't pray," I said, trying to pull him from the floor, but he was planted there. He grabbed my arms, forcing me down to my knees. "Mark."

"Father, I ask in the name of Jesus's blood that you restore this marriage," Mark pleaded, pulling me closer. I struggled against him. "Claire, no. Claire." He paused, trying to catch his breath. "Claire, don't let the devil destroy us. Claire, I was wrong. Please forgive me. Claire, you're my wife!"

"You betrayed me!" I cried, continuing to pull away. I had hardened my heart and worked my way up to being able to hand him the divorce papers as if it had no effect, but the truth was, I loved him. I loved him with every piece of me. However, he had ruined everything we had, and so I couldn't stop myself from pulling away from him.

"Jesus, I ask that you don't take this woman from me," he prayed, tightening his grip. "I won't let this ruin my marriage. I won't allow the devil to take my marriage! Jesus, find a way!"

"Let go, Mark!" I screamed, prying his fingers from my arms. He finally let me go, lowering himself even more in prayer. I hated being the woman who walked away in a moment like that, when he was calling on Jesus. I felt like the devil himself.

A part of me wanted to stay, to tell him that it would all be all right, that I'd find a way to forgive him and accept his child. That I'd learn to love her, no matter the color of her skin. To admit that maybe her skin color hadn't bothered me as much as I'd let on. That what had really got to me was the fact that he had had a child with someone other than me.

The only thing I could do was walk away. I couldn't be-lieve I was the type of woman who would leave a praying man in his misery . . . but what about my misery? I wasn't done being hurt. And so I forced myself to believe I was doing the right thing as I left him crying on the floor.

Chapter Thirty-one

MARK

I couldn't believe Claire had left me there, that she'd walked away, like her heart had been turned to stone. I couldn't blame her; it was my fault. I had sealed my own fate, and yet I still couldn't believe she had been so coldhearted. The Claire I once knew was kind and loving. She held herself up to high standards and wouldn't hurt someone just because they'd hurt her. I had broken her, shattered her world, and the effect was a woman scorned.

It was Ciara who found me hours later, curled in a ball, sleeping on the living room floor. I felt her tap me, but I just couldn't find enough strength to respond. I continued to lie there in defeat.

"Daddy," she called. The name sounded so sweet coming from her little mouth. It reminded me of when Sarah was a small child, and how she used to call out to me. "Daddy, wake up. I'm hungry."

I still didn't move. I didn't want to. Everything I knew had changed. It was as if I was living someone else's life, and I had no choice but to stay in that body and take every beating coming at me.

My wife wanted a divorce. Darn right I couldn't move. I could barely breathe.

"Daddy, I'm hungry," Ciara said again, shaking me with an impatient moan. "Wake up."

I opened my eyes and saw her kneeling beside me, worried. It only added to my misery. I wished I could reach out and touch her, tell her that I'd be up shortly, but my arms weren't working. In fact, my whole body was opposed to movement. Instead, I closed my eyes and welcomed blackness.

"Dad!" I heard a distant sound, and it awakened me from my slumber. Then something slammed against my cheek. I winced as the searing pain on that side of my face. "Dad, wake up! What the heck!"

I could make out Sarah's voice clear as day now. I opened my eyes and saw her standing over me. Ciara was at her side, with the same worried expression. I was afraid, and so I forced myself into a sitting position, squeezing my eyes shut as a headache intruded.

"I come home to find Ciara sitting on the couch, staring at you, and you're passed out! Were you drinking, Dad?" Sarah asked, and I responded with a shake of my head. "Then what's the problem?"

I said nothing.

"You've been crying," Sarah said. I watched Sarah's eyes travel to the stack of papers strewn about on the floor. I tried to grab them before she could, but I was much slower in my state of mind. It didn't take long for Sarah to figure everything out as she stared down at the papers.

"A divorce?" she asked with an incredulous expression written all over her face. I was too ashamed to admit it to my daughter. I couldn't stand the way her shoulders sank, as if she was defeated. It was because of me that she felt that way. "Dad, you can't get divorced!"

"It was your mother's decision," I said, closing my eyes due to the pounding in my head.

"Where is she?" Sarah asked. "I need to talk to her."

"She's gone," I said.

Sarah's face turned red, as if she was fighting back some sort of urge. She began clenching and unclenching her fists in anger, and then she let out a grunt. "I hate this! I hate this house, I hate this family, and I hate my life!" Sarah stormed out of the living room, leaving me stunned. I looked over at Ciara, who wore the same expression. She probably thought our family was more dysfunctional than Sarah did.

I managed to get myself up. I made Ciara some pancakes and sent her to bed early. After Sunday's fiasco at church, I had at least eighty voice mail messages and e-mails to go through. Most were probably from church members, either offering their condolences or biting my ear off. I was also backed up with paperwork and clients. I had only two cases I was working on at the moment, but I had neglected them once I'd learned of my love child. I didn't know when life would right itself, if it ever would.

I went to my study and took a seat at my desk. As always, I prayed to God for the strength to deal with my work. My desk was stacked with papers and files I needed to sort through from previous cases, but instead of dealing with that, I chose to listen to the voice mails. I picked up my phone and dialed my voice mail. Thirty new messages. Not as bad as I'd thought. I began to listen.

"Mark, this is Eric Gusto." I could hear the hesitation in his voice. "We've decided to rescind your membership here at Gusto's Golf Course. We don't condone your behavior of late. It's bad for business. Hope you understand." Eric sighed. "I'll . . . I guess I'll see you around."

I quickly deleted this message and moved on to the next one.

"Hey, Mark. It's your mother. I know about the child. Claire called me. Mark, give me a ca—" I deleted the message and continued.

"Hey, Mark. This is Mr. Dawson with the law firm Dawson and Dawson, wanting to schedule an appointment. I have public records showing a divorce has been filed, and we are interested in represent—" I hit DELETE.

"Mark? Hi. It's Jessie Carlton." I nodded to myself, recognizing her voice. She was one of the clients I represented. "I'm sorry, but my husband and I have recently decided that we don't want you representing us. I do hope everything works out with you and your wife—" I pushed DELETE again.

"Mark! My man! It's Jonathan from college," a voice shouted enthusiastically. I was hoping for some good news finally, after the previous messages I'd deleted. "Look, man, I heard about the thing with you and your wife. Dude, that's so unfortunate. Well, look at it this way. She didn't cut it off." Jonathan laughed so hard, it sounded like he was barking. "So if you're going to be joining the bachelors' club again, I'll be down at Smokey's tonight. Drinks on me, man!"

I remembered Jonathan perfectly. He had long bleached-blond hair, olive skin, and ripped muscles. He was the type of man who refused to grow up. I hadn't seen him in years and didn't plan to see him. I went on to the next message, which happened to be another client who had decided to fire me as their lawyer.

By the time I got through all the messages, I had lost five clients. And the very last caller informed me that a board meeting had been held, and due to a unanimous vote, I needed to step down as preacher over my church, the very church I had helped build. People stuck around when things were great, but the moment things went sour, those same people were quick to leave.

The church shouldn't be that way. There were always other routes, whether it was counseling or confessions. The church should work the way a marriage should.

Meaning all members should stick together in moments of happiness and crisis. I wanted to lead a church that didn't cast a member out without the congregation at least trying to help. Jesus hadn't thrown me away, and yet His church had. It wasn't right to me, but it also wasn't my decision.

I wanted to pray, but what would I say? "Father, I have sinned. Make everything better"? Faith was believing that even when things seemed upside down, God was still working to turn them upward. I had done my part by praying continuously over the situation, and I knew I needed to have faith in my Lord to see my prayers through. Even when everyone else had abandoned me, I knew He was still there, fighting for me. That fact alone would be enough to get me through the night at least. Tomorrow might be a different story.

Chapter Thirty-two

SARAH

I couldn't breathe; I could barely even think straight. As soon as I learned about my parents' divorce, I stormed out of the house and called Alex. Even though we weren't on the best of terms, I knew he would be there for me. I needed a friend who would hold me and promise me everything would be okay. Sadly, Alex didn't answer his phone, which made me even more frustrated.

I sat down on my porch steps and cried. I was angry at the world, and especially at God, who I thought was supposed to be the one to comfort me in my time of need. I didn't feel Him anywhere near me or my family. It felt like He had turned his back on us, left us to deal with our family's sins alone. My blood was boiling.

I wanted to run back into the house and hit my father, curse at him for ruining our family. I wanted to call my mother and tell her all the ways in which she had ruined my life. No one understood what I was going through. My mother hadn't even taken the time to talk to me about everything. I thought that was what parents were supposed to do: sit you down and explain that a divorce was imminent. Instead, I had found my father passed out on the floor, with divorce papers all around him. I had found his youngest daughter sitting there, afraid and worried. Who knew how long Ciara had been sitting there?

I pulled out my phone and dialed my mother's cell phone. My call went straight to voice mail, and my anger got the best of me as I left a message. "Hey, Mother. It's your daughter, but I bet you forgot you had one. Seems to me you're more concerned about the daughter that isn't yours. Well, Mom, I'm all alone in this! You just left and didn't tell me. You gave Dad divorce papers, and you didn't tell me that, either. What about me? Huh, Mom?" I paused to wipe my tears and collect myself. "It's cool, like, whatever. I'll just vent some other way, since my *mother* isn't here to get me through this. I hope you get this message."

I hung up, feeling more alone than ever. I just wanted to jump off a bridge and end everything. I'd read about girls who cut themselves due to family issues. I had never understood what could drive a girl to hurt herself, but now I understood. Sometimes, the pain inside got so bad that the only outlet to relieve the pain was to hurt outwardly. I wasn't that damaged, but I couldn't lie and say I hadn't thought about it.

My phone rang, and my spirits lifted. My mom was calling me back! I'd never imagined a day where I'd be happy just to hear her voice. Without looking at the caller ID, I picked my phone up and answered it. "Mom, I knew you'd call me right back."

"Um . . ." Ryan's voice echoed in my ear. "Definitely not your mom."

"Oh, Ryan." I instantly felt stupid for not checking to see who had called before answering.

"You don't sound happy to hear from me," he said. "What's up?"

"It's just . . ." I sighed, shaking my head. I didn't want to cry anymore. I was tired of being disappointed and angry. I needed a distraction. A big one. Something that would definitely take my mind off my parents and their divorce.

"Ryan, can you come pick me up? I want to stay the night with you."

"Oh yeah, definitely," he said too quickly. I could hear the excitement in his voice. "Where are you?"

"In front of my house," I told him. "And hurry up."

I hung up the phone.

Ten minutes later, Ryan's black truck pulled to a stop in front of my house. I jumped up quickly and ran straight to his truck. As soon as I got in, I planted a wet kiss on his lips while holding his face between my hands. He sighed with pleasure when I pulled back and buckled my seat belt.

"You must have really wanted to see me, baby."

"Just go," I said, and he stepped on the gas without hesitation. I watched my house turn into a blur as we sped off. We ended up at his house.

"Here we are again," Ryan said, allowing me to enter his bedroom first. He hit the light switch, illuminating the single bed and the nightstand that completed his room. "I don't have to worry about an angry best friend ruining our night again, do I?"

I flopped down on his bed and looked out at the full moon that shone into his room through his bare window. I knew he lived on his own, but couldn't he afford curtains? "Nope."

"Good," Ryan said, taking a seat next to me. The look he gave me said, "I want to devour you," and it both frightened and excited me. "I don't want anything to ruin tonight." He leaned in, placing a soft kiss on my lips. Everything tingled inside, and I felt my bad mood begin to lift. I knew he wanted me badly, but did I really want this? With him?

It was almost as if he had read my thoughts when he said, "We can go slowly." He kissed me again, then pulled away and cupped my chin in his hand. He followed that by brushing my nose with his nose, which was the cutest thing ever. I instantly melted. "I really like you, and I've been waiting patiently for this."

"How much do you like me?"

"More than a full moon," he said, looking out the window behind me. He smiled, as if he was impressed by his corny comparison to the moon. "I never told you how I became this bad boy everyone makes me out to be. My mom died when I was young, and my father was a drunk who couldn't take care of me, and so I ended up in a foster home. I went from home to home, and a lot of times I got kicked out of those homes. They said I was bad, but I wasn't. I had ADHD and couldn't control how hyper I got. It hurt, though, having families give up on me on a whim. It made me never feel loved.

"So I did what any kid would do in my situation. I stopped caring. I completely shut down. I started getting into trouble, smoking cigarettes, as well as other things. I got into a lot of fights to earn respect. I used girls and earned my womanizer title." He stopped to laugh. "But you made me look at things differently. When I saw you, I saw innocence. I saw the person who I should still be, but life took my innocence, if that makes sense."

"It does," I told him, hanging on to every word he spoke.

"I wanted to get to know you so I could understand why you are the way you are. I wanted to decode you, and now I think I have."

"How so?" I was lost in his words, feeling as if I were on a page of a romance novel, listening as my knight in shining armor confessed his undying love to me.

"Family. You have a strong family. I never did. Well, when I was fifteen, my dad came back into the picture, but he was still a drunk, and so I fought to get emancipated."

"My family is broken," I told him, feeling the pain of my reality making its way back into my heart.

"But it used to be whole, right? That's something I never had. I didn't have a mom to be strict with me or a dad to be my role model. You've complained to me in the past about how you hated your mom, and I used to think, *Dang, if only I had a mom.* You had it made, and you didn't appreciate it. Now it's gone."

"Gee, thanks." I was offended. "So you're saying everything that has happened is my fault? My parents are about to divorce because of me?"

"No," he said, shaking his head. I could tell he saw his error by the horrified look on his face. "I'm just saying, sometimes things happen to make us appreciate what we have. It can all go away in a second. It irritates me when fortunate people can't see their fortune."

I nodded, finally understanding what he meant. Maybe he was right. Maybe I didn't appreciate what I had. Sure, my mother was a pain, but she was my mother. She had always been there, sometimes too much, and I couldn't wait for the day when I got to escape her. And after my father's sin, she had barely looked at me in the past week. I miss it. I truly miss my mother.

"Come here," Ryan said, pulling me closer. "I don't want to make you sad."

I smiled, resting my head on his shoulder. "Alex is wrong about you."

"How so?"

"He thinks you're wrong for me . . . that you're going to hurt me or something." I closed my eyes and inhaled Ryan's scent. "I just think you're misunderstood."

"I don't know. You might want to listen to your friend," Ryan said, pushing me back against his bed. "I'm just a charmer."

"More like Prince Charming," I said and giggled. My giggling quickly ceased as Ryan began to climb over me. The way he looked down at me, as if he wanted to devour me whole, frightened me. I hadn't really thought this through.

There was no Alex to stop us. Ryan had been emancipated and had been on his own for a year, so there were no adults around to break us up. We were completely alone, and I started to feel uncomfortable and afraid. Was this really what I wanted? Did I truly love Ryan enough to lose my virginity to him?

As Ryan began lifting up my shirt, I caught a glimpse of my tattoo. *Rebel.* I ran my hand over the peeling skin. That was what I was now. Rebels didn't question their actions; they did whatever they pleased. A rebel wouldn't worry about losing her virginity, but instead would dive face-first into the unknown, refusing to conform to beliefs about waiting until marriage and celibacy.

I was a rebel now, or was I? Either way, I allowed Ryan to undress me, hoping I wasn't making the biggest mistake of my life.

Chapter Thirty-three

TAMARA

I lay on my side and watched Dominique as he lay in my bed, snoring softly. It was his second day in the house, and it had passed without one outburst of anger. I had purposely made macaroni and cheese and put it on the first rack in the oven, just to see what he'd do. I wanted to make sure he wasn't the same monster. Surprisingly, he had shaken his head, had gently moved me to the side, and had put the baking dish on the second rack.

I had also done a few other things to test him. He had tried to blast Tupac in the house, and I had turned it off. He'd wanted to "make love" at midday, and I'd rejected him. He'd seemed upset, but it was nothing compared to how he used to be. I still didn't buy his act, nor did I want him there. Sure, the ways in which I had tested him were tricky, but I'd rather know now if he would try to kill me, verses finding out while Ciara was around.

He must've felt me staring, because his eyes opened.

"Planning to kill me in my sleep?" he asked, but I could hear the hint of humor in his voice.

"How did you know?" I joked back, but I caught myself, not wanting to give him my smile.

"That's what I'd do if I was you," he said, but this time, all humor was gone. He got out of bed and headed to the bathroom, leaving me to contemplate the meaning of his words. Was he warning me to get rid of him now? If only I knew how.

It was about time I stopped being afraid of him, but how? When I thought about having the courage to tell him to leave, my mind instantly went back to all the beatings I'd endured for things that were less complicated. If I suggested it, who knew what he'd do?

Maybe killing him was a great option.

I shunned the thought when he returned to bed and pulled me against his chest. God knew I was a Christian woman, and killing a person was the devil's play, but sometimes when someone was pushed far enough, things could happen. I prayed for the best.

With the little courage I had, I sat up in bed and turned to Dominique.

"What if I told you that I wasn't interested in getting back with you?" I asked, bracing myself for the worst.

Dominique looked slightly hurt; his dark eyes seemed to darken more as he took in my words. With a sigh, he pulled me closer. "I deserve that from you, so I'd leave peacefully."

I was shocked. "For real?"

"Yeah," he said. "I don't deserve you."

I couldn't believe the words coming out of his mouth. The Dominique I knew would never say those things to me. Either he had changed or he was putting up a good front.

I'd heard about men who pretended to be one thing but turned out to be something totally different. Once they were confident they had the woman right where they wanted her, they changed up. I couldn't allow myself to believe him. I was still on edge. So I decided to press the matter farther.

"Dominique, I think you should leave."

He sat up on his elbow to see me fully. "What?"

"You can't just show up somewhere and think things will go back to how they were," I explained.

"But we ain't going back there. We're moving forward. Baby, I changed."

"That doesn't erase everything you did to me!" I screamed, and instantly I regretted it. I was prepared for him to hit me, but he didn't. He only lay there, confused and hurt. I saw no traces of anger on his face as I searched it. "When you touch me, I think about every time you hit me. When you move, even the slightest, I jump." I sighed. "I'm a Christian woman now. I'm not supposed to have a man lying in my bed or shacking up. That's not my lifestyle anymore."

He instantly pulled the covers back, which scared me, but he got out of bed and took a few steps back. "You're a Christian, and so am I, so I get that and respect it. I'll sleep on the floor."

"We're still shacking up!"

He groaned. "Fine. I'll leave, if you want that." He turned to head out of the room, stopping to grab his clothes that sat on the chair near the bed. Before leaving, he turned around, facing me. "We were nineteen, Tamara. That was nearly seven years ago. I was still trying to be a young thug in the streets. I ain't have no daddy to tell me how to raise my family! I learned from my mama's boyfriends, who always hit on her to keep her under control. When I went to prison for something I didn't do, I figured that was God punishing me for the things I did do. I believe in God too, Tamara, and I believe in second chances. I believe in forgiveness."

His words began to touch my heart, and before I knew it, I began crying. I cried because I wanted to believe he had changed and he wanted nothing more, but I still wouldn't allow him to get close.

"Dom—"

"Maybe I shouldn't have run up in here like I did. I should've respected your space. I ain't perfect, but I'm working on it. I'll show you, though. I'll get myself all the way together, just to show you I've changed. Let God be my witness." And with that said, he left.

I stared at the door for a few minutes, processing everything he'd said. There was a time when I used to plot to hurt him. I would think about having him jumped by my cousins. Once, I saw him walking down the street a few weeks after the incident, and I had the biggest urge to run him over with my car. I felt guilty for having these thoughts, being a Christian woman, and yet I couldn't help but replay all the ways I'd avenge myself over and over again. I finally had a chance to get back at him, and yet my anger had vanished. Instead, I felt myself snapping.

I didn't know how I was even living at that point, having lost my best friend and spiritual sister. I was having a difficult time adjusting to Ciara's new lifestyle, while also dealing with the abusive boyfriend from the past. The only thing I knew how to do when times were hard was to fall to my knees and pray.

That was exactly what I did.

Chapter Thirty-four

CLAIRE

When I walked into the house, I was thankful that Mark had left early with his daughter. He had probably taken her to school. And now he was probably dealing with his downfall. I could only imagine the number of calls he'd received from clients who were firing him for what he did to me. He didn't deserve to have anything, anyway. I searched through the morning newspaper for any stories of the event but found none. Mark must've figured out a way to keep his sins from being printed. Lucky for him.

I had expected to feel more relieved once I gave him the divorce papers, which, I noticed, were sitting on the living room end table, unsigned. But I only felt worse. This woman, who had gone out of her way to make her husband fall on his face after he hurt her, this woman, who had neglected her own daughter due to the stress of the divorce, was not a godly woman, or at least she wasn't acting how one should act. I was that woman. I didn't know who I was anymore.

I had played Sarah's voice message over and over again in my head, hating myself for being neglectful. I hadn't told her about the divorce; I hadn't sat down with her and explained why things were happening. I had thought she hated me, blamed me somehow, and I just couldn't face her. I had thought that by giving her space, I was helping.

That was the only reason I'd come home this morning. If I had it my way, I would've stayed longer at the hotel. I'd sent Sarah a text, letting her know I'd be the one to drop her off at school, not her father. I could hear her rustling around in her room, most likely throwing clothes around in a fit in order to find something stylish enough for school. It seemed as though she hadn't started caring about her appearance until a few months ago. I wondered if it was because of a boy. However, I didn't worry. Sarah was a good girl. She was often disrespectful when it came to me, but she wasn't a wild girl, like other teenagers I knew. She cared more about her books than boys. She loved and served God even better than I did at times. I couldn't have asked for a better daughter.

I understood how things were at sixteen. You hated your mother and tried to be anything but like her. You tended to get the blunt end of peer pressure. You experimented and learned through errors. Self-image was everything, and so that meant low self-esteem, having to always compare yourself to the other girls around you. Sixteen was a hard age, especially if you were dealing with your parents' divorce on top of all of that.

I understood Sarah's anger toward me. At times, when I wasn't busy hating my husband, I hated myself for the same reasons. I was hoping this time with her would be a good time to clear the air. I hadn't even thought about how to approach her. What did I say to a daughter who would only hate me more, no matter what I said? I guessed the truth was enough.

Five minutes later, Sarah jogged down the stairs. She didn't even bother greeting me. She walked right past me to the side of the couch to grab her book bag. She then turned and headed out the door. I sighed, stood up, and followed her out.

Sarah sat in the passenger seat, with her arms folded defensively, staring straight ahead. Everything about her posture told me she wasn't up for conversation. I sat next to her, put my seat belt on, and started the car. I put the car in reverse and began backing out of the driveway.

"Dad could've taken me to school, you know," she said the moment we drove away from the house.

"I know," I said, clutching the steering wheel for support. "I got your message last night."

"Figures."

"Sarah, I don't mean to be neglectful," I began.

"But you are!" Sarah yelled and then quickly began taking deep breaths to calm herself. I wanted to do nothing more than to pull her into a hug. However, I knew that was out of the question.

"I'm sorry," I stated quietly, not knowing how else to respond. She was right, after all.

"For what, Mom?" she asked, turning toward me, opening up slightly. I knew that if I met her eyes, I'd see the challenge there, and so I kept my head forward as I focused on the road.

"For neglecting you during all of this," I said.

"You disgust me," she spat, turning back in her seat. "You ruined Dad's life! You're the one behind everyone knowing what he did! He told me this morning that he lost a lot of clients and had to step down as the preacher. You're breaking him too!"

"What about me?" I shouted, matching her tone. "How would you feel if one of those little boys at school cheated on you after you gave them everything? Am I supposed to pretend that I'm not hurting just as much as everyone else? You always blame me for everything, Sarah, but this one was your father's fault. He brought all of this on us, so stop blaming me! I'm not sorry!" I shouted.

Sarah didn't say anything for a while and simply turned to stare out the window. I was glad for the moment of silence. It was enough for me to correct my approach.

"Sarah, more than anything, I'm sorry you're hurting. I wish I could take it away."

"Then don't divorce Dad!" she cried. "Work it out, please! For me!"

"It's not that simple—" I began, but Sarah cut me off.

"It's very simple! Aren't you the one who taught me about a forgiving God? I remember when I was younger and got into trouble for something, and you said you forgave me because God forgave you. It took me a few years to understand what you meant, but it always stuck with me. If God can forgive Dad, why can't you?"

"Because," I began, but I was defeated. Sarah was right. I could forgive if I wanted to, and I just wasn't ready to. I wanted to be angry; it was better than feeling hopeless and lost.

"Oh, wait. I know why. It's not Dad's mistake you can't accept. It's his daughter, and you know it! If she was a little white girl, you would've swept it under the rug and forgiven Dad. You racist."

"Sarah, don't you start with me," I said, feeling my anger rise. I knew it was because she was right, but I didn't want to hear it. I pulled up to the school and put the car in park, then turned toward my daughter as she spoke.

"You're a racist! How can a godly woman be a freaking racist?" Sarah began shouting over the soft music that played in the car. Her words rung in my ears, causing a headache. "You can't call yourself a Christian and discriminate against others, especially innocent people. Jesus rejected no one. That's nothing but the devil!"

I wasn't thinking when I smacked Sarah across her face. As soon as I'd done it, I instantly regretted it. The look of hurt and confusion that stretched across her innocent face broke my heart. I was just so angry.

Sarah slowly met my eyes, holding on to her red cheek as tears ran down her face. "I hate you," she said and then turned to open the door.

"Sarah, wait," I called out to her, but she was already gone. I watched my daughter walk up to the school building and eventually drown in the sea of students. I pulled off, knowing I'd hate myself forever.

Sarah was right. What kind of Christian woman hated the innocent?

I didn't deserve to be a godly woman.

I didn't deserve any of God's forgiveness.

Neither did Mark.

Chapter Thirty-five

SARAH

I stormed into the school, needing to find anything to distract me from that car ride. I couldn't believe my mother had slapped me, as if I was wrong. My cheek still stung, and I held it, afraid that it would be red and swollen. I ran straight into the bathroom and went to the mirror. Thank God it was only slightly red, as if I had been blushing. I smacked my other cheek a few times to bring color to it so that it would match. When that didn't work, I dabbed some foundation on my cheek and left the bathroom.

As soon as I rounded the corner, I ran into Alex. His nose was still slightly swollen from when Ryan had punched him. I instantly felt bad. All my previous anger toward Alex had vanished, and I missed him. He was the one person I could go to who would comfort me through this. In fact, he'd tried to, but I had pushed him away, like I did everyone who was close to me. Well, everyone except Ryan.

Last night, I'd opened up to Ryan in ways I'd never opened up to anyone. My body hurt in weird places, but I felt alive! I was in love with the perfect guy. Everyone thought I was stupid for dating him, but he had opened up to me yesterday and had shown me that underneath it all, he was good. Even though my home situation was bad, it was nice knowing something was going right in my life. I felt elated, and as I basked in the thought of Ryan, the sting from the smack earlier was washed away.

"Hi, Alex," I said with a big smile.

"You're smiling. What changed?" he asked.

"I'm just a girl in love, is all," I explained as I began walking down the hallway, knowing Alex was close behind. I noticed a bunch of students staring and laughing, but I didn't care. I wouldn't let my family's drama ruin this newfound happiness.

"Let me guess. Your boyfriend finally told you that he loves you?"

"Better," I said, not wanting to give away the secret. I didn't kiss and tell. As I continued walking, I started hearing people shout at me, call me sexual names. I began to slow down, wondering what they all meant. One girl, a cute blonde with a seemingly bubbly personality, was brave enough to walk up to me and Alex.

"Tell me, is bagging Ryan as good as everyone says?" she asked with a bright smile. I couldn't tell if her smile was genuine or not. What caught my attention more though, was what she'd said about Ryan and me.

I stopped walking. "Excuse me?"

"Half of the school says he is the best," the girl continued, flicking her long blond hair. A few of her friends stood behind her, giggling. I realized that she might have been bubbly, but she was far from warm. "But my guess is that Little Miss Perfect would know best since you were the last to have him."

"I don't understand. . . ."

"What's to get?" She laughed. "Half the school already knows what you did last night. You can blame your blabbermouth boyfriend for that."

I stormed past her, completely embarrassed by her accusations. I couldn't wrap my head around what she was saying, or maybe I didn't want to. All I knew was that I needed to find Ryan.

"You slept with Ryan?" Alex asked, keeping up with my pace, even though the flooded hallways made it nearly impossible.

Down the hall, I saw Ryan chatting with a few boys, laughing at some joke. I ignored Alex and pushed my way through the last of the students. I grabbed Ryan's shoulder, turning him toward me. When he saw me, all the amusement on his facewashed away.

"Half of the school knows, Ryan?" I asked, but I didn't wait for him to respond. "You promised you wouldn't say anything! You said last night was special!"

"Ah, well, yes, anytime you take a girl's virginity, it's special." All the humor came back in his voice as he spoke.

"You told half the school!"

"Wouldn't you if you nailed the Jesus freak?" He laughed, earning him a few pats on the back from his friends. "You won me over two hundred bucks."

"There was a bet?" I was near tears.

"Yeah," he said matter-of-factly. I hated how he looked at me as if I meant nothing. As if I was some joke. "See, I was bragging to Joseph here," he said, pointing to his friend behind him. "I told him I could sleep with any girl in this school. He didn't believe me. I told him to pick the least likely girl and I'd sleep with her within three months. See, everyone betted against me. Said they went to church with you, knew your mother and father, and said that you wouldn't crack. I almost believed it too. You were a tough one. I was just about to give up, but then your daddy's scandal got out, and you clung to me like never before. I saw the perfect opportunity."

"But all those things you said to me last night . . ." I let the tears roll down my face without any shame.

"I'm good with words." He laughed and then turned to his friend. "I had her eating out of the palm of my hand."

Watching Ryan and his friends laugh at me, humiliating me in front of the entire student body, set off rage inside of me. In that moment, I knew what it felt like to want someone to pay for hurting me. I wanted him to suffer.

Before I knew what I was doing, I punched Ryan as hard as I could. The sound echoed throughout the hallway. He was surprised as he stumbled back, lifting a hand to his bloody lip. I went to hit him again, but a hand grabbed me. Alex quickly pushed me behind him and lunged at Ryan, shoving him into the lockers. They both fell on the floor as the growing crowd cheered them on. Alex managed to get on top of Ryan and punched him whenever there was an opening. The old me would've been begging Alex to stop, but I was enjoying every second of this and found myself cheering him on.

I wanted the whole school to see Ryan get beat up over me. I wanted him to feel as stupid as I had felt when that girl came up to me and told me she knew about last night.

In that moment, I understood my mother and her pain. She was simply a woman responding to the hurt and embarrassment of her husband's infidelity. Was she wrong? Was I wrong? Could I truly blame her, now that I understood what wanting revenge felt like? I wasn't so sure of that just yet. I was still enjoying watching Alex beat the crap out of Ryan.

All too soon, a few teachers parted the crowd and made everyone back away as they pulled Alex away from Ryan. Then they escorted all of us to the principal's office.

A half an hour later, my father walked into the front office of the school, looking solemn. He marched right up to the front desk and spoke quietly with the secretary. Alex had already had a meeting with the principal and had been sent home with his mother, having gotten suspended for three days. Ryan had managed to get off the hook, claiming he was the innocent victim who got attacked.

I was still awaiting my fate, which was about to come. The principal came out of the office, greeted my father, and beckoned us both into his office.

I quietly took a seat, trying to be as small as possible in my chair. My father, however, sat tall, but he didn't look in my direction, letting me know the extent of my crime. He avoided direct eye contact only when I was in serious trouble. He had once told me it was because he needed to focus on keeping his cool. I was practically shaking, hoping by some miracle that my father didn't find out what had caused the fight.

After Principal Harris closed the door to his office, he took a seat behind his desk, looking at both my father and me expectantly. "Nice to see you, Pastor Douglas, or Mr. Douglas," he said, correcting himself. Seemed as though even my principal knew my father had got fired. I hated the outer suburbs of Chicago. "It's unusual to see Sarah in here due to bad behavior."

"Exactly what happened?" Dad shot me an accusing look. I was surprised he even looked at me.

"She punched a student, which led to another fight breaking out," Principal Harris said. "I'd have given Sarah a stern warning and sent her back to class, but this isn't the first thing that has happened that has caused me to question whether something is going on with her."

"Please explain," Dad said, sitting up in his seat, as if he was hanging on my principal's every word. I couldn't sit through this another minute. Principal Harris began looking through a stack of papers on his desk and then handed it to my father.

"This is a compilation of Sarah's homework, class performance, and test grades over the past two weeks. See how they begin to drop? She went from being an A plus student to a C minus student in every class." Principal Harris sat back in his seat and joined his hands together in his lap. "This raises a bit of suspicion. When we see these things happening, it's usually due to stress at home. And now she's getting into altercations even before school starts. We have to then ask, what's going on at home? However, we already know."

I snapped my head in my dad's direction just as he began to lose color in his face.

"Mr. Douglas, I would like to suggest school counseling with you, your wife, and Sarah. Sometimes divorces and things such as infidelity affect children more than us adults. We have an excellent counselor who can help Sarah get the support she needs and—"

"Are you saying we don't support her?"

"Not at all, Mr. Douglas—"

"It's Pastor Douglas," Dad said, still holding on to his title, although I was sure Principal Harris already knew about my father's title, given that he'd corrected himself earlier.

"Pastor Douglas," Principal Harris said, shifting in his seat, "I am not saying that you, as a parent, are incapable of helping her through this. But sometimes a teenager needs an outsider's help to see things clearly."

I blocked out the rest of the conversation as I thought about Ryan. My heart hurt worse now than it did when I found out what my father had done to my mother. Ryan had told me he loved me. He had told me that one of the things he admired most about me was my innocence, and then he'd taken it from me.

Every kiss, every smile, every praise had been a lie. He had never cared, had never loved me, not even a smidgen.

It was all for a stupid bet. I wished I could erase every moment with him. I'd take back every kiss. I'd remove this tattoo, which I'd gotten with him.

I suddenly felt claustrophobic. I tried to suck in huge amounts of air, but it didn't help. I wasn't in control of anything in my life. No matter what I tried to do to fix things, they always seemed to get worse.

In that moment, I no longer wanted to be alive. I no longer wanted to feel pain.

Everyone around me had failed me in some way.

And my only question was, *Jesus, is this too much for you to fix?*

The real question, was why would He even want to put His hands on a family that was so damaged?

Chapter Thirty-six

MARK

Sarah and I drove half the way home in silence. I had to wrap my head around the fact that she'd just gotten suspended for three days for initiating a fight. Not to mention her poor grades. I was disappointed in her, but I wasn't angry. How could I be? It was because of me that she had begun to act out.

Before the affair, before the divorce and everything else that had happened since then, Sarah had been a great student. When I looked over at her as she sat in the passenger seat, intently staring out the window, I barely saw my daughter.

Did she still pray the way she used to? Did she still hold on to her faith? Did she still sleep with her Bible next to her, as she always had? I didn't know the extent to which she was suffering, but it was clear she was. I only hoped that she kept as close to God as she had before. Judging by her latest actions—first, being caught with a boy and then getting into trouble at school—I wasn't too sure, but I knew I needed to fix it. I didn't want to ruin my daughter any more than I had.

"I'm sorry," I told Sarah. From the corner of my eye, I noticed her head turn toward me in surprise. "Almost seven years ago, I headed over to the beach by myself. I was supposed to be at the office, working on cases. Around that time I was more stressed. I had a child and

a wife I needed to provide for, and I was just starting off
as a lawyer, so I wasn't getting paid a lot. On top of that,
I was spending more than I was making on adding to the
church. I wasn't in the highest place with God, either. It
was as if I was just going through the motions.

"I was walking on the beach, and this woman caught
my eye. It was Ciara's mother, Candace. We laughed
and had fun on the beach, and the night ended with me
committing a sin. I don't even know why I did it. I didn't
even know Candace, and I definitely didn't love her. I
guess it was a moment of weakness and poor judgment.
I was weaker in spirit, and thus the enemy was able to
attack successfully."

"Dad," Sarah began, exasperated, but I pushed on.

"No, you need to know this. You need to understand
the consequences of bad actions. That one mistake may
cost me my family . . . you." I broke down as tears began
to flood my face. "Regret is one of the worst types of
pain. You spend the rest of your life hating yourself for
something you did. Regret slowly eats at the spirit, until
you look up and don't even know who you are anymore.

"I was a preacher, an amazing father, and a providing
husband. I was a darn good lawyer and represented
clients only for justice! Now? I'm not a preacher. I'm not
an amazing father, because I don't know how to connect
with my youngest and my oldest. You can't even stand
being in the same car with me. Most of my clients fired
me, meaning I have no wages to pay for our home or to
provide the way a husband is supposed to provide.

"So you see what the result of one sin can be? Do you
see everything I'm losing because of that mistake? I see
you are starting to make mistakes of your own, which
is okay, as it's how you learn, but you don't want to do

anything that'll cost you your future. You're no longer in the running for valedictorian, and your grades have dropped. Say good-bye to law school. What you do now can profoundly affect your future. Learn from me." I pointed at my chest with passion.

I went on. "I know I am responsible for how you are feeling, and I'm trying to right my wrongs. I'm trying to fix our family, but you won't let me in. Sarah, I'm your father, no matter what I did. I love you, and that hasn't changed. Can you find it in your heart to forgive me?"

"Dad," Sarah said, but I continued.

"When you choose to hold on to things, it wears you down. We have to move on as a family, or we will stay stuck in the past. I don't want that for you! Sarah, I'm asking for you to find it in your heart to forgive me. Not for me, but for you. We can get through this, but only as a family."

"But Mom wants to divorce you," Sarah said wearily.

"We'll make her stay."

"We?" Sarah asked, looking confused.

"You, me, and Ciara," I told her.

"Mom hates Ciara."

"That can change," I told Sarah. "With Jesus, anything is possible. Are you willing to move forward with me and begin healing our family?" Sarah looked away, her mouth opening and closing, as if she was hesitant about speaking. I could see the tears in Sarah's eyes as she slowly turned back to me and nodded her head.

"I'm still mad at you, though, Daddy!" she confessed. "I'm so angry."

"I know, baby, and it's okay to be mad. I'm angry at myself too. But at least we will be angry together, as a family." I reached my hand out, hoping Sarah would take it. Slowly but surely, she linked her hand with mine.

"Together," Sarah said, but she sounded as if she was unsure of what she said.

"Now, let's go be a family," I said, feeling victorious for the first time since I'd learned about Ciara, and I had a reason to feel that way.

I finally had my daughter back.

Two hour later, Sarah, Ciara, and I stood at the entrance to an amusement park located an hour from where we lived. It was barely even noon. We'd decided to pull Ciara out of class and have a fun day bonding as a family. It had been Sarah's idea to go to the amusement park, and I'd agreed, just happy to see a smile on her face.

"I wanna get on that ride and that one and that over there. See it, Daddy?" Ciara asked, jumping up and down as she held my hand. I laughed, because she'd pointed to all the big roller coasters, which she was too little for.

"We'll start off small," I told her as we walked to the line to buy tickets.

I took a deep breath, mesmerized by the smell of cotton candy, funnel cakes, elephant ears, and fresh lemonade. If I closed my eyes, I bet I could see myself again as a child, happy and running through a carnival as if my life depended on it. Ciara looked as if she was ready to do the same.

Once we were inside the amusement park, Ciara wanted to ride the Ferris wheel. After that, she took off, wanting to ride everything that she could get on. Sarah was content with staying by my side, watching as Ciara enjoyed everything.

"Go on. Get on something, and we'll meet up," I told Sarah, wanting her to enjoy herself, but she shook her head.

"This is better," she said, watching Ciara ride the merry-go-round. "Just look at her. She's so happy."

"Yeah," I agreed, waving at Ciara as she circled back around on her pony. She waved back, with a bright smile.

"I can't believe I have a sister," Sarah said, marveling. "She's so beautiful too." She paused, looking as if she was in deep thought. "I was afraid for her at first, Dad. She had it worse than all of us. She lost her mom and then had to go to a new home with a new family who argued over her in her face. And now look at her up there, smiling as if nothing happened. It gives me hope, you know. Like, if she can recover, so can I." Sarah turned toward me. "So can *we*."

The merry-go-round stopped, and seconds later Ciara came running toward us.

"Was it fun?" I asked, grabbing ahold of her hand and heading off to the next attraction, which happened to be a photo booth.

"Yes!" she said, noticing the photo booth as well. "Oh, a picture!"

"Let's go take one, the three of us," Sarah said, and we walked up to the booth and waited in the small line. An elderly woman standing in front of us turned around and smiled. Her eyes traveled down to Ciara, who seemed to catch her interest.

"Such a pretty girl," the woman said and then looked at Sarah. "And such a beautiful young lady."

"I'm a lucky father," I replied, which caused the woman's mouth to form an O.

"You've adopted?" she asked, seemingly thrilled by the idea.

"No." I shook my head. "They are both my biological daughters."

"Ah," she said, understanding. "Well, you have a lovely family. Don't let anyone tell you otherwise."

"Thank you," I said, appreciating the word of advice. My wife was afraid that people would shun us due to our diversity, and maybe in a way she was right, but in that moment, she wasn't. Our family was beautiful, indeed.

We got our picture taken, the three of us, and as I looked down at the picture, I felt a pang of sadness, wishing Claire had been present for it. I said a silent prayer, asking God to allow us to have many more family pictures, ones that included Claire, and wishing that she'd be just as happy as we were in this little picture taken at the amusement park. After my prayer, I had a feeling that a blessing was soon to come.

Chapter Thirty-seven

CLAIRE

I returned again to the house that I had once called my home. It was amazing how everything in my house could be in order and yet feel so out of place. The maid had still been showing up early mornings, cleaning. The lawn was nice and kept, thanks to the workers we paid, although their jobs would be at stake unless Mark found another firm or church. From the outside, people would think this was a happy home, but they had no idea just how upturned everything was on the inside.

I was surprised when I walked into the house and heard my daughter's laughter. This joyous sound came from the kitchen, and it was followed by Mark's barking laughter. I was slightly confused, knowing how much my daughter hated both Mark and me, and yet they were laughing. I quietly walked toward the kitchen, eavesdropping on their conversation.

"It would be fun if Ciara was here, making pizza with us," Sarah said.

"She's spending some time with Tamara for now, but we can look at this moment as a father-daughter one. Just the two of us." I heard Mark pause. "Why are you looking at me like I'm crazy? I'm just putting the cheese on the pizza."

"No, Dad. You put the sauce on the pizza first." Sarah laughed.

"What if I like my pizza with cheese first? Never heard of an upside-down pizza?" Sarah laughed in response, and Mark continued. "It's when you make the pizza backward."

"Even then, you forgot the pepperoni! The pepperoni comes last, so in this case it would go first."

Mark was silent for a moment. "Good point!"

I heard Sarah laugh as they continued to make their pizza. A minute passed before Sarah spoke again.

"Dad, how bad is it? You know, with losing your job?"

I heard Mark sigh. "Not too bad, yet. I was smart enough to save for a few rainy days. The worst would be us having to move."

"That might be a good thing." I could hear the sadness in Sarah's voice.

"Why is that, honey?"

"It's just . . ." Sarah sighed. "School . . . and boys . . . normal teenage girl stuff."

"I bet you wish you had your mom to talk to," Mark said. His suggestion made my heart ache for my daughter. I wanted to be there and show her that I would always support her, no matter what. I was about to walk into the kitchen when Sarah responded.

"No," she said. "She's the last person I could go to about this. You see, I'm not even telling you."

"Is it that bad?" Mark sounded afraid, which was different than how I felt at that moment. I felt rejected, as if my daughter didn't believe in me enough to trust me with her problems, and yet she was making pizza with the man who had hurt our family the most. What was I missing?

"No, Dad. It's normal stuff, girl stuff, though," Sarah sighed. "I had a boyfriend who turned out to be a really big jerk."

"Sarah Ann Douglas, who told you that you could date?" Mark joked, but I could hear the truth behind his words. What father wanted his sixteen-year-old daughter dating? "Was it that guy Alex warned me about?"

"He happens to also be the same guy Alex beat up and I punched today."

"That's my girl," Mark told her, and I couldn't believe he had cheered her on for punching a kid, one who was her boyfriend.

"Dad, you're supposed to be a godly man. You can't cheer your daughter on for punching a guy," Sarah teased.

"I could say the same to you for punching that kid," Mark retorted. "Truth is, no one is perfect. Some of us claim to be close to perfect, and even try to be, but we aren't. Even preachers make big mistakes. The key is to find forgiveness in Jesus Christ. I don't know how many nights I have lain awake, asking over and over again for God to forgive me.

"When I found out about Ciara, I thought that I was being shunned by God. I thought He was finally punishing me for that one thoughtless night with Ciara's mom. I could barely even look at your sister, because all I saw were my mistakes. Somehow, through those sleepless nights, God put it in my heart to accept the things I couldn't change and to change the things I could. I made it my goal to welcome my daughter in my family and to rebuild my relationship with you and with my wife."

"But Mom wants a divorce," Sarah said, causing a few tears to escape my eyes.

I pressed my hand against the wall, thankful that they couldn't see me. I was going to break down.

Sarah continued. "She's one of those types of people you mentioned, you know, the kind of Christians who think they are perfect, when they aren't. She gossips with her church friends, puts more value in money than her Bible, and she's racist. I could go on!"

"Sarah," Mark said. "Why do you dislike your mother?"

"Because she's flawed! She's flawed, and all she wants to do is point out other people's faults! I was never good enough in her eyes. 'Sarah, you can play soccer better than that!' 'Sarah, this A needs to be an A plus. Looks like no Harvard for you!' 'Sarah, sit up straighter. Remember grace is everything. We don't want these people thinking you're from the ghetto.' You didn't do that, Dad. You showed me how to behave by encouraging me to follow your footsteps and by how graceful you acted. You didn't make me feel like I was less than who I was. I always looked up to you, not her." Sarah paused.

"And then, when I learned that you had had an affair, I went downhill right with you," she added. "Now that you're getting better, I see myself getting better too. We work on the same wavelength, Dad. Mom?" Sarah sighed. "Maybe you should get a divorce."

"Don't you say that," Mark replied, and I could hear his love for me in his voice. "I am going to do everything in my power to make sure that your mom and I don't divorce, I promise. When you love someone, you never stop fighting for them. Remember that, okay?"

"Sure thing, Dad."

"Now, let's get this pizza in the oven."

I quietly excused myself from the house. Having heard everything that Mark and Sarah had said, I couldn't bring myself to face them. I got in my car, and I drove for miles, gathering my thoughts, praying, crying, asking for forgiveness, and generally picturing the life I was willing to leave behind.

I had a choice to make. That was either stay with my husband and accept his child, or leave and say good-bye to my daughter as well. It wouldn't be an easy choice, but I knew what I was going to do.

Chapter Thirty-eight

TAMARA

I was excited when Mark dropped Ciara off, and by her sweet, warm greeting, I knew she'd missed me. Ciara wasted no time telling me all about her new school and friends. She spent extra time telling me about her new room, which had princesses and castles painted on the walls, and all the dreams she had of being a princess one day. She ended her report by telling me all about her day at the amusement park with her dad and sister.

Afterward, I sat her down at the kitchen table as I cooked dinner. She pulled her crayons and paper out of her bag and began drawing a picture and humming. After a few minutes, Ciara began to speak.

"What do you think Mommy is doing in heaven, Auntie Tamara?"

Her question shocked me, but I didn't let her see it. With a lighthearted voice, I said, "Mommy is probably looking down and watching you with a smile. And she probably likes your picture too."

"I know she does. I'm making it for her."

I stopped cooking and walked over to where Ciara sat drawing, and was amazed as I stared down at the picture.

"This is me," she said, pointing to the little brown girl in the picture. "And this is my sister, Sarah." She pointed to Sarah, whom she had colored in with a pink crayon. "And this is my daddy and his wife, and that's you!" All the figures in the picture stood in front of a big house and a tree that resembled a weeping willow, with raindrops under it. I found it a bit odd, since there were no raindrops anywhere else besides under the tree.

"Why is it raining only under the tree?" I asked.

"It's not rain. It's tears. The tree is crying. Daddy called it a weeping willow tree and said it weeps like God weeps when we sin," Ciara said matter-of-factly. "That tree must always be crying. I should water it."

"Why hearts?" I asked her, watching as her small hand began drawing little red balloon hearts all over the tree.

"It's balloon hearts, and they are filled with love. When the heart grows, it bursts open and waters the tree with love," Ciara said.

I was completely taken aback by how powerful her words were and how deep her imagination ran. The fact that she knew that love was the answer, and that showering a weeping tree with love would cure it, melted my heart and touched me to the bone. The Lord did say that love was the greatest gift we had. It was love that kept fallen marriages together, love that put a child in a good home, and it was going to be that same love that would heal Ciara's family. I was almost near tears, until I felt a presence behind me and turned around.

Dominique stood in the entryway to the kitchen, with one hand hidden behind his back. I blinked a few times, not really sure what to do. The last time we'd spoken, he'd left with the understanding that we wouldn't be together. I looked over at Ciara, who was still coloring quietly. I hoped she wouldn't eavesdrop on our conversation as I headed over to where Dominique stood.

"What are you doing here?" I asked, trying to keep my voice low.

Dominique pulled a bouquet of flowers from behind his back and held them out for me to grab. I didn't. I could see the hurt in his eyes when I rejected him. "I wanted to show you that I changed."

I peeked around him and saw that the front door was open. "By breaking into my house again? Normal people don't do that."

Dominique sighed and rubbed his face, and I could make out the veins in his neck, which was a sure sign that his anger was peaking. "I can't get nothing right!"

"Shut up. You're talking too loud," I said, looking back at Ciara, who still colored and hummed, unaffected by his outburst. "I'm busy, Dominique. You should leave, and we'll talk about it later."

"Tell me what I gotta do to get you back, baby," he begged, clutching the flowers as if the bouquet was his life support.

"You can leave, and we'll talk about this later."

"No," he responded with urgency. He took a step toward me aggressively, and then, as if realizing what he'd done, he stepped back. I saw it then, that thing I was trying to find. It was still there, deep inside of him. It was a monster, and it was just waiting for the right moment to show itself. I was truly afraid, and I hoped I could find a way to calm him down enough to make him leave. I decided to take the flowers, but he pulled them away from me. My plan was to tell him anything to calm him down.

"You can stay," I said. He seemed to relax, judging by how his shoulders fell, but I could tell he was still on edge. Maybe he wouldn't put his hands on me, but I didn't want to take that chance. I reached for the flowers again, and this time, he gave them to me. I felt slightly victorious, as if I'd successfully tamed a lion.

"Auntie Tamara, can I have some cookies?" Ciara asked from the table, and I instantly stiffened.

"Auntie?" Dominique asked. I'd hoped he hadn't noticed. *Too late.* "I thought she was your daughter."

"My mommy died," Ciara said, still facing the same direction in her seat but obviously listening to us.

"Ciara, go upstairs," I said, trying to avoid meeting Dominique's eyes.

"But I want a cookie," she argued.

"You'll get one later. Go upstairs!" I hated yelling at her, but I had no choice. I was caught in a lie, and who knew how Dominique would respond? Ciara pushed the chair back, stood up, and stomped out of the room. The moment I heard her door shut upstairs, Dominique spoke again.

"I thought you said she was your daughter?"

"Not biologically. Her mom died. I'm her guardian," I said, still not meeting his eyes. I knew that if I did, I'd cower at what I found there.

"No, you intentionally lied to me," he said in a menacing way, which made me back up. "That wasn't your husband, either. So you lied to me to keep me away, huh?" He laughed. "I can't be mad, though, not when I've been lying too."

"What do you mean?" I asked, watching as he advanced. I backed into the sink, a common mistake I had made in the past with him, but I was stronger now. I had the strongest thing a person could have. Jesus.

"I ain't changed," he said, pushing me against the sink. "I just wanted you to think I had so you'd take me back. I know you ain't want me here. You was plotting to get me out from the beginning. I ain't stupid. I felt you watching me in my sleep, like you wanted to kill me. Did you want to kill me?"

"I ain't have to do nothing to you," I said bravely. "God will handle that all on His own."

"Oh yeah." He laughed. "You're a Christian now. Tell me, where is your God now?" Dominique pushed me again, this time hard enough to make my head jerk back. I gripped the counter for support.

"He's always watching," I said, taking a quick glance behind me at the knife in the sink. I wouldn't be afraid to use it if I had to. God didn't always work in direct ways, but He'd always provide a way out. I wasn't comfortable with the idea, so I kept talking to buy myself some time.

"It's funny how you thought I'd let you back in, even after everything you did," I said, moving my hand closer and closer to the knife in the sink. I wrapped my hand around the handle of the knife and held on to it tightly. "I was too afraid to tell you no, but I let you stay until I found another solution. You ain't nothing, Dominique. And that's probably why you chose to hit on women, because you ain't nothing but the devil's pawn. I was stupid to let you hit me, but knowing my worth, I'd never let you do it again."

Dominique flew into a rage and reached out to choke me. I struggled against him, losing my grip on the knife as he pushed me even farther against the counter. My hands instinctively clawed at him as he choked me, stealing my air. I could barely think as my throat and chest burned from oxygen deprivation.

"I'll kill you," he said, shaking me as he choked me. His own sweat dripped onto my forehead as I stared into his eyes in a panic. I started to see darkness around the edges of my vision, and I tried to pry his hands from me, but he was too strong. "And then I'll kill your so-called daughter."

That did it. The fear his words engendered in me made something inside me snap. I'd lost myself to him, but I wasn't going to lose a child to a man's temper. I stopped fighting him and lowered my hand behind me in the sink, reaching for the knife.

I couldn't find it. I kept patting the bottom of the sink, moving my hand all over it, but the knife was gone. I had just had it in my hand, so it had to be there! My energy was slipping, and I knew this was it. My life was going to end, which also meant Ciara's would. *Jesus*, I silently prayed. *Give me the strength.*

I was so numb that I could barely feel my hand as I continued patting the sink. I willed myself to keep searching as pain seared my lungs. I finally found the tip of the knife sticking out of the drain in the sink. I quickly picked it up and was grateful I still was able to grip it. The knife almost slipped out of my hand, but I managed to tighten my grip in time. With the last of my strength, I drove the knife toward Dominique's neck. Everything around me went black.

The last thing I thought about was Ciara.

Chapter Thirty-nine

SARAH

I was surprised that my dad took my suspension from school lightheartedly. I was pretty sure that my mom would blow a gasket. The last time I had spoken with her, we'd argued and it hadn't ended well, so I definitely wasn't up to explaining how I had put my hands on a boy, and I didn't want to explain why.

My dad was right in saying I needed to build a better relationship with her and forgive her for her ways. I guessed if I could forgive him, I could patch things up with my mom, but not until she destroyed those divorce papers.

After my dad and I ate pizza, we decided to watch an action-packed movie, so we turned on the fireplace and got cozy on the couch. I wanted to watch a romance, but Dad was adamant about seeing something that was more entertaining. After a five-minute battle, he won. I was just happy to have some normalcy in my life.

I wished Ciara was there with us, making backward pizza and watching movies. I knew she'd like it, but it was a good thing that she still had her other home to go to. In a way, I wished Mom was here, sitting on the other side of Dad, with a bowl of popcorn in hand, pressuring him into picking the chick flick and crying during the movie.

I remembered when I used to laugh at the sight of her wiping her tears away, wondering how she could be so sensitive. As I got older, I started to cry with her, understanding how heartfelt those movies were. Dad would just shake his head, probably wishing he had a hero movie to watch instead.

Now it was just the two of us, but hopefully, it would soon be the four of us—Dad, Mom, Ciara, and I—all sitting on the couch, debating which movie to watch while sharing a bowl of popcorn.

I once didn't understand why life had to change so much, but sometimes, things happened for the better. I hadn't really lost anything; I still had a mother and a father, and now I also had a beautiful half-sister. Sure, my dad had lost his clients and his position at church, but we'd find a way to pick up where we'd left off. We just had too.

After the movie, I retreated to my room and decided to call Alex. There were still some things we needed to discuss. Although I was afraid to broach the subject, I knew I needed to. I was thankful he picked up on the first ring, or I would've hung up.

"Don't yell at me," he said, answering the phone.

"I'm not." I laughed. "I actually wanted to thank you."

"Oh?" he said, going silent. "Really?"

"Yes. What you did was brave, and you did it for me. How could I be mad?" I asked, not really expecting an answer. "You kicked his butt!"

"Well, he did tell the whole school that you gave him your virginity," Alex said, and all the lightness in the conversation disappeared, like I knew it would. "I warned you."

"I know you did."

"I told you that he was bad news. I said he wanted only one thing!" Alex barked. "And you went and gave it up. Not to mention how he almost ruined our friendship. I was only trying to be a friend, and you just kept pushing me away, Sarah."

"I'm sorry," I said, and I was being honest. "If I had listened, I would've avoided all of this. You wouldn't have gotten into trouble for fighting him, and we'd still be best friends. I changed so much over the past two weeks, and I regret it. When I found out what my dad did, I lost who I was. I rebelled."

"I'm not mad at you, Sarah, just disappointed. I can't blame you for acting out. I probably would've done the same had my dad done what yours did. But you pushed me away, and I showed you how faithful I still was to our friendship by still fighting for you. I still am."

"Me too, Alex. That's why I wanted to apologize for how I treated you. I was wrong."

For a while Alex was silent, and I guessed he was trying to wrap his head around my apology. I was afraid he never would, and so I spoke up again.

"It was so cool how you beat him up. I didn't know you had it in you!"

Alex laughed, but it didn't sound genuine. "Yeah," was all he said. Even though he didn't accept my apology outright, I knew it was a done deal. I decided to move on to the hard part of the conversation, the thing I had been meaning to ask him.

"Alex, do you like me?"

I heard him suck in air.

"Of course. You're my best friend," he finally answered.

"No, not like that," I said. "I mean, like more than friends."

"Are you trying to hit on me, Sarah? Because if so, I refuse to be a rebound," he joked. "No, but seriously, Sar, you're my best friend. Besides, I'm in love with Jesus."

I laughed, a little relieved. "That you are."

"And I like virgins. If your name were Mary, maybe we could date."

"My feelings are hurt," I joked.

"And I like blondes."

"I'm pretty sure Mary wasn't a blonde."

"Hey, now," Alex joked. "Did you live when she did? No, so you don't know."

"You're too much." I laughed, but somehow, deep inside, I felt a little disappointed that Alex didn't like me in that way. I was almost sure he did. Maybe he was just that good a friend, the kind who would always have my back, no matter if it meant getting suspended from school.

After seeing Alex defend me, I had a deeper appreciation for him. Maybe that fondness contributed to my disappointment that he didn't like me romantically. I wasn't even sure I even wanted him to. Alex and I had played in the sandbox together, wearing diapers and drooling. He had been like family since day one.

Maybe it was the idea of knowing that someone actually liked me for who I was. Maybe I wanted to feel loved, like, really loved by someone. So much hate and confusion had torn my life apart over the past two weeks, and I just needed a breath of fresh air. I guessed that air wouldn't be coming from Alex's mouth. That was okay. But I was happy that he cared nonetheless.

"The good thing is that me and my dad are back on good terms," I told Alex after a long pause.

"God is good!" Alex responded. "All you had to do was trust in Him, and He would've guided you from the beginning."

"That's true," I agreed. "I feel like a huge weight has been lifted off my shoulders. It's so much easier to think now with less anger and hatred building up. Don't get me wrong. I haven't completely forgiven him, but we're getting there."

"And your mom?"

"That's a different story," I sighed. "She's just so . . . I don't know, but—"

"Your dad did worse, and you forgave him, so forgive her too," Alex said.

"Not until she accepts my sister," I told him. "Not until she forgives my father."

"At least tell her that. Sit down and talk to her, let her know how you feel without yelling at her, because then she may get defensive and shut down. What would you have accomplished then?"

I thought about it, knowing he was right. "Sheesh, Alex. When did you get so wise?"

"I don't know," he said. "It isn't me. Has to be Jesus."

I heard pounding on my door. Most likely, it was my dad. I sighed.

"Alex, I'll call you—" Before I finished my sentence, Dad burst through the door, looking anxious.

"Get up. There's an emergency."

Chapter Forty

MARK

I spent most of my evening in thanksgiving, praising God for restoring my relationship with my daughter and asking Him to restore my relationship with my wife. I knew that would be a hard one, but I was hopeful, so much so that I didn't cease praying about it. When I saw those divorce papers, everything had shattered for me.

I was surprised I hadn't sunk into a deep depression as I mourned the loss of my position at church and the retreat of my clients left and right. I was left wondering how bills would get paid, how the divorce would get paid for. Wondering what all Claire would try to take from me in the divorce, knowing I'd probably end up with nothing and be deemed unfit to even raise my youngest. Every possibility flew through my head, creating a whirlwind of chaos, one big enough to throw me into a deep depression, and yet I was still standing. I attributed that to God, because I should've fallen. Looking at it all now, I realized it was Jesus who was holding me up, and so I thanked Him even more.

Sometimes life hit so hard, it was easy to believe God wasn't in it with me. I thought He was somewhere on the sidelines of this game of life, watching passively, with no intention of helping. However, God had promised that He'd go before me on my path and clear the way. Surely, God knew my sins would resurface, and I had to have faith that He had already cleared the path and fixed my marriage. I was already seeing evidence of this with my daughter. Now I was waiting on my wife.

My phone buzzed in my pocket. Tamara's name popped up. I quickly answered it. "Hello?"

"Daddy?" It was Ciara.

"Hey, honey. Miss me already?"

"Auntie Tamara won't wake up," she said, crying. "And the man."

"What do you mean, honey?" I sat up, feeling my heart rate increase.

"She's hurt, Daddy! I'm gonna call nine-one-one."

"Ciara, wait!" I said, but she'd already hung up. I tried to piece together what she'd said. Tamara wouldn't wake up, and there had been mention of a man. Ciara had just lost her mother, and now something was wrong with Tamara. I jumped up, grabbed my keys from the counter, and ran upstairs. When I reached Sarah's door, I pounded. I didn't wait for her to respond; I opened the door and rushed inside.

"Get up. There's an emergency."

"With Mom?" she asked, hanging up her phone and jumping out of her bed. I wanted to ease the pained look on her face, but I'd explain everything later. "I'll tell you in the car."

Once we were on the highway, Sarah turned to me, shaking.

"Okay, Dad. What's up?"

"Ciara called and said that something was wrong with her aunt and that she wouldn't wake up," I explained. "She said she was going to call nine-one-one, and then she hung up. We need to get there as soon as possible."

"Do you think she's dead?"

"I don't know," I answered honestly. "Ciara can't afford to lose anyone else."

"I'll pray," Sarah said and then leaned over, closing her eyes and focusing.

I decided to pray as well and lowered my head. "Lord, please allow everything to be okay, not for myself, but for my daughter."

When we pulled up to Tamara's house, an ambulance was parked in front. Three cop cars were parked behind it, and officers stood around talking. I parked across the street and jumped out of the car, watching as the police began putting yellow caution tape around the house. Someone had died. *Oh no! Tamara,* I thought to myself. *I need to find Ciara.*

I ran up to a police officer, who seemed focused on a notepad as he jotted things down.

"Excuse me," I said. "I'm family of the person who lives here. Where are they? There's a little girl! Six years old . . . curly hair . . ."

"Please calm down," the officer said, finally glancing up from his notepad. He looked up at me, but then his eyes darted past me, toward the house. His forehead creased. "Hey! Don't go in there!"

I turned around and saw Sarah running into the house. I left the officer standing where he was and started running up toward the porch. I took the steps by two and entered the house. I heard soft voices coming from the living room and decided to investigate. As I made my way into the room, a paramedic passed me, pushing a stretcher out.Unable to see who was under the sheet covering the body, I began to panic. *Oh no,* I thought, feeling the deepest type of pain. I needed to find Ciara.

I walked into the living room, taking everything in. Sarah had kneeled down next to Ciara and was holding her hand. I could tell by Ciara's face that she had been crying, but she seemed to have calmed down. My heart eased a little, until I remembered the body being taken out on the stretcher.

"Where's Tamara?" I asked, trying not to panic. Tamara and I hadn't known each other long, but we shared Ciara, and so she was important to me. I couldn't bear the news that she had passed away, knowing what it would mean to my daughter. She was dead. I just knew it.

"I'm right here," a familiar voice called from behind me. I turned around and saw Tamara standing in the doorway, with an officer close by. She had a white blanket covering her, but she was still shivering. Her hair was all over the place, and her neck was dark and swollen, as if she'd been choked.

I was immediately relieved, knowing she was okay, but if she was alive, who had died?

Tamara took a seat on the couch, and I followed behind, taking a seat next to her. "What happened?"

Tamara looked over at Sarah and Ciara. "Can you take her upstairs for a bit?" she asked Sarah, who nodded and stood.

As soon as they left, Tamara broke down and started to tell me everything about her crazy ex from her past and how he had shown up uninvited and had wanted to be a part of her life again. She ended the story by describing the fight that had taken place in the kitchen and how she had managed to stab him in the last seconds before she'd passed out.

She had managed to puncture his carotid artery, which had made him bleed to death. Tamara then explained that after she'd passed out, Ciara had found her lying there and was finally able to wake her up right before the ambulance came. Tamara was horrified that Ciara had found her passed out next to a dead man, with blood everywhere. This was the second time Ciara had witnessed an adult who had passed out.

"I should've ended it the moment he showed up at my house," Tamara observed. "But I was so scared."

"You had a right to be," I said.

Tamara nodded, but it was clear that she was deep in thought. "As he was choking me, I just kept thinking about Ciara and how he would kill her next. Or how he would leave her unharmed, but how she'd spend the rest of her life mourning my death and the death of her mother. It was the grace of God that gave me just enough strength to stab him. Thank you, Jesus!" Tamara leaned over, praising God, shaking and crying all the same. "Thank you, Jesus, for sparing my life! Thank you, Jesus, for your grace! My God! I didn't know what I was gonna do or how I would get him out of my house, but you provided a way! You protected me against my enemy, as you did for David! Lord, I am thankful!"

I let her have her moment with God, giving Him my own thanks. He was a God who had nothing to prove, and yet every day He proved His undying love and mercy. An hour later, the house was cleared out and the crime scene cleaned. Tamara spent most of that hour testifying to the police, and she also brought Ciara down to give her story. They told Tamara that the evidence supported her account that she'd acted in self-defense. Afterward, they made her sign a statement, and then they left. Sarah and I stayed behind to help Tamara get settled again. The paramedics suggested she get seen by a doctor, but she refused, saying she was okay and there was nothing the doctor could do to take her bruises away.

Tamara asked me to keep Ciara for a while, and I didn't reject her offer. She had just been through something traumatic and needed her space. I offered to stop by daily to check up on her, but she refused. She was strong and was obviously trying to reassure us that she was okay, but I was still unsettled. I said a prayer over her and her house and then left with my girls.

"Daddy, how long am I staying at your house?" Ciara asked as we walked to the car.

"Until your aunt gets better," I responded. "Does that upset you?"

"No. I miss my room," she said with a smile. It amazed me how well she was adapting. It amazed me even more that she was mine. I also couldn't wait to see the day when Claire was amazed by Ciara as well.

Chapter Forty-one

CLAIRE

I walked into the house, thankful that no one was home. Mark's car wasn't in the driveway. I needed some peace to reflect on the decision I was going to make. After eavesdropping on Mark and Sarah's conversation, I felt different. I saw that my family was beginning to heal, and without me. It meant I was the only one holding on to the past and not giving it all to God.

When I saw Mark and Sarah together, making pizza like that the night before, I felt left out, as if I belonged in that picture, and I did. I was no longer fueled by the same anger that had made me visit that lawyer for the divorce papers and reveal the infidelity. I no longer wanted revenge; I no longer wanted to tarnish Mark's reputation. However, there was still one thing I wasn't able to accept.

Ciara.

If the saying was true that everything happened for a reason and it was all in God's hands, then what was His reasoning for bringing a child of color into my marriage? I guessed that some would say that He did it to teach me how to love people who were different than me. I figured some would say that God did it to make me a better woman, since most women would crumble under that amount of stress. Whatever the reason, I didn't understand it. I hoped I would one day.

"Sarah," I gasped, not expecting her to be home on a school day. I'd assumed that since Mark's car was gone, so was she. Sarah sat on the living room sofa, watching TV with a blank stare. She looked up and saw me standing in the entryway.

"Oh, right," she said, looking nervous. "I got suspended from school."

"What?" I screamed, dropping my purse. I thought back to the conversation she had had with Mark while making pizza. She'd mentioned punching an ex-boyfriend. Was that why she had been suspended?

"I knew you'd be the dramatic one," Sarah huffed, getting up from the couch and storming out of the living room. I followed her into the kitchen, watching as she poured herself something to drink.

"How am I supposed to react to something like that? You've never been suspended before. You're not even the type of child to get suspended!"

"Well, I'm glad you think so highly of me." The sarcasm was evident in Sarah's voice.

"Why were you suspended from school?"

"Because I punched my ex-boyfriend in the face," she told me smugly.

"Since when did you have a boyfriend?" I was bewildered.

"Well, he's not my boyfriend anymore, and you'd know these things if you were here!" Sarah fired back, and then she sighed, taking a seat at the square island. "Dad says I need to learn how to talk to you without getting so upset. So here's my attempt." She paused, as if she was gathering her thoughts.

"I wish you were around more, which is funny, because I used to hate how close you were to me, and would beg for distance. Now that I have it, it sucks. But you picked the worst time to be distant. During this whole thing, I learned that I need you. When I found out about you and Dad, I literally closed up. I found ways to vent that ended up hurting me even more."

"What do you mean?"

"Please don't yell," Sarah said wearily. "Besides the tattoo, I smoked a cigarette this girl offered me. I lost my virginity to my ex, who went back and told the whole school, which caused me to punch him and get suspended." I blinked and said nothing while concentrating on not raising my voice.

"Okay, um . . ." I nodded quickly, almost too animated. My heart was racing, and I needed to have a seat. *Cigarettes? Fighting? Sex? Sarah?* "This is a bit much to take in." I paused again as I began thinking of STDs and pregnancy. "When you lost your virginity, did you use protection?" I asked as calmly as possible, but I knew she could tell that I was anything but calm by the way she fiddled with her fingers nervously.

"No," she told me, looking down.

I lost it.

"What's wrong with you? You know better. You could get pregnant or worse!" I clasped my hand over my mouth. "You're getting tested! I'll call the doctor and schedule an appointment as soon as possible. Oh, Sarah, look at you!" I started crying and took a seat across from her. "I could've prevented this. It's all my fault."

"Mom—" Sarah tried to interrupt my rant, but I raised a hand to silence her.

"You should've been the first person I worried about. Instead, I ran to my own little world. But, Sarah, you can't blame me completely for my distance. Every time I tried to open up and talk to you, you ended up pushing me away! What was I supposed to do?" I started to breathe heavily, feeling a panic attack coming on.

"You're right," Sarah admitted. "I blamed you. I get that it's not your fault, but there's more, Mom. Like Ciara. If the color of her skin is the only thing keeping you from tearing those divorce papers up, then you are a terrible person. Mom . . ." Tears started pouring out of her eyes as she tried to find her words. "That little girl is the best thing that has happened to this family."

"How can you say that?" I asked, offended.

"She does something to Dad. Like, there is this spark in his eyes now. Like, even though everything is going downhill for him, he brightens up when he sees her. We went to an amusement park and had so much fun, just the three of us, and it was like there was nothing wrong. We were a family. Ciara completes us, Mom. I wished you could see it. She's so smart and alert and beautiful—"

"And what will people think if we walk about with a black girl in public?" I asked, cutting her off.

"Who cares?" Sarah asked. "'For do I now persuade men, or God? or do I seek to please men? for if I yet pleased men, I should not be the servant of Christ.' Galatians, chapter one, verse ten. Mom, you care too much about what other people think about you and not enough about what God thinks, and that's not the type of mind-set a former first lady should have. So what if people stare? Let them! The whole town knows about her, anyway! The damage has already been done!" Sarah stopped and sighed, but then her expression completely changed, as if she'd stumbled upon something wonderful.

She went on. "I think I get it. What's the worst thing that could happen to a white woman who felt that way? A new addition that would change the outside image of her family. What better way to do that than to bring a biracial love child into the picture? Now your perfect family isn't the idealized picture-perfect unit anymore. But, Mom, that's not a bad thing. Sometimes, God does things to check our ego. I'm not saying He put it in Dad's heart to cheat. That was Dad's fault. What I'm saying is, God could've let Ciara remain a secret, but He allowed for her to come into our lives, not to torture us or reprimand Dad for his sins, but to humble us, especially you."

"So, you're saying God wanted to destroy our perfect family?"

"No," Sarah sighed. "We were never perfect! We are never going to be perfect. Only God is! He just needed to realign us. Sometimes we don't always understand how God works. Mom, our family was falling apart, no matter how perfect you thought we were. What if Ciara is what brings us all back together again?"

I had to laugh. How was my daughter smart enough to reveal God's great mystery and yet stupid enough to lose her virginity, without using protection, to a boy who she was no longer with? Maybe it wasn't her speaking to me, but God speaking through her.

I felt a change in the air, as if my suspicions had been confirmed, as if God Himself was present, watching quietly as we chatted, deciding to take over the conversation in order to break through to me. In that moment, I knew Sarah was right. As much as I wanted to be stubborn, I couldn't help but acknowledge the truth. God had found an opportunity to strengthen our family when we were on the verge of falling apart. That was His nature, after all, to restore what had been broken down by the devil. His main goal was to restore mankind's relationship with Him through the sacrifice of His only begotten son, Jesus.

I thought back to how life was before we learned of Ciara. Mark stayed locked away in his study, barely acknowledging me. We were drifting apart, and I hated myself for it. Around that time, I thought that making myself even more perfect would make him love me again. My daughter, she'd drifted away from me, hating that I was trying to make her as perfect as I wanted people to believe I was, although she knew just how imperfect I was.

Had I kept it up, it could've been Mark who was the one asking for the divorce. Had I kept it up, I could've lost my daughter more than I already had. I had once thought that being perfect was what God wanted, but that wasn't necessarily the case. God knew just how imperfect we were. What He wanted us to know was that we must trust in Him and His perfect love, and that the blood of Jesus covered us when we repented.

If I had had faith in God from the beginning, I would've known to trust Him. I would've understood that there was sunshine after every storm. Instead, I had chosen to see only the storm. I had chosen my pain, and I had reacted according to that pain. I think we all did. But my daughter was right. It was time to accept the things I couldn't change, even if it meant finding a way to accept my husband's love child.

Chapter Forty-two

TAMARA

I didn't go to work the next day. Instead, I lay on the couch, going through old photo albums, laughing and reminiscing about easier times. Like how Candace found out she was pregnant with Ciara shortly after I had moved in after Dominique nearly killed me. I remembered it like it was yesterday.

I knocked lightly on Candace's door, which she'd left open a crack. I could see where she sat on her bed, concentrating on something in her hand. I couldn't make out what she was reading. She was too distracted to notice the sound of her door opening wide.

"What are you doing?" I asked, but she still didn't look up. Alarmed, I took a seat next to her and peeked over her shoulder. It was a pregnancy test, with a blue plus sign hinting that she was pregnant. I gasped, which caused her to blink a few times and look over at me, as if she hadn't noticed before that I was there.

"I'm pregnant," she said sadly as a single tear escaped.
"By who?"
"This guy I met once during the summer," she told me.
"And I take it you ain't seen him since. One-night stand?" I asked, shocked that she'd do something like that. Candace wasn't the type of girl to sleep around randomly.

"No." *Her tears picked up. "And I don't really know anything about him."*

"You ain't the first," I joked, but she glared at me. "I'm not helping none. Okay, sorry. We can find him."

"Tamara, he was a middle-aged white man, and I was probably his black fling. Do you think he'd approve of our baby?" she asked me.

"Well, it's the twentieth-first century," I told her. "There's all types of mixed races."

"My whole point is, I'm alone in this," she said, crying into her hands. I wrapped an arm around her, wanting to make her feel better, knowing it wouldn't help much.

"You have me to help," I told her. "Besides, I owe you!"

"How?" she asked, lifting her face from her hands.

"You saved me from Dominique, remember?"

Candace nodded in response.

"He could've killed me."

"He almost did," she said.

"And thanks to you, I'm out of there. So let me help you. I'll be like an auntie! I always wanted a niece," I said, delighted.

"You'd be her godmother," Candace replied, correcting me.

"She's still going to call me Auntie Tamara."

"How do you know it's a girl?" Candace laughed.

"I'm hopeful," I said with a smug smile, pulling Candace close for another hug.

I'd done exactly that. From the moment Ciara was born, she was my niece, and I treated her no differently than family. I remembered the day she was born. . . .

I held Candace's hand as the doctor told her to push. Up until that moment, Candace was calm and collected and had barely let the pain get to her. Now, as she prepared to push, she squeezed my hand, cutting off my circulation.

"*Ouch,*" *I said.*

"*You can't say ouch!*" *Candace began breathing heavily.* "*That's my line. You say that everything is going to be okay.*"

"*Everything is gonna be okay,*" *I said, still trying to pull my hand away, but she wasn't letting go.*

"*Oh, gosh, this hurts so bad!*" *she said, relaxing after her first push.*

"*Relax for a moment,*" *the doctor said.* "*I'm going to have you push again. Okay?*"

Candace nodded.

"*One . . . two . . . three . . . push!*"

Candace pushed, scrunching her face up as she did so. After a few seconds she stopped and let out a loud groan.

"*That's good. You're doing great. I can see the baby's head. Let's push again,*" *he said.* "*That's it. Yes.*" *A second later, the doctor held a crying baby up.* "*It's a girl.*" *The nurses moved quickly. They put some type of liquid in her eyes, wrapped her in cloth, and then handed her to Candace, who was in tears.*

The baby was so beautiful, with the lightest complexion, and when she opened her eyes, they were a beautiful hazel color. She had a head full of straight black hair, and she cried in bouts, staying quiet long enough to stare up at Candace.

"*She's beautiful,*" *I said, wiping the tears from my eyes.*

"*She's a blessing,*" *Candace chimed in.*

"*What are you going to name her?*"

Candace looked down at the baby with a smug smile. "*I'll name her Ciara.*"

I closed the photo albums, feeling the weight of everything bearing down on my shoulders. I'd nearly escaped death last night. That was a hard thing to adjust to. I had kept looking up at the bedroom door last night, expecting to see Dominique walk in and charge me. This morning I had taken a shower with the shower curtain open, afraid he'd pop up and attack me.

Another thing that weighed on me was the fact that I'd killed a man. I'd prayed to God, asking for some sign that I'd done the right thing. I knew the answer to that question, since I felt that it was God Himself who had given me the strength to do it. But I still felt terrible for taking a person's life, no matter what they'd done to me.

There was a knock at the door. I jumped, feeling panicked as the image of Dominique's face popped up in my mind. I made my way to the door and peeked through the peephole, shocked by who stood there. How did she know where I lived? I straightened my back, which was what I did when I felt threatened, and opened the door.

Claire stood at my door, slightly turned so that she could look at the other houses. She still looked elegant and stuck-up, with a tan designer dress, a designer purse, and heels that looked fit for a queen. Her blond hair looked coiffed, as if she'd just stepped out of a salon, and it blew with the wind as she turned her head toward me.

She smiled. However, the smile didn't meet her eyes. It was almost as if she was slightly pained to be at my house. Judging by our first encounter, I knew this wasn't going to be the best conversation.

"Sorry for just showing up. I saw what happened on the news this morning. I got your address from my daughter Sarah. I hope you don't mind. May I come in?" she asked hesitantly.

My mind instantly ran through the different things she could possibly want to discuss with me. I pictured her sitting down on my couch, pulling out a wad of money, and declaring her wish to pay me off to keep Ciara out of their lives. When I invited her in and we took a seat on my couch, it became apparent that buying me off wasn't her intention. At first, she glanced around the living room cautiously, and I could tell by how she sat with her butt barely touching the couch that she was uncomfortable.

"Would you like something to drink?" I offered, knowing that was what white people usually did when they had guests.

"No," she said, resting her hands on the purse on her lap. "Sorry to show up unannounced. I'm here because I've come to apologize for how I treated you that first day."

I sat back, shocked and amused at the same time. I had expected anything but an apology, but exactly what was she apologizing for? Her bad attitude? Her racism? Being wrong?

"I judged you and Ciara with no real grounds," she said. I nodded, watching as tears built up in her eyes, willing to spill out at any moment. "Just imagine how you'd feel if a stranger dropped a child off at your doorstep and said she was your husband's child. Pointing out to you that she was black was the first thing in my mind, as that would prove you wrong, or so I thought. I didn't want to accept it. But I think I am close now."

"According to Mark, you are going to divorce him," I said, crossing my arms.

"I'm debating about just tearing those papers up," she said. "Depending on a few things, which is another reason I came." I unfolded my arms and sat up, intrigued by her words. Claire seemed unsure of herself, as she opened and closed her mouth multiple times in an attempt to speak. "Tell me about Mark and Ciara's mom's relationship," she finally said.

I nodded. Of course she wanted to know the specifics. "Well, it was a one time thing, from what she said. They met at a beach, laughed, and ended up together that night." I went on to explain how Candace had felt when she'd learned that she was pregnant, how she'd known she'd be in it alone, and how I'd promised to be there with her.

"Can I see another picture of her?" Claire asked, and I agreed. I opened one of the photo albums and flipped through a few pages until I saw some pictures that would satisfy Claire's curiosity. I handed her the album, pointing to a few pictures.

"This was her before she was pregnant." I showed her a picture of Candace standing in front of her house, wearing a long white maxi dress, smiling at the camera. I flipped to another picture, one of Candace holding her belly. She was around seven months pregnant at the time, and I remembered taking the picture. "That wasn't a good day for her." I laughed. "She felt fat and was always uncomfortable. I think toward the end of her pregnancy, she had a hard time accepting that Ciara wouldn't have a father. She never seemed happy, not until she saw Ciara for the first time." I turned the page to reveal a photo of a beautiful baby girl, curled against Candace's chest as she smiled at the camera.

"Being a mom was the best thing that happened to her. To both of us," I told her. "Not everything is black and white. There's always the gray. The white would be you and your family, the black would be our side, and the gray is where we all come together as one family." I reached over and put a hand on Claire's. She seemed shocked by the intimate gesture. "Our families are one now. Even if you decided to divorce him, you'd still have to be a part of your oldest daughter's life, which means you'll never really escape everything.

"You should feel lucky that you have a husband, ma'am. Nowadays, staying married seems impossible. Candace always wanted the white picket fence and husband, but she wasn't given the chance. After Candace died, I learned to appreciate everything. One day you'll look up and see your world has been changed."

"Mine has been changed, and I'm trying to get it back," Claire said, and I shook my head.

"You can't go backward, only forward. You came here to find out as much about the past as possible, but you're looking in the wrong direction," I said, impressing myself with my own wisdom.

Claire nodded once, but she didn't seem convinced.

"You shouldn't be here. Being here means you're holding on. You should be with your husband, trying to forgive and move on."

Claire nodded again, wiping her eyes. She stood up, and I showed her to the door.

"Thank you," she said, turning to leave.

"Claire?"

She turned back to me.

"Even preachers mess up. Forgive him."

She didn't nod, but she smiled weakly and walked to her car. I didn't know what came over me, giving her advice like that, when only two weeks ago, I wanted to slap the racism out of her.

Maybe it was Jesus.

Maybe? It was always Jesus.

Chapter Forty-three

SARAH

It was as if I was a celebrity. When I walked into school three days later, the students in the hallway cried, "Welcome back!" I was shocked by this welcome, as I did not feel deserving of such praise when three days ago, everyone was laughing at my expense. A girl who I didn't know walked up to me and wrapped an arm around my shoulder.

"Who knew you could be so feisty?" she asked, smiling back at those in the crowd as they watched us walk down the hall. "Ryan hurts so many girls, but no one ever does anything about it. You and Alex really gave it to him."

"I'm not proud of it," I told her.

"And that's cool and all, but you really put him in his place, and it meant a lot to at least twenty girls here."

I stopped walking. "He's been with twenty girls?"

"Well, yeah . . . I thought everyone knew that," she said, laughing, but then her face turned serious. "Well, I mean, I guess you wouldn't know, because you were all saved and stuff, so you were never involved in all the gossip and stuff."

"I am still saved," I told her.

"You're better than me. I couldn't ever be saved. You have to live this perfect saved life and—"

"God accepts us as we are," I explained, interrupting her and not even caring about the crowd. I saw an opportunity for Christ. "You don't have to be perfect. You just have to have faith in Jesus and know that He forgives our shortcomings."

"I guess." She laughed.

"Seriously," I said. "I have a tattoo, and obviously, I lost my virginity. My freaking dad had an affair, and the whole town knows. We are far from perfect, but we still walk with God. If He can accept me and my flaws, why wouldn't He accept you?"

"Really?" She was surprised. "You think?"

"I know so," I told her. "You should sit with me at lunch. I'd be glad to explain it more."

She laughed. "Yeah, sure, I guess. Catch you later."

I watched as she walked off, disappearing down the hallway. I felt Alex before he even spoke. I could always feel him when he was near me. I turned around and saw him leaning against my locker, with an amused expression.

"It's funny how you turned that conversation into a godly one," he said with admiration in his eyes. "That's the old Sarah I know and love."

"Oh, what? You don't like the new Sarah?" I asked, laughing. "She kicks butt, from what I hear."

"Well, I'm sure I could fall in love with her too." He was smiling, but that smile quickly dropped when he realized what he'd said.

"I thought you didn't see me in that way," I said, stunned by his revelation. He crumbled.

"I lied. Or maybe I didn't lie. Okay, I was confused." He took a deep breath. "I knew I was in love with you at first, but then you started dating Ryan. I told myself that I didn't like you, but then, when I saw you guys together all the time, I got jealous. I didn't want to act out of jealousy, knowing it was a sin, so I told myself I was protecting you because of my loyalty to your dad. But I was protecting you because . . . I love you. In fact, the only reason I was ever close with your dad was that I wanted his blessing for when I worked up enough nerve to ask you out.

"I told you I didn't like you on the phone, because at that time I was unsure. It's like you changed right before me." He paused, deep in thought. "I used to imagine us getting married and you still being a virgin, thanking God that girls like you still existed. You were a breath of fresh air, so different from all the other girls. Ryan saw that too, and he wanted to ruin you."

"Do you think I'm ruined?" I asked, feeling the weight of my rebellion, as if ten worlds sat on my shoulders.

"I think you're imperfect," he said. He lifted up one finger, indicating that I should wait. Suddenly, he pulled me close and planted a sloppy kiss on my mouth. I was too shocked to speak. "My first kiss, which would be a sin. So I guess I'm imperfect too."

I laughed, although I felt more than amused. It now made sense that I had felt disappointed when Alex said he wasn't interested in me. I was interested in him. It wasn't because he was safe or even saved; it was because he was always there, supporting me, being what I needed, even if I didn't know I needed it.

He was other things too, like funny and attractive in a modest way, and he had the most amazing smile. He was simple, unlike Ryan, and predictable. Some girls liked wild boys, but it took me dating one to understand that I'd much rather date the quiet type.

I leaned in to kiss him, and this time our kiss was less sloppy and more passionate. When I pulled back, he was smiling from ear to ear.

"We're imperfect for each other," I told him, and I watched his mouth curl into a smile. I smiled back and grabbed his hand, and we headed in the direction of our class.

I didn't know what this meant for Alex and me. I wasn't sure whether we were dating or not, but something had definitely changed, and fast. It was as if I couldn't wait to see what happened, like how I skipped to the end of my favorite book just to find out if the guy and the girl ended up together.

I was glad he was holding my hand, because the looks we got were murderous. Most definitely, some of the girls wanted to rip my head off for being with the guy who had beat up Ryan. Obviously, Alex wasn't interested in those girls. They'd always tried to date him, but he had always been unfazed by them. I started to wonder if I was the reason behind that as well. Alex was the type of guy who believed that God had only one woman in the world for him and that all the other women didn't exist. I was surprised that he still wanted anything to do with me based on how I'd treated him. I guessed good guys were like that.

As we walked to class, I saw Ryan standing by his locker, staring at Alex and me like he wanted revenge. I looked right in his eyes, which happened to be black and swollen, and laughed. I hoped he'd learned that he couldn't shame a child of God. In the end, he'd always lose. I felt a change in myself coming about. It was almost like I was maturing into a woman. I had made mistakes and was definitely going to continue to make mistakes, but as long as I had my family and God, I could get through anything.

There was another issue pressing on me, though.

My mom.

Chapter Forty-four

CLAIRE

I was still staying at the hotel. I needed to be away for just a few more days so that I could really think about the decision I was going to make in regard to staying with my family. Tamara's words had really helped, and I actually thought I could really like her. She seemed to have everyone's best interests at heart, when the only thing she really needed to be concerned about was Ciara.

I didn't really know why I'd felt I needed to know about Candace, but I was glad I'd asked Tamara. And I guessed I had felt I would get a more unbiased opinion of Mark and Candace's relationship from Tamara rather than from Mark himself. I didn't trust him enough to tell me everything that I wanted to know. Had it been a continuous affair, I probably would have called Mark right after meeting with Tamara and forced him to sign those divorce papers. I could forgive a mistake that happened once. And maybe I could forgive the fact that a child had resulted from that one mistake.

My family meant everything to me, and that meant I needed to be a woman who fought for her family when the storms came, and who did not run and hide. I owed it to my daughter to try. I owed it to God.

God.

The very one whom I had also hid from. He should've been the one I reached out to first. It was amazing how He still helped us in our time of need even when we thought we could handle our storms on our own. God could've shunned my family, turned His back on us, but He didn't. I knew deep inside that His love still kept us moving forward.

There were things I still couldn't fully forgive and accept, but I prayed that night that the Lord would help me see my situation differently and accept my new stepdaughter.

Early the next morning, I checked out of the hotel and drove home in a rush, wanting to arrive there before either Mark or Sarah was up. I stepped inside the house, and all was still. There was something peaceful about quiet mornings in the house, and I needed to be in a familiar place. I went to my bedroom, quietly opened the door a crack, and peeked inside. Mark was sleeping on my side of the bed, wrapped up in thin blankets. He was sleeping like a baby. The sight filled my heart. The fact that he was sleeping on my side while I was gone let me know he missed me and still needed me.

I closed the door and then headed to Sarah's room. I quietly opened her door and chuckled at the sight of her half hanging off the bed as she slept. It reminded me of how she had slept as a child—all over the place. I could barely stand when she slept with me, and some nights, Mark had had to sleep on the couch because Sarah had literally kicked him out of the bed. But seeing her lying there now let me know that she was sleeping more peacefully. Sarah slept in such odd positions only when she was in a good, deep sleep. I chuckled to myself again and closed the door.

As I turned to head back down the stairs, I noticed a sound coming from the third bedroom. I walked toward the door, noticing that it was already open a crack. I looked inside the room and saw Ciara sitting on the floor by the window, with two Barbie dolls in her hand, talking quietly.

And then I noticed the walls. Someone had ripped all the paper off, but I didn't even care. It was the magic that lay hidden behind all the paper that caught me by surprise. I instantly thought about Sarah when she was eight years old and about how obsessed she was with princesses. Mark and I had thought it would be a wonderful idea to paint her walls, each wall telling a different fairy tale.

And now it was Ciara's room.

I walked into the room, moved by nostalgia. When Ciara noticed me, she put the Barbie dolls down and stared. I knew she was unsure of me, and I was unsure of her as well, but that didn't stop me from experiencing that moment with her.

"I painted these walls," I told her, looking around the room. Everything looked as it had when Sarah used to play with dolls in her room. "It was for your sister." I walked the length of one wall, running my hands along a castle and then through a blue sky. "I haven't painted in years. Life kind of happens that way."

"I like to paint," Ciara said shyly.

I took a seat next to her, leaning against the wall. "Do you? That's nice. It took a whole month to complete this room," I told her. "Once Sarah became a teenager, she wanted the bigger room, and so we covered up the walls in here, just in case we had guests. I like it much better like this."

"Me too," Ciara agreed, picking one of the Barbie dolls up.

"Can I play?" I asked, completely shocking myself. She seemed shocked too, but she nodded and handed me a doll.

"This doll is Kendal, and her name is Ashley," she said, pointing to the doll in my hand and the one in hers respectively. "Kendal doesn't like Ashley, because Ashley took her man."

I had to laugh outright. Sarah used to make up stories when she played with dolls. It was like a little soap opera or a play.

"Well, why does Ashley want Kendal's man?"

"Because he's a prince with a lot of money. He lives in that castle," she said, pointing to the wall with the biggest castle painted on it. "She wants to be his queen. But Prince Averly loves Kendal. He's always loved her, but his father, the king, doesn't want them to be together."

"Why?"

"Because she's not a true princess. But she is a true princess. She just doesn't know it yet. A dragon took her away when she was a baby, but her home is that palace over there." Ciara pointed to another castle. "The blue one with pink flags."

"How will she find out that she's the princess?"

"Well, she has to take a long journey to Old Willow. It's the tree of knowledge." Ciara stood up and looked out the window at the willow tree. "Daddy said it's God's tree, so I know the tree will help her."

"That's . . . a very good story," I told her, truly meaning it. Mark had an imagination like that. He had obviously passed it on to Sarah, and now to Ciara. A day ago, the thought would've disgusted me, but now it made me fond of Ciara. She was a smart little girl.

Ciara and I sat there for some time, playing with her dolls and bringing her story to life. I felt like a child again. I felt surprisingly happy, which was something I hadn't felt in years. At some point, we must've gotten loud, because I looked up and saw both Mark and Sarah in the doorway, watching us. Sarah had a smile on her face, as if she was about to open a Christmas present, and Mark looked like he was on the verge of tears.

I quickly stood up, straightening my pencil skirt. "Sorry if we woke you."

"No need to apologize," Mark said.

"Um . . ." I hesitated. "I think I'll go make breakfast for everyone. Mark, would you like to join me?"

"Sure," he said, picking up the hint that I wanted to talk to him. "Sarah, you should hang out with Ciara for a bit."

"Sure thing," Sarah said, walking into the room. She took a seat next to Ciara and picked up the doll I had been playing with. I headed out of the room with Mark.

Once in the kitchen, I moved to the refrigerator and began setting items on the island for breakfast. Mark leaned against the counter with his arms folded, patiently waiting for me to get my thoughts together. I didn't speak until I began cracking eggs open.

"I visited Tamara yesterday," I told him. "She showed me pictures of Candace. It amazed me how much Ciara looks like you, more so than her mother. Ciara also has your imagination, and I can even sense a deep determination in her. She's strong, like you, and very smart. Sarah is more like me, and maybe that's why we don't get along much, but Ciara . . . There's no doubt that she's yours. We didn't need the DNA test to prove that.

"She's a part of you, a huge part. So I guess that also makes her a part of me. And I tell you, Mark, I wasn't excited about the idea of raising a child that wasn't mine, especially one of a different race . . . or at least part of a different race. But the funny thing is, when I look at that little girl, I no longer see her light brown skin or curly hair. I see you. I see Sarah. And maybe I even see my own innocence inside of her."

Mark blinked rapidly, as if trying to fight back tears. I could tell my words were touching him. It made me smile.

I went on. "And as we played, I thought about the possibility of playing dolls with her every day or just hearing these amazing stories that she comes up with inside her head. I'd like to hear those stories throughout the week or play with her in the mornings. I can really see it. Who knows? Maybe we need another child. It'll definitely lighten the mood around here. And none of this excuses what you've done to me, but I think I'd like to try to forgive you and work everything out."

I felt all my emotions surface. I felt as if I'd crack like the egg in my hand. I looked down, not realizing I'd squeezed the yolk out due to my anxieties. I still had more to say.

"Mark, you gave another woman what was mine! You shared yourself with another woman!" I couldn't stop the tears. "Do you know how worthless I felt? How low you took me? I hated the person I became because of what you did, but then I learned I needed to take some ownership of my actions. I didn't have to tell the church or my friends. I could've taken everything with dignity. So I owe you an apology, Mark. I'm sorry for—"

"Don't apologize," he said, cutting me off. His face was sad and serious and almost seemed to age in those few minutes, and yet there was something else there, behind his eyes, a spark—something I hadn't seen in ages. Mark was looking at me, really looking at me, and it took me back to when we were eighteen and in love and he couldn't get enough of me. I hadn't seen that look in the past ten years, but it was here now, as if he was just waiting to love me again.

And maybe the look in my own eyes was what caused him to take a few steps toward me, cup my head in his hands, and pull me into a passionate kiss. His kiss said everything without him even having to speak. His kiss apologized to me, patched up my broken heart, dusted away my pain, and enlightened me to the real possibility of us staying married and in love. His kiss broke chains and made my heart sing to God in thanksgiving.

I pulled him closer, hoping his kiss would never end, but soon it did. Mark pulled back, searching my eyes for confirmation that I'd truly forgiven him, and I nodded.

"It's going to be hard, and some days I might wake up and hate you, but I'm willing to try." I laughed through my tears. "I tried to picture a single life, but it held no value or hope. Everything that I am is right here with you. We made vows to stick together through thick and thin, in sickness and health, through our ups and downs. I promised before God and said, 'Until the end.' Well, this isn't the end of our book, just the end of a chapter."

"Thank God there's always a new chapter." Mark laughed, pulling me in for another kiss.

And I let him.

Chapter Forty-five

TAMARA

For some reason or another, I felt depressed. I woke up in the morning and tried to get out of bed but couldn't. Instead, I lay in bed, thinking about Candace and Ciara. Sometimes, I thought back to when Dominique used to be a good guy, and that thought made me mourn his death. Even though he was crazy and had tried to kill me, I'd once loved him. His death meant something to me.

When was life going to get better? When would I be able to move on and start my own family and have my own children? The only family I had was Ciara. I never knew my father, my mother died when I was fifteen, my brother lived across the country, and we never spoke. He had his own life, and I didn't blame him.

Sometimes I thought about him and missed him. I wanted to visit with him and get to know his children. After my near-death experience, I learned that life was short and that it was wise to spend it with those who mattered most. I decided I'd write him a letter, letting him know how I'd been and informing him of my plans to visit.

After I wrote the letter, I forced myself to eat something and then got dressed. After I got dressed, I talked on the phone with one of my girlfriends from work. During the conversation, my mind wondered off again, putting me back in a deep funk. After I got off the phone, I decided to play some gospel music. I turned on some Mary Mary to get my spirits up, and even that didn't help.

Maybe it was the fact that I was all alone in an empty house with my thoughts. I decided to get up and go run a few errands. Anything that would distract me. Once I got out of the house, I decided to walk instead of drive.

It was a beautiful day, one that would make anyone happy, but I wasn't. Too much had happened in a short period of time, and it was all starting to catch up to me.

I barely escaped death, I thought. *I could be dead right now. . . .*

"Excuse me, miss."

I turned around and noticed a man running toward me. I tried not to pay attention to how attractive he was as he came to a stop, breathing heavily. He wore a dark gray suit and slick black dress shoes, which hinted that he'd been in church. I looked down the street and saw a church sign down the way.

"You dropped this." He handed me a letter, which must've fallen out of my purse.

"Thank you," I said, feeling insecure as he stared at my bruised neck. I absentmindedly touched my neck.

"How did that happen?" he asked.

I felt uncomfortable talking about it, and I was in a bit of a rush. "Big fight," was all I said.

He shook his head in sympathy. "I go to church down the street. Church of United Faith. Do you know Jesus?"

I laughed. "Of course I do."

"Do you have a church home?"

"Yes," I said, growing impatient. I didn't go to church every Sunday, but I was a member of the one Candace used to go to when she was alive. She'd invited me several times before I finally went. Eventually I joined. I hadn't been back since Candace's death, but a couple members had called to check on me. "I don't mean to be rude, but I have places I need to get to."

"Well, if Jesus stopped on the side of the road and wanted to have a conversation, no matter where you were or what you were doing, you'd stop. Right?"

I smiled, understanding what he was getting at. "Yes, I would."

"Well, why not stop and have a conversation with one of his brothers?" he asked.

"Well, brother . . ."

"Larry."

"Brother Larry, when you put it that way, how can I reject you?" I smiled, extending my hand. "I'm Sister Tamara."

He took my hand, with a huge smile, and shook it. "It's not every day you get to meet a beautiful woman of God. Whoever did that to you didn't understand the woman of God that you are."

"The person who did this to me is now dead." I didn't mean to sound harsh. "Self-defense. I was blessed to have survived."

"God is good," Larry said with a nod. "Some men don't know the Lord, and a lot of Christian women tend to forget that they need to be equally yoked to a man."

"I never said it was a man who did this," I told him, wondering just how much he knew about me.

"You didn't have to," he said. "God did. See, as I was coming out of the church, God began to whisper to me. He said, 'See that woman? She's going to drop something. Take it to her,' and I obeyed. Once you dropped your letter, I picked it up and took it to you. Then God whispered again and told me to ask if you knew Jesus, and you did. So I was a little stumped about why He told me to go to you. Well, I was confused until I saw the scars. When I blinked, I saw a man's hands wrapped around your neck as you tried to fight. You should've died that night." He paused for a moment. "And then it all made sense to me. God wants me to minister to you."

"Wow," was all I could say, but I didn't need to say much more, because Larry began speaking again.

"She's going to be okay with her new family," he said, and I dropped the letter again. "The past catches up with you, because you tend to stay stuck in the past. You never let that man go, not really, and so he came back. Old doors must close. You must also let go of your worries and know that your goddaughter is with a good family."

I thought about how Mark's household had been falling apart, and I didn't understand how they could possibly be a good family for Ciara, but Larry was right. I had been stressed ever since Candace died, and I hadn't been the same since.

Larry continued. "God also says there will be a new man who comes into your life, a man of God, but you won't be able to accept him until you let go of the past and make room for the future."

"Sweet Jesus," I said, ready to praise Him in the street. Everything Larry was saying was spot on, meaning he was a true prophet and a man of God, meaning God was using him to speak directly to people. He was God's messenger, and I could believe in the message he had for me.

My feet started moving, my lips started going, my hands rose in the air, and I shouted in victory. I had lost my best friend, but I was still surviving. Had to give Ciara away and felt alone when she wasn't with me, but I was still surviving. I had almost got killed, but I was still surviving. I had almost lost everything, and yet the Lord still kept me. He could've let me die that night, he could've put Ciara in a foster home, but He didn't, and I praised Him for His grace, mercy, and everlasting love.

I looked up at the sky and caught sight of a red balloon floating near a weeping willow tree. I watched the balloon as I thought about Ciara's drawing and about how she'd drawn hearts filled with love so the tree no longer cried.

I realized that in many ways, I was that tree, hanging low and always weeping over the things I couldn't change. When I saw that red balloon floating near that tree, I knew God was speaking to me. I knew His love was strengthening me, making me whole again.

I continued to praise Him, knowing everything was going to be okay.

Epilogue

MARK

The Fourth of July came in a blur. Sarah was on school vacation and had been spending as much time as she could with Ciara, building their relationship while working out her issues with her mother. It was almost as if things had returned to normal. However, we had all changed.

I'd learned to value my wife and my life far beyond the physical pleasures this world could bring that were apart from God's commands. I had learned how to trust in Him, had learned that all bad worked together for His good, and even though we didn't understand our storms as we endured them, we could know without failing faith that God was in control. When Peter called out to Jesus to silence the storms, Jesus said, "You of little faith, why did you doubt?" I imagined Jesus saying that to me at least a hundred times as my family faced our biggest trial.

Most marriages fell apart when faced with such obstacles, but God had revealed to me that no man could tear apart what He built. No devil could break the covenant God had set on a man and a woman. He had shown me through my own marriage just how powerful He was. Everyone had seen the worst in me. They'd shunned me, hated me, fired me, and talked behind my back, but the Lord, He had seen the best in me. He had forgiven me my wrongs and had set me back on a path that would bring glory to His name.

Recently I had founded my own business, aiding elderly people, whether it be sitting with them and reading the Bible or bringing them warm meals with happy smiles. Most of the time, I'd minister to them, which was more fulfilling than anything I'd previously done.

On the weekends, my daughter and her boyfriend, Alex, volunteered to help out. Even Ciara came along and kept my clients company a few days during the week, now that school was out. Claire had picked up a secretary job to help out with the bills and was actually happy about having actual work outside the home to do.

Any chance I could get, I'd share my testimony about how one man, a strong Christian man, could succumb to temptation and sin against God, and how that one sin could lead to the destruction of his family. But with a God who was always faithful, even when we weren't, we could be assured that if we trusted in Him, He would make straight our paths and lead us to redemption.

Not every family was as lucky as mine was, as we had suffered and had pulled together and had turned out even stronger than before, but I knew that God had used our family as an example to those other families that might be suffering from adultery, lies, abuse, or other methods the devil used to destroy families. Anything was possible through Jesus Christ. Families could stay together.

I'd said before that I thought Ciara was my biggest curse and was sent to destroy my family. At one point it did seem that way, but as time passed and the Lord began to complete His purpose through it all, I began to realize that Ciara was my blessing.

It had been seven months since Ciara was dropped at my doorstep. For the first few months, it was an obvious struggle for my wife to accept Ciara, but she tried. Claire would wake up in the morning and start her day off by making sure Ciara had everything she needed for her day.

She stepped into a mother figure role quite naturally. There were days when Claire and Ciara would take off on a fun adventure and not return until evening. Ciara would come running up to me with new toys, shouting in excitement as she unveiled her day's events.

Today Ciara sat in Claire's lap as Claire talked to a few of her friends while they sat around the picnic table. I stood by the grill, watching with a smile as my friend Daniel set a plate of meat down. It was nice to have our remaining friends, the ones who had stuck by us through our storms, at our barbecue.

"Beautiful family," Daniel said, staring at the view. I nodded but didn't say anything. "I mean it."

"I know," I told him. I looked out over the yard and saw Alex and Sarah having a squirt gun fight. Sarah's screams caused Ciara to turn in their direction, and her eyes lit up. She jumped from Claire's lap and ran out into the yard. When Sarah saw her, she gave Ciara her squirt gun, telling her to get Alex for squirting her.

Ciara charged at Alex with no fear, and it reminded me of how she'd been throughout everything. She'd lost her mother, met me and my family, witnessed Tamara's near-death experience, and she had still continued on, seemingly unaffected. She was a fearless child, and I told myself I'd be more fearless like her.

"I have arrived!"

I turned around and saw Tamara enter through the side gate. She held a container of potato salad and was dressed in a yellow sundress that seemed to match her attitude. Behind her, a man entered. He wore a nice pair of slacks and seemed really put together. Tamara approached, giving me a hug.

"Sorry I'm a bit late. Colored people's time," she joked.

"It's fine. We're all family," I told her, and I reached out to shake her guest's hand. "I'm Mark."

"Pastor Larry," he said, firmly shaking my hand, and I knew instantly I'd like him.

"Well, Pastor Larry, feel free to make yourself at home. We have brats grilling now, and the chicken is over there, on the table. We're throwing on some steaks and hot dogs." I pointed behind him. "There's water and soda in that cooler over there."

"Thanks," Pastor Larry said and walked away to greet my wife and her friends at the picnic table. Tamara stayed beside me, watching him with a wide grin.

"You're in love," I said, reading her expression.

"I am," she responded. "God is so good to me. Pastor Larry is everything I could ever wish for in a man. Mark, do you believe we have to sometimes go through a process to get our blessing? Well, that's how I feel, anyway. I wondered why it seemed like so many bad things were crashing down on me at once, but it's hard to see the rainbow in the middle of a storm. I didn't know what God was up to, and had I known then that He was preparing me for my blessing, I would've praised Him throughout that storm."

"I should've done the same," I admitted. "In storms, we tend to lose faith. However, the storm is meant to build our faith and to remind us of who is in control. God is. After the storm, we finally see why everything happened the way it did. I'm glad to see you found someone."

"Thanks, Mark," Tamara said, looking on the verge of tears. She smiled and wiped the loose tear that escaped from one of her eyes. "Earlier you said we're family, and I really do feel that way. If it hadn't been for you, I wouldn't have known what to do with Ciara or even myself. It was a rough road, but surprisingly, we are all so close."

At that moment I thought about the many times Claire had invited Tamara to tea and about how they had seemed to build a sisterhood once they came to an understanding.

It was as if they both shared the role of mother in Ciara's life, and they worked together to make sure Ciara had love from both sides.

Eventually, it came to a point when we asked Ciara if she'd prefer to stay at both houses or if she wanted to live full-time with us. Ciara said she wanted to keep things the way they were, and so she spent four days with us and three days with Tamara. It seemed to work wonderfully, and if Ciara was happy, so was I.

Sarah was doing great. She and Alex had officially started dating a few months ago, and I had given them both my blessing. I knew Alex was a good boy, far different than that Ryan guy. Alex loved the Lord and would be a great head in his marriage one day, and hopefully, that would be with my daughter. I only hoped he didn't make the same mistakes I had, but judging by his character, he'd never let the devil that close.

As Christians, we must wear the armor God is providing us with, which protects us from the devil's attacks, I thought. *We can have a great offense, but without a good defense, we are easily pursued by the devil. The armor of God is His Word, which He has freely given us. However, His best gift is salvation, which is atonement for our sins through Jesus Christ. Even when we haven't put our armor on and we fall into temptation and sin, God's salvation covers us when we come to Him for forgiveness. However, even though we are forgiven, He will still discipline us, so that we do not make the same mistake twice.*

I had been disciplined for my adultery, but God's great love had brought a new peace into my life, and I had everything to be thankful for.

I grabbed Tamara's hand and squeezed it.

"God is good," I told her.

"Always." She squeezed my hand back.

She then headed over to the picnic table, sat next to Pastor Larry, and joined the conversation they were having. I stood back in awe of God's work in all our lives. If there was something I had truly learned through all of this, it was that nothing was greater than God's love, which covered all His children in their time of need. Everything was well in the Douglas house.

All glory to God.

Questionnaire

1. Did Tamara exhaust all her options when she dealt with finding Ciara a home? If not, what could she have done differently?
2. There were times when Ciara was subjected to arguments she shouldn't have heard. How would you have handled a six-year-old child during a trying situation, such as what took place in *When Willows Weep?*
3. Based on everyone's description of Candace, what type of woman do you believe she was?
4. Would you be able to forgive your preacher if you learned of his infidelity? Why or why not?
5. What is the greatest lesson that Mark learned in the novel? (Give details.)
6. What is the greatest lesson that Tamara learned in the novel? (Give details.)
7. What is the greatest lesson that Claire learned in the novel? (Give details.)
8. Sarah seemed to spiral out of control after learning about her father cheating. Whose fault was it? Her own? Mark's? Or Clair's? Or was it all inclusive?
9. At what point did Claire learn to let go of her racist beliefs and accept Ciara?
10. It is evident that God was working on each individual in the novel. List five ways in which God's hand moved in the novel.

UC HIS GLORY BOOK CLUB!

www.uchisglorybookclub.net

UC His Glory Book Club is the spirit-inspired brain-child of Joylynn Ross, an author and the acquisitions editor at Urban Christian, and Kendra Norman-Bellamy, an author for Urban Christian. It is an online book club that hosts authors of Urban Christian. We welcome as members all men and women who have a passion for reading Christian-based fiction.

UC His Glory Book Club pledges its commitment to providing support, positive feedback, encouragement, and a forum whereby members can openly discuss and review the literary works of Urban Christian authors.

There is no membership fee associated with UC His Glory Book Club;however, we do ask that you support the authors by purchasing their works, encouraging them, providing book reviews, and, of course, offering your prayers. We also ask that you respect our beliefs and follow the guidelines of the book club. We hope to receive your valuable input, opinions, and reviews that build up, rather than tear down, our authors.

What We Believe:

—We believe that Jesus is the Christ, Son of the Living God.

—We believe that the Bible is the true, living Word of God.

—We believe that all Urban Christian authors should use their God-given writing ability to honor God and to sharethe message of the written word God has given to each of them uniquely.

—We believe in supporting Urban Christian authors in their literary endeavors by reading their titles, purchasing them, and sharing them with our online community.

—We believe that everything we do in our literary arena should be done in a manner that will lead to God being glorified and honored.

We look forward to online fellowship with you.

Please visit us often at:

www.uchisglorybookclub.net

Many Blessings to You!

Shelia E. Lipsey,
President, UC His Glory Book Club